Praise for *The Joke a[t]*

"★★★★ 4
Hard to [Put Down]"

"A unique sci-fi novel. The[re is an] exceptional narrative full of twists, mystery, engaging stories, and well-developed characters."

—*Online Book Club*

"Fun ... A Good Story, Worth Reading"

"A quick and easy read that was tongue-in-cheek about the modern day ... social commentary in a tone that reminded me of Terry Pratchett and Neil Gaiman."

—*Reedsy*

"Great Read ... A Real Page-Turner"

"One thing that I find is the best form of entertainment—and it's very hard to find nowadays—is not knowing what will happen next. There's a lot of lazy storytelling. *The Joke at the End of the World* was almost a real time commentary on what was going on. It's nostalgic, it's kind of heartwarming, it's fun, it's interesting. It's not a bleak recap of 2020. Definitely seek out Scott Dikkers' new book ... Honestly, I can't say how much I enjoyed it enough."

—*KXSF radio, San Francisco*

"Brilliant"

"Full of twists, turns ... eerily real and immensely enjoyable. Things are not what they seem. Keep reading to see why."

—*Goodreads* review

Praise for *Our Dumb Century*

"The Funniest Book Ever Written"
—*The Baltimore Sun*

"Hilarious"
—*Forbes*

"Riotously Funny"
"Succeeds with every turn of the page."
—*Pittsburgh Post-Gazette*

"This Is Terrific Stuff"
"Even the graphics and asides have bite."
—*Library Journal*

"Oddly Beautiful"
—*The New York Times*

Praise for *Jim's Journal*

"Delightful"
"You need neither a higher consciousness nor irony specs to find pleasure in "Jim's Journal" … Jim's serene unchangingness is hypnotic, clever, poignant, sublime and, oddly enough, funny."
—*Salon*

"Fresh, Quiet Humor … Refreshing"
—*Oakland Press*

"Fun — and Funny!"
—*Comics Journal*

Praise for *Trump's America:*
Buy This Book and Mexico Will Pay for It

"A Must Read"
"Scott Dikkers is a brilliant satirist."

—*The Huffington Post*

"Scarily Prescient"
"Scott Dikkers' new book is a necessity."

—*Vice*

"Damned Funny"
"The satire is relentless and consistently spot-on."

—*Kirkus Reviews*

"The Definitive Comedy Takedown"

—*The Washington Post*

Praise for *You Are Worthless*

"A Breath of Fresh Air"
"A self-help book with the vinegar and grit to tell it like it is."

—*The Austin Chronicle*

"Dikkers' Humor Is Strong Stuff"
"Pastel Sweet Tarts with a cyanide kick."

—*Salon.com*

"Bitterly Funny"
"On par with The Simpsons and The Onion ... an endless string of guilty laughs.."

—*Daily Mirror*

Scott Dikkers
The Joke at the End of the World

Copyright © 2020 by Scott Dikkers. All rights reserved. In accordance with the U.S. Copyright Act of 1976, no part of this book may be used or reproduced in any manner whatsoever without written permission from the author except in the case of brief excerpts in the context of a review. To contact the author or to find more information, visit www.scottdikkers.com.

The characters and events depicted in this book are fictitious. Any similarity to any real persons, living or dead, is coincidental and unintended by the author.

ISBN: 9798695741476
Printed in the United States of America.

The Setup

1

It's Saturday, June 8, 1957. My name is Patrick Stoodle, I'm 12 years old, and I'm standing alone in the middle of the desert with no sign of human civilization in any direction. To be exact about it, I won't turn 12 until tomorrow, but I learned about rounding up in math, so I decided, why can't I round up my age? I don't like math, but I'll use it when I can get something out of it, like being 12.

But that's not important because once the Reds drop the H-bomb, nobody will care about me turning 12. They won't care about birthdays or presents or parties or cakes or singing the birthday song or any silly stuff like that. They'll be fried into ashes with the snap of a finger, and then they'll blow away like snowflakes.

Can you even imagine how much that would hurt? Your skin would boil off. And that's not even the worst of it. Imagine how scary it would be. You'd be screaming with pain, and what would make it worse is that you'd know you're a goner. The last thing you'd remember is getting cooked alive. It's tough to get that thought out of your head. I've tried. It gets stuck in there. "Sixteen Tons" gets stuck in my head a lot too. It's one of the worst songs there is.

But the only thing stuck in my head right now is sand, because today was the first day I tried to figure out what's wrong with my life in Cordial Falls, Nevada. That's where I live, with my dad, in a house on Pine Street. There are no pine trees on Pine Street. There are falls in Cordial Falls, though. The falls are in some woods that a little creek runs through. It's called Humboldt Creek. There's crawfish in there, but they don't pinch you unless you try to rile them up. And why would you want to do that? Imagine if they grew into giant monsters as big as station wagons. You'd be the first one they'd chop in half with their giant pincers.

The falls are down the hill after you go by Winneman's Grocery, just past Cordial Falls Elementary, where I learned how to "duck and cover" from Bert the cartoon turtle.

I tried to tell Mrs. Pasternack that an H-bomb would vaporize the desk, all us kids, everybody else, and everything in the whole town, so what's the point of "duck and cover"? She told me not to talk without raising my hand and to mind my manners. I figured I outsmarted her on that one.

But then she said, "We do the drill to protect us against an H-bomb that gets dropped on a big city close to us, like say, San Francisco, because that might cause tremors in Cordial Falls, Nevada, which could shake our school so much that you're liable to get hit on the head with a piece of the ceiling. And that's why we hide under our desks. We don't have to worry about an H-bomb vaporizing us because the Soviets probably aren't going to bother dropping an expensive bomb on an insignificant place like Cordial Falls, Nevada."

The class had a good snicker at me after that. And you can guess I felt pretty lousy for trying to be a smart aleck. But I knew from talking to my dad that there would be nuclear winter afterwards, even if the bomb dropped far away, and we'd all die eventually from radiation. I just couldn't come up with the words for all that just then to answer Mrs. Pasternack.

My dad knows science. He's definitely a notch or two smarter than Mrs. Pasternack. I learned a lot from him. My whole life, I believed everything he told me. But that's starting to change. I'm starting to get wise to what's really going on.

My first step to gathering clues was to head out of town on my bike and get as far away from Cordial Falls as I could. I needed to find out what's outside of the town. We never take any trips, so how would I know? Turns out, there's nothing but desert.

It was starting to get hard to pedal. The wind was picking up, blowing sand in my face. It was everywhere. My eyes, my ears, my mouth, my nose. I stopped to pee and looked around. That's when I realized all I could see was flat desert every way I looked. It was like I was the only person on Earth.

I bet I biked ten miles. And I'd been going for at least an hour. That means I had to bike another whole hour just to get home.

I wanted to keep going to see what I would find, but I was tired and thirsty, so I made the tough decision to head back. Once I got my bike turned around, I thought about how nice it would be to drink a tall, cold glass of milk when I got home.

Our house isn't a big house. It's not a small house either. It's about the same as all the houses in Cordial Falls. There's no upstairs, but it has a basement. There's an attic too. My dad let me look up there once. It's hot, stuffy, dark, and full of cobwebs. If you ever wanted to hide something, like treasure, or a dead body, or a secret pet monster, that would be a good place.

When I'm not out on my bike trying to piece together clues about the real story behind my life in Cordial Falls, you can usually find me reading, especially comic books like *Star Rangers*, *Weird Fantasy*, and *Weird Science Fiction*. And when I get tired of reading, I watch television, if there's anything good on. At night before bed I listen to the radio. I like *X Minus One*. I also like *Dragnet* and *Sam Spade*, but especially *Night Beat*, which is brought to you by special transcribed disc. It's my favorite show because reporter Randy Stone tries to dig up the truth. Sure, Sergeant Friday and Sam Spade go after the truth too, but reporter Randy Stone gets to the truth *and* the heart of the matter. And then he writes all about it on the front page of *The Chicago Star*.

I'm Randy Stone out in the desert. I thought maybe I'd discover there are no other towns in the whole world besides Cordial Falls. Next time I go exploring, maybe I'll find out some evil scientist shot the town with a shrink ray to fit it all on a tabletop.

I'll get to the bottom of it one way or the other. I'll get up first thing tomorrow and hunt for more clues, and I'll ask my best friend Walt to come along. Walt has so many freckles I think if you took them away he wouldn't have a face. I haven't seen him much this summer. I don't have any other friends. I do just fine by myself most of the time. I used to play cowboys and Indians with Walt and the other kids on the block. But they'd always just shoot each other, and then everybody would argue about who was dead and who wasn't.

"I shot you dead to rights—square in the gut!" somebody would say.

Then the other person would say, "Uh-uh, no way, you missed. I shot *you!*"

And that would get boring real quick. It made me want to go inside and eat lunch. And once I was inside I wanted to stay there. Especially after we got our window air conditioner.

One kid I could do without is Tommy Haddigan. He's a square-shaped seventh grader who always wears farmer's gloves because I guess he burned his hands when he was a kid and doesn't want anybody to look at them. He calls me "puny" and "shrimp" and "Patrick Stooge." And he calls me "weird." He leaves me notes on my desk saying he's going to kick my teeth in after school, and then when the bell rings and I walk out of school, he makes me wonder where he is with my legs shaking and my back all sweaty. I get on my bike and zoom home, never knowing if he's going to jump out of the bushes and kick my teeth in. On the last day of school he promised he would kick my teeth in this summer for sure. So far I've been lucky and haven't seen him, so I still have my teeth.

After I biked a while, the trees and rooftops of Cordial Falls came up on the horizon. I had the wind behind me now, so I felt like I was pedaling at super speed. I was Superman on a bike. With my super strength, I could square off against Tommy Haddigan. I could punch him in the face and he'd land in the dirt. Or I could punch him in the face and he'd go flying off a cliff. Or I could punch him in the face and he'd fall into a horse trough full of dirty water. If I was a space hero, I could punch him in the face so hard he'd go flying into orbit where he'll die slow and alone.

I imagined telling Dad about my daydreams, and I heard his voice as clear as if he was saying it himself.

"Just be chummy to people and they'll be chummy back. That's how people work."

But that's not how Tommy Haddigan works. Dad hasn't factored him into his formulas.

I'd never tell anybody about my daydreams. Why would I? I might be dead tomorrow from the H-bomb, and I bet dying is even worse when you make a fool of yourself right before. Anyway, I don't think I could ever punch anybody in the face in real life. I think I'd feel bad for hurting them, even if they were a terrible person like Tommy Haddigan.

The best punchers are in the matinees. *Cody of the Pony Express* and *Flash Gordon* are my favorites. I ride my bike to the movie house on Saturdays, if I behave. And I usually behave. I only got into real trouble once, when Dad left the keys in the car when it was sitting in the driveway. I got in and tried to drive it. I moved a big lever like I'd seen him do, and the car started moving backwards. Our driveway is only about two or three cars long, so the car rolled into the street. The bottom bounced off the pavement with a terrific clunk that almost threw me off the seat. And then the bumper knocked over the Garbers' trash cans when it hit the curb on the other side. I was 8. Driving looked easy, but it had a lot more dials and levers than I thought.

Dad grounded me for a week after that one.

He always says, "In the final analysis, you're a good boy." He says I'm so good he doesn't have to worry about me most of the time. But sometimes I wish he'd worry about me a little bit. *Good boy.* Isn't that what you call a dog?

I wish I had a dog, but Dad says he doesn't want to end up being the sucker who has to take the dog out for walks every day. He wants me to show that I can be responsible first.

Thing is, I'm one of the most responsible kids there is. I do chores, like taking out the trash and cutting the grass. I even help out Mrs. Cummings. She's old and her knees hurt, so she doesn't get around so good anymore. I cut her grass too, and I bring in her newspaper and milk bottles and feed her cat, Cleopatra. Cleopatra is an old orange critter who has a bad eye and a flap of blubber hanging off her belly that swings from side to side when she walks.

Today wasn't one of my regular days to check in on Mrs. Cummings, but after I got home and put my bike in the garage, I heard her calling for me out the back window.

"Patrick!" she yelled, but also kind of whispered, like she was trying not to be so loud. "Psst. Boy!"

I could tell she wasn't just saying hi. She was worked up about something. I made my way over to her yard and asked what was the matter.

She pointed to the grass a little ways away from the window and said, "There's a varmint in the garden! Get that thing out of here! Lordy!"

Her garden looked normal to me, but she pointed again and seemed in a panic about it, so I looked more closely. Then, between the green beans and the squash, I saw a little garter snake slithering around having a swell old day.

"It's a snake," I said.

"Boy, get that awful thing away from my house!"

Mrs. Cummings is starting to forget things. I explained to her before that some snakes are good for a garden because they eat bugs and mice that can tear up the plants. That's scientific. But she forgot, I guess. My grandma used to forget my name, so I know how it can be with old folks. She died when I was 7.

I told Mrs. Cummings again about how this snake wouldn't hurt anything, but she shook her head.

"No, mm-hm. You get that varmint out of there." She was dead set against that snake. So I picked it up by the tail and flung it into our yard. It'll probably come back, but I figured at least Mrs. Cummings will feel better.

"Lordy." She shook her head.

She backed away from the window and I couldn't see her so good anymore. But I heard her talking still.

"You come in here now, boy."

I came inside through her back screen door. Her house always smells like butter frying in a pan. I like how every house has its own smell. Except mine. But the thing is, I figure if somebody else came into my house, they'd probably smell my house just as clear as I smell Mrs. Cummings'.

Mrs. Cummings has a scrunched up little face with dark brown skin and a tight batch of hair on top of her head with little gray strands sticking out. She was wearing a gray dress with orange flowers on it today. I noticed some white spots and dark spots on her legs as they shook, carrying her over to her big old chair with the faded flower patterns on it. She got herself into position over it, and then she sat down and let out a big breath.

Every now and then Mrs. Cummings will offer me a piece of butterscotch and chat with me awhile. She tells me stories from the Bible mostly and asks if I'm saved. I tell her I go to church most Sundays, so I figure I'm in good with Jesus. Once she told me the terrible story of her great grandfather, who was a slave. I learned in school that her ancestors got kidnapped from Africa and sold into slavery right here in America, just like the Israelites in Egypt. And I learned that in some states in the Union, her people still get treated rotten because of prejudice and discrimination. We learned those words in school.

Can you imagine being a slave? I hear the whip crack in my head and I feel how much it would cut into my bare skin. It makes me shiver.

"Go ahead, have a piece of butterscotch," she said with a little laugh.

I unwrapped a piece of candy from her little bowl and popped it in my mouth. It didn't hit the spot like that glass of milk I wanted, but when you're seconds away from dying of thirst in the desert, you take what you can get.

She had a lot of chuckles in her today for some reason. I didn't know why at first, but then I noticed on the table next to the candy was a box wrapped in newspaper with a ribbon around it.

"Oh, what's that there?" she said. She was smiling big at me and sort of winking with both eyes at the same time.

I looked at the box and it had "Patrick" written on it. That's when I figured out she was giving me a birthday present. I wanted to say "thank you" because I knew it was the polite thing to do, but I'm not sure if one came out. I started tearing the wrapping open, and I heard her chuckling some more.

It was an ant farm. The tin box was bright red with a funny black drawing of an ant on the front. It said, "See the ants building bridges! Digging subways! Moving mountains!" Mrs. Cummings probably got the idea from my dad. He thinks I like things like this.

A bunch of thoughts went through my head while I looked at the box. I told Dad I didn't want a birthday party this year. It's too many people. That means this ant farm might be the only present I'll get besides Dad's. And his present is still a big mystery that he hasn't told me about.

"It's your birthday, isn't it?"

I nodded. I could feel the redness rushing into my face. I felt bad for her, giving me a present that I didn't really want. With her knees, she would have been better off staying at home than going out to Fawber's Department Store, which is surely where she bought it. I never know what to say when somebody gives me something I don't want, especially when they sit there in their comfy chair with the old-lady patterns on it and their set of little glass figurines of poodles and Bible characters on the shelf behind them, and their face glowing like a heavenly angel because they're so happy to give me a gift that they think I'll love to death.

Grown-ups have this way about them where they seem to be trying real hard to be nice to me. It's like they're nervous around me and want me to like them. I don't know what it is, but I never felt it from another kid, only a grown-up. Except my dad. He acts normal. Well, he acts like my dad, if you can call that normal.

Mrs. Cummings sat there smiling.

"Do you like it?"

I felt a pain in my chest, like I was short of breath. I couldn't bring myself to lie and say I liked it because I can't lie that good. So I just looked down and tried to say, "Thank you, Mrs. Cummings" like a good boy and get out of there as fast as I could.

That night I sat in bed and read *Strange Adventures* with my flashlight. It was the one where Captain Comet fights the Air Bandits from outer space. I've read it before, of course. I was mostly just looking at the drawings.

Dad's footsteps came past my door every now and again, but I couldn't tell what he was up to. My door was closed and the little "Do not disturb" sign I made was hanging on the doorknob. He used to knock on my door and say goodnight. One time he did that after I already went to sleep.

His little knock woke me right up, and I said, "You woke me up!"

That's why I made the sign. We don't really say goodnight anymore. We just sort of go about our separate business.

I had my radio on. There was a show about a midget who plays major league baseball. I wasn't paying too close attention to it, but I liked the sound of the baseball announcer and the fans cheering in the stands. It reminded me of when I went to a real baseball game. It was at the high school. Dad got me a hotdog and I remember I didn't squirt quite enough mustard on, so it was almost too dry to eat. We sat together, and he didn't say much because he said he had some thinking to do. But it was nice being there with him.

Let's see if I live through the night to make it to my actual twelfth birthday. Because if the Commies drop the big one, this is the last you'll ever hear from me.

2

I must have survived, because there I was wiping peanut butter on a Popsicle stick and setting it on the curb, even though I'd rather be thrown into an atom smasher. It was a nice summer day. It wasn't too hot. A perfect day to get pulverized at near light speed. Would that hurt less than radiation? I think so. Because you'd die faster.

The ant farm came with a little booklet called *The Ant Watcher's Manual*. This is where I learned about the peanut butter trick. Pretty smart, I guess. But it takes an hour! That's enough time for the Reds to launch a full-scale nuclear attack. If I got a spade from the shed and found an anthill by the sandbox out back, I could get ten times the ants. But who wants ants anyway? Not me. They're not even that fun to watch.

I didn't feel like doing the ant farm anymore, so I dropped my last Popsicle stick, ran over to Walt's, and banged on the screen door. His mom is a small lady with orange hair just like Walt, but without as many freckles. She answered with the regular how-do-you-dos even though she seemed nervous, trying hard to be nice, like I was saying about grown-ups.

I asked if Walt could ride bikes. She called into the house

for him. She invited me in, but I stayed outside, just scratching the bottom of my sneaker on the concrete step, not minding anything.

I heard Walt's voice inside.

"Aw, Ma, don't make me play with Patrick!"

My stomach felt like somebody dropped poison in it, the kind a spy uses to kill himself in eight seconds after he's captured by the enemy. But I should have known it was coming.

His mom lied and said he was busy with chores. I guess she didn't think I could hear him, but I have good ears.

I ran off. She called after me.

"Come back again, Patrick!"

She was more interested in me coming over than my so-called friend was. I wouldn't mind it if once in a while a kid would be as nice to me as the grown-ups. And someday I'm going to figure out why grown-ups like me but kids don't.

I grabbed my Schwinn from the garage and hopped on. I also grabbed the spade so I could do some digging. My plan was to go down to the falls to think. It's my favorite place to do that. And if I can find a place in the woods with good soft ground, I'm going to dig to see if I eventually hit the metal hull that the town of Cordial Falls was put on when aliens carved it out of the Earth and set it up in their lab onboard their spaceship that's as big as a planet and hiding behind the sun.

I tried this same experiment in the front of our house, but Dad made me stop.

"Patrick, don't dig up the whole yard! What are you, one of the mole people?" he said.

Before I got halfway across the yard, Dad popped his head out the door.

"You sure you don't want a party tonight?"

"Yeah, I'm sure."

"Okay, but Walt and Missy are going to be crestfallen."

"What does that mean?"

He pointed at me when I asked that. And I knew what he meant. He meant if I didn't know a word, I was supposed to look it up in my dictionary.

"I'm on my bike, Dad. Just tell me this one?"

He pretended to zip his lip and walked back into the house. I groaned and headed down the road.

It's hard to believe my birthday is today. It doesn't feel like a birthday. I guess because I'm getting old, birthdays aren't as special as they used to be. I used to like parties too. But there's too many people. And I have more important things to worry about. After all, I don't have much time left. The Reds have their finger right over that big button, I know it.

Walt is going to have a grand old time at home tonight playing with somebody else.

Missy used to be my friend. But she walked up to me in school the other day and said, "There's nothing special about you, Patrick Stoodle."

What am I supposed to say to that? She walked off in a huff like she'd given me the business. I'm never much for words. I can think of smart answers, but I usually don't think of them until later. I especially couldn't think of anything to say to Missy. What she said stuck. It turned into sticky worm guts inside my skull and gummed up every part of it. I felt like a dying worm that day, just slithering home from school, slouching at the dinner table, slurping up my peas and carrots like it was my last meal of worm food, Dad asking me, "How was school?" and me mumbling, "Fine," without looking up.

One of the best feelings is the warm summer wind hitting my face, blowing my hair back while I whiz my bike through the curved streets, passing all the houses. They all look the same. Yellow, light green, light blue. If I go fast enough, they blend together and start to look like swirled up candy-apple ice cream. The air goes past my ears and makes a big sound like rushing water that drowns out everything else.

I thought of the time when Walt probably decided he didn't want to be my friend anymore. I should have remembered before I ran over to his house just now, but I guess I was hoping he forgot.

He was outside with his magnifying glass looking at the sidewalk. I asked what he was doing, and he looked at me, smiled, and said he was burning ants alive.

I asked why he was doing that. Inside I was hurting. I kept imagining what it would be like to be burned alive, especially with that thin beam the magnifying glass makes. It would be like a hot bayonet going in, piercing the skin real slow. I couldn't help but feel it. I knocked the magnifying glass out of his hand and told him to stop it. I asked why he would want to hurt an ant.

He said, "What do you care about a stupid ant? You're weird."

There was the word again. I hear it a lot. It always feels like a punch in the nose. But I've gotten used to it.

The truth is, I don't care about an ant. I just couldn't stand the idea of somebody strong having fun torturing somebody weak. It seemed to me like the worst thing you could do, like something Tommy Haddigan would do, or Ming the Merciless. Flash Gordon wouldn't stand for it, and neither will I.

I didn't tell Dad what happened. I knew what he'd say because he always says the same thing.

"Weird means different, and different is an advantage in the marketplace. If it were up to me, I'd want *everybody* to be weird."

Somehow he didn't make me feel any better about being called "weird." It still felt like a punch in the nose.

I whooshed down the hill past Winneman's Grocery and turned onto the road that goes to the falls. I even skidded a little and kicked up some gravel.

Along the wooden fence just before the woods, a crow started following me. It was squawking and flying right over my head. Maybe she was scared I was going to mess with her nest.

"Gee whiz, crow! Go easy," I said. "I'm not going to bother you."

I rode low and tried to pedal faster.

Once I got to the end of the road, I dropped my bike in the tall grass at the end of the fence and headed down the path to the falls. The shade was nice after the ride. Sometimes I ride my bike and I don't realize how hot I am because of all the air on me while I'm moving. But as soon as I get off my bike, I realize I'm sweating and burning up like I'm on fire.

I hopped up on some of the bigger rocks on the path. One of them had some nice-looking moss patterns on it. Lots of white and dark green and black mixed in. The falls made a faint trickling sound in the distance. And I heard a few frogs in the brush. I thought maybe I'd get lucky and catch one. It's fun to hold them in my hand and look at their little fingers, but I always let them go now after they pee. I learned my lesson when I brought one home to make into a pet and it died after two days. I felt bad for that little frog. He didn't want to be a pet. I named him Freddy. He was grayish brown and had yellow squiggles on his belly.

Then I remembered I left the spade in the basket on my bike. I turned around to get it when I heard another noise along with the falls. It was voices. It was some boys laughing and talking. They sounded older, maybe seventh or eighth graders.

There was no sign of them coming up the path from the falls, so I didn't know who they were. I know just about everybody in Cordial Falls, but they were too far to make out by just their voices.

I got hit just then with the thought that this was Tommy Haddigan and his friends. My whole body started buzzing at the idea.

What are the chances?

There's two thousand people in Cordial Falls, so whatever that comes out to.

Even though that's good odds, I couldn't help thinking about the danger I'd be in if it was him. I remembered what he did to Ronald Fikema. He hit him in the mouth in fourth grade and Ronald had to go to the hospital. His mouth still doesn't look right. Word was they almost sent Tommy to military school because he couldn't learn how to treat people in a regular school.

In case it was Tommy, I wanted to make a break for it and run back to my bike and get out of there as fast as I could. But they'd see me if I went back on the path. I slid down the rock on the brush side and crouched, trying to stay still. My chest was thumping fast. I had a rabbit heart all of a sudden. I could hear my own breath. My whole body was sweating.

As the voices got closer, I heard what they were saying. They were talking about girls in the seventh grade. And they were cussing and talking dirty. My dad would wash my mouth out with a whole bar of Lava if he heard me talking like that.

"Cheryl's got some nice bazongas on her, for a seventh grader."

The others snickered and hooted.

"What do you think she looks like naked?" one of them asked.

"In your dreams, Russell."

"Tommy, check this out. Look at me."

Tommy.

My insides crashed into the rocks.

It's funny how sometimes when I think of someone, they show up. Does that only happen to me? I wonder if there's a scientific explanation for it. This was the strange little thought that ran through my head just then. Mostly I was trying not to breathe so loud.

They all jeered, and I could hear them play-punching, jumping around, and laughing, their feet scuffling on the dirt. They were close, right on the other side of the rock. I was sure of it.

"It's the eighth and ninth graders I want, like Alice Anderson. She's not a little girl anymore. What I wouldn't do to get her alone behind the church on a Friday night."

"You'd pop her cherry!"

One of them made the mouth-pop sound with a finger. The others giggled. As much as they talked about girls, I thought it was kind of funny that they didn't have any girls with them.

I realized when they got to where the path opens up they would probably see my bike. Would they take it? Would they slash my tires? Tommy probably had a switchblade. He was liable to do anything. He was like a real-life Mortimer Black. Or even one of the Air Bandits.

I snuck a look around and saw them walking away, toward where the fence starts. I saw Tommy's head with his hair that looks like a dirty horse mane. He wasn't wearing a shirt. One of them had a handkerchief tied on his head. They were lollygagging, so I thought if I went into the brush and ran along the path, I could run faster than them and get to my bike before they did, and then hightail it out of there. I was wearing my white T-shirt, so I wasn't going to blend in so good with the trees. But I thought if I went in deep enough, maybe they wouldn't notice me.

I got myself up and started heading into the woods. A few yards in, I could still hear them, but I could barely make them out through the trees. My socks and cuffs were snagging tons of burs, and the pricker bushes were tearing up my arms and legs. The brush was too thick to move fast in, but I moved through it best I could.

I tripped over a dead branch that was covered in moss and landed right on my face. I got a mouth full of moss and dirt, and I'm sure I scraped my cheek pretty good on some thorns, but I got up and kept going. My heart was pumping so fast I could hear it over the sound of my bushwhacking.

The sun poked through the trees ahead. I knew I wasn't far from my bike. I ducked down and looked toward the path. The boys weren't looking my way. They were still walking slow, and I was getting ahead of them.

Once I came out of the woods and into the clearing, I ran as fast as I could toward the path to grab my bike.

"Hey, who's that?" one of them said.

I looked back. They stopped talking, and one of them was pointing at me.

"It's Patrick Stoodle."

"That little pecker."

One of them laughed. Hard footsteps hit the gravel and came towards me.

I stood my bike up and got on. My panting wasn't just breathing anymore. My voice was wheezing out with each push of air. Sweat was pouring off my forehead. I wobbled on my bike at first, but as soon as I got balanced, I started pedaling as fast as I could. The footsteps got closer.

"Get him, Glen! Tackle him!" one of them yelled from way back.

A big rock hit the gravel next to me. Then another one in front of me. Then something hard and sharp hit me right on the side of the head, by my ear.

"Got him!" one of them laughed.

I kept going.

My ear got warm fast and then went numb. I tried to shake off the feeling and keep pedaling. With each pump of my legs, I panted more and might have cried. I saw a drop of blood land on my handlebars. I didn't dare look back.

If only I had a shield on my back like when Captain America rides his motorcycle.

"Schwinn, don't fail me now!" went through my head. It was like something Bill Cody would say about his horse when he's being chased by a band of Indians. For a second, I was the calm hero in a movie instead of a scared kid in real life.

I got to the part of the path that dips down and I was able to pick up speed. I couldn't hear the runner anymore.

"I'm going to kill you, you stupid brat! I don't care what anybody says!" one of them said from far off.

When I turned off the gravel and onto the main road, I was still panting hard. I was worn out from pedaling. I was even more worn out by the thought that I barely escaped the situation with my life. It was a gift from the heavenly angels.

When I got home, I put my bike in the garage and went to the bathroom to see what my face looked like. It felt like I got beat up even though they didn't lay a hand on me.

"Holy peanuts. What happened to you?" My dad said over his newspaper.

"I fell. In some bushes."

My ear was all bloody, and sure enough, I had two good scratches on my cheek.

"You need to be more careful. You're riding a death machine out there."

I rinsed with water and held a washcloth to my head. Then I came out into the living room and stood in front of the big front window. I realized the Popsicle sticks out on the curb would be swarming with ants about now, but I didn't feel like collecting them. Let them have their peanut butter, I figured.

"So you know I've been keeping your birthday present this year pretty close to my vest," Dad said.

I wasn't sure what he meant by that. After my brush with death at the falls, I pretty much completely forgot about my birthday. A moment ago there was a fair chance I'd be dead before I ever saw a full twelve years on this planet.

"You mean like not telling me about it?

"Precisely."

He put down his newspaper and looked at me square. He said, "Well, it's time to spring it on you."

I was disappointed that I didn't get to test out my theory at the falls, digging for metal. I admit it's one of my more outlandish theories, but you never know. I learned from Randy Stone you have to keep digging and keep searching because sometimes the truth comes out in places you'd never expect. But now I thought maybe this birthday present, whatever it was, would give me a clue about why my dad is so strange, and why everyone in Cordial Falls is so strange, and none of the kids like me, and why something just doesn't feel right.

"You're about to get the best birthday present ever. And I don't mean ever for you. I mean, ever for anybody. Ever. In the history of birthday presents. Brace yourself, because this present is going to be absolutely, undeniably incredible."

This is how my dad talks, but he never promised anything this big before. My first thought was that he probably didn't buy it at Fawber's Department Store.

3

DAD EXAGGERATES A LOT and gets excited about things he thinks are amazing even though, when all's said and done, they're no fun. Like if he was trying to get me to clean my room, he'd say, "How would you like to play a critical role in the maintenance of the home?"

It's the old Tom Sawyer trick, and I'm wise to it.

I thought of trying it on him, saying, "Hey Dad, let's see who can pull more burs and prickers off my trouser cuffs." But I knew it would never work on him. You can't out-Tom Sawyer Tom Sawyer. I knew picking burs off my clothes was going to be my exciting night and no one else's.

My dad isn't going to win any fathering contests against the *Father Knows Best* dad, that's for sure. There are even real-life dads who are better than my dad. They take their boys fishing or flying kites. Or they play catch after school. My dad is too busy for any of that. Sure, he's taken me on a walk down to the falls once or twice, but that's like a golden birthday plus Christmas on Jesus' actual birthday rolled into one.

He has an important job. I know a little bit about it, but not much. He says the things he does at his work would be boring for me, so he's pretty tight-lipped about it. He explains things he doesn't want to talk about by saying "it's boring grown-up stuff." And I have to give him credit because that shuts me up pretty good. I want to find things out for myself, but it seems like whenever I ask a grown-up who knows the answers, they always give me the runaround and don't tell me straight because they don't think I'm old enough to know things. But the Randy Stone in me knows they're hiding something. Especially when it comes to my dad.

I see other kids with their dads and moms and brothers or sisters playing tag in their front yards or going on walks with their dogs or taking Sunday drives together. Since I don't have a dog and my dad doesn't like to take a drive without a purpose, where does that leave me?

I asked if we could go for a drive once, and he said, "What's your ideal outcome?" He was washing the car when he said it.

I was playing with my paddle ball next to him. "Ideal outcome? I just want to drive around."

"Just drive around!?" he said like it was the craziest idea ever.

After I bugged him for a long time about getting a dog, he got me a turtle instead. I named him Myrtle and he lived longer than Freddy the frog, but not by much. I felt sorry for him because all he ever seemed to do was try to get out of his little aquarium. I let him out sometimes, but Dad would always tell me to put him back in. He was trapped, like a prisoner in a frontier fort, waiting to be hanged. Sometimes I would lie awake in bed at night thinking of Myrtle right next to me on my shelf in the dark. I would hear him scratching around on his rock in his little pool of water. Or maybe I was just imagining it. I would feel trapped too, in my house and in Cordial Falls.

I would whisper. "Myrtle, let's bust out of here, you and me, tonight. I have a plan." And then I would explain my detailed escape plan to him.

The one thing I know about Dad's job is that he makes gadgets like air conditioners, washing machines that you don't have to crank, the Flash-matic wireless remote control for our television set, and our no-stick frying pan. He didn't make *those* things exactly, I don't think, but he makes things like that, and he gets excited about scientific and technological things. One time he showed me the no-stick pan and explained the chemicals on it and I wasn't impressed.

I said, "Dad, it's a pan."

He laughed at that.

Dad's main job, though, is telling people what to do. He told me he's the boss at work. That's the one time he gave me a straight answer when I asked him about his job. And he acts like a boss too. I've seen it. Everybody does what my dad says, and everyone pays attention to him special. I can't tell what it is about him. He always seems to be in charge, and people go along with it. He's not especially bossy. Not like Norma Barnes from my class. She's taller and louder than the other kids, and I guess that's why she thinks she can boss everybody around. Dad is different. He has a quiet voice, and he's not as tall as most grown-ups. He's a little hunched over, with his head down a lot, working or reading. But he doesn't have to yell orders like Norma Barnes. People do what he wants anyway. I notice it when we're at a picnic or at church or places like that. One time I saw Mr. Reinhardt reach into the fire on the grill to try to rescue Dad's hamburger patty when it fell through the grate. Why would somebody risk burning his own hand just so my dad wouldn't have to wait a few more minutes for another patty?

Maybe beings from another dimension kidnapped my dad and they're using mind control to lord over all the people of Cordial Falls. And maybe I'm like his turtle!

Dad gets excited to listen to *X Minus One* with me sometimes. He'll play it on the big radio in the living room. He'll sit in his chair, and I'll sit or lie on the floor.

When it's over, he'll say, "Well, gosh darn it, that was a good one, wasn't it?" and things like that.

I remember we listened to the one about the family in the bunker who had to ration their air in the future. They couldn't go outside because they couldn't breathe the atmosphere. That *was* a good one because the main character was a boy about my age.

Today Dad sat down on the couch next to me and touched his knuckle on my cheek to nudge my head to one side.

"You crazy ruffian, you really got banged up. Are you going to be okay?"

I pulled away because I don't like when people touch me. I told him it was just a scratch. It still hurt a little, but it wasn't that bad. I didn't want to get into it with him because I didn't want to tell him the whole story. Also, "It's just a scratch" is like something Bill Cody would say after a fight to the death, and that's how I wanted to be. Can you imagine being so strong that when you get a mortal wound it only feels like a scratch?

The thing about my dad is, he'll ask about my cuts and bruises, but he isn't really interested. He doesn't care that I almost got killed by a gang of hooligans. He prefers to work, read his newspaper, or maybe on a good day, talk about science.

"You ready to find out about this birthday present?"

I stared at the stitching on the seat cushion while he was talking. I could barely make out the patterns. From a distance our couch looks solid green, like an olive. But close up it has these gold patterns that look like doilies. Do we have an old-lady couch like Mrs. Cummings? I never noticed before.

He explained again how great this present would be, how it would be nothing like any other birthday. But before he could get too far into it, I started guessing, mostly to get my mind off almost getting my head busted open by a rock. Normally I would just sit there and not say anything, but I had a lot of energy, and I thought up a lot of possibilities.

"Is it a race car?"

"How would that be the greatest present ever? You can't even drive."

"A trip to Disneyland?"

"That's nothing special. A lot of people get that for their birthday."

"A million dollars?"

"Money can't buy happiness."

"A trip to the moon?"

"It's impossible to go to the moon."

This line of questioning reminds me of a conversation my dad and I had about my mom. She went away a long time ago and I don't remember her. My dad knows more about all of that than he lets on. And he's good at dodging questions. I asked once if he had any pictures of her and he said, "I think I do somewhere," but he never coughed them up. And when I'd bring it up again, he'd always change the subject. One day I had some questions thought up ahead of time and I let him have them, one after another.

"Did she join the circus?"

"She wasn't the circus type."

"Did she join the French Foreign Legion?"

"She wouldn't want to kill anybody."

"Did she become a nun?"

"She's not a Catholic."

"Did she join a cult?"

"Where did you learn about cults!?"

I keep wondering why somebody's mom would leave her family. If there's one thing I know about mothers, it's that they care about their kids more than anything. This is how it is, even in the animal kingdom. Dogs. Lions. Heck, even ant queens care about their larvae. What kind of child-hating monster was my mom?

I don't even know where to look for clues about my mom. Even when I ask the straight question, "Why did she leave me?"

he just says, "That's not exactly how it went." Nothing but half answers, dodges, and lies. Dad never gives you the whole story. He gives you just enough to keep you confused. He'll hide some important detail and I won't know what it is. I'm tired of all these grown-up secrets. I want to be Sam Spade and piece together the clues of my life, roughing up deadbeats down at the saloon, shaking them down for information so I can solve the case. I'll go outside the law if I have to.

I started thinking about the time he gave me my Schwinn when I was 10. He opened the garage door and there it was. I got super excited because I was asking for a bike for a long time. And the BB gun he gave me when I was 11. That was fun. He let me shoot at a target we hung off the sapling in the back yard. But birthday presents don't give me the same thrill they used to. Also, I've wised up. Why does he want to give me such a great birthday present this year? When people are extra nice to me, I get a distinct feeling they're trying to get something from me, like with all these grown-ups. The way I figure it, people are always trying to get something from you. If somebody wants to do something really nice for you, watch your back. But if somebody wants to give you the best birthday present ever in the whole history of the world, dig a hole to China and hope you burn up in the Earth's core.

I thought about the telescope I got when I was 9. It was fun for a while until Dad took it away. I saw a strange streak of light next to the moon and he couldn't explain it. He said it must be an experimental Russian satellite. I told him that was pretty farfetched. And then I saw more of them, and he said maybe there was a defect in the glass. There was definitely something fishy about that.

I put my hand up to my ear and got blood on my fingers. That snapped me back to reality, and I noticed my ear was hurting. The numbness was wearing off.

"Oh, Patrick, let's take a look at that. You got the old noggin banged up good."

Dad took me into the bathroom and had me lean my head over the sink. He rinsed water on it and gave it a rubbing. It hurt like getting hit by the rock all over again. I yelled for him to stop.

"Aw, stay still now. The wound's not going to clean itself."

I heard him take out a glass jar from the medicine chest and open it. Next thing I knew a cold liquid spilled onto my head and it stung like a thousand hornets. That's when I knew it was hydrogen peroxide. He always pours that stuff on bad cuts.

I tried not to cry, so I just stayed angry.

"Dad, this hurts!"

He cleaned my head about as careful as you'd shuck an ear of corn. It should be obvious why Dad's not the town doctor.

"There, there, buddy. That'll do with the bellyaching. It's going to be okay. We don't want it to get infected."

I calmed down pretty quick after he eased off. I kept my head down over the sink and felt his warm hand resting on my back. Just then I didn't mind him touching me. It was like he really cared about me, like he was a genuine dad. But only for a fraction of a second.

"Is it a toy rocket?"

"No, you could lose a thumb with a toy like that."

He took a Band-Aid out of the tin and taped it to my head. My hair is trimmed close on the sides, so I could feel it stick pretty good. Or maybe it was sticking to the strip of skin behind the ear where hair doesn't grow.

"Is it a horse?"

"No, it's not a horse. You can go riding any time you want at the Womacks'. You don't need a horse."

He lifted his hand off my back with a pat, and I stood up and touched around my ear to feel the Band-Aid. I also took another look at my cheek in the mirror. The scratches weren't bad. They were just pink and weren't even bleeding.

"Good as new," he said.

He gave the top of my head a little rub, making my whole body lose its balance. I tried to duck it, but he wasn't having it this time. It was like he was trying real hard to be a dad tonight even though I could tell he'd rather be reading his newspaper about now.

We went back to the living room and sat on the couch.

"Patrick, I've been working on this gift of yours for a long time." He looked me in the eye. "And I'm excited to give it to you."

I looked at him good. His face was real familiar to me, but just then, all of a sudden, it looked like a stranger's face. The eyes were sharp. There were lines shooting out the sides of each eye. There were a few white whiskers among the brown. I could see each separate strand of hair on his head, all thin lines. I don't remember ever looking so closely at him, smelling his aftershave and feeling his warm breath.

"Son, we're going to travel through time."

I got confused at first when he said it. Did he mean we were going to get older, and travel through regular time like everybody else? Was this present going to be some awful science lesson about how time goes by?

"Do you remember the episode of *X Minus One* where hunters went back in time to hunt dinosaurs?" he asked.

I thought for a second and then remembered it. It wasn't the best episode. I nodded.

"The men used a time machine, remember?"

"And I know *The Time Machine*. We had to read it for school."

"Of course! For sixth-grade literature."

I tried to think of how my dad got his hands on a time machine, because as far as I knew, time machines hadn't been invented yet. They were only in science-fiction stories.

"So, what are you talking about? Who has a time machine?" I asked.

"I do."

"Dad, stop fooling around!"

"Not fooling."

"Where did you get a time machine? Fawber's?" I was razzing him now.

"No," he laughed. "I built it. In the basement. It's behind the water heater."

The idea wasn't squaring with me. My dad built a time machine, and he was going to take me traveling through time? How could he hide something like that? Our basement wasn't that big. None of this seemed real, but I played along.

"Can we go to the Old West?"

"No, as a matter of fact, we can't."

"Why?"

"Do you remember on that *X Minus One* episode, about the time paradox?"

I shook my head.

"If you go back in time, you can change things and they can affect the future, maybe even prevent us from being born. That's what 'paradox' means. I'll give you that word for free."

"So where can we go?"

At this moment I was wondering why he didn't give me a puppy or a pogo stick like a normal dad. Everything had to be complicated with my dad, and I still didn't know what the gag was here. He obviously couldn't take me traveling through time.

"We're going to the future. The year 2020."

4

Was I really going to travel to the future? The idea was nutso, but just in case it was on the level, before I got into any time machine, I wanted to change my pants. No way was I going to spend the rest of time picking burs out of my other ones.

After getting dressed, I started to imagine that traveling through time was possible, and even though it was one of those things Dad gets excited about, maybe I wouldn't be bored by it. Maybe it could even be fun! I was disappointed we couldn't go to the Old West, but I got over that pretty quick. I don't want to be responsible for any time paradoxes, after all. I don't want to prevent myself from being born. And I would feel terrible if somebody in Cordial Falls got eaten by a dinosaur.

My mind started imagining what it would be like to go to the future. Would there be food pills, flying cars, robots, and ray guns? If there were flying cars, would I get to ride in one? Would they fly to colonies on other planets in our solar system or even other star systems? Other star systems would be amazing, but from what I know, it would take a lifetime to get to another star system, never mind setting up a colony there. I've thought about this stuff. By 2020 there must be colonies, at least on Mars and

Venus. Would I see myself in the future? I added up the years in my head and figured I'd be 75 years old in 2020. I'd be wrinkled and weak like Mrs. Cummings. Would my knees still be good? Well, even if they weren't, it would be the future, so I could get robot legs. Or I'd fly myself around in rocket boots.

My mind was going the speed of light, and I couldn't catch up with myself. As soon as I thought of a question to ask my dad, a hundred more popped into my head. I stammered and stuttered and had trouble thinking straight. I couldn't tell if I was excited, nervous, scared, confused, or all of it wrapped together. I still wasn't even sure this was happening.

Dad was calm, just sitting there, smiling at me.

"Take your time. We'll go zip-zip whenever you're ready."

"We're leaving now?"

"No, when you're ready."

"I want to go now."

"Are you sure?"

"I think."

"Do you have any questions for me about traveling through time?"

"I have a million questions—a hundred trillion million."

Dad chuckled at that. He tried to put his hand on my shoulder, but I pulled away like a reflex. He held his hand back at the last second because he forgot that it makes me uneasy. That's how it usually goes.

"Take a deep breath, son."

I tried to breathe slow. In, then out.

"Are we the first to go? Did you go yet?"

"Yes, I had to go by myself first to make sure it was safe to take you."

A new flood of thoughts took over. I never considered that the future might not be safe. Suddenly I wasn't thinking of flying cars or rocket boots. I was thinking of atomic wars, rationing buckets of air, and falling into caves swarming with Morlocks.

"Is it dangerous?"

"No, it's safe."

"But what did you find out? Could I get hurt?"

"You'll be safe."

"Are there Morlocks?"

Dad laughed at that but tried to stop himself. He was doing that thing again where he knows something that he's not letting on, something he thinks I'm too young to understand. But I understand more than he thinks, most of the time. I'm sure of it.

"No Morlocks. We're not going that far into the future. Besides, Morlocks aren't real. H. G. Wells spun those out of his head. This is real life. You'll be safe."

I looked at his face and tried to pick up any clue about what he might be hiding. I looked at the basement door. It was closed like normal, but it looked different to me now. It wasn't just a door to our basement anymore. It was a door to the future. It seemed like it was glowing or vibrating with time waves coming out of it.

I got impatient and tried to pull him by the hand toward the door. I told him I wanted to go, that I was going to die of curiosity if we didn't go right this second.

He got up from the couch.

"Okay, let's skedaddle."

Another thought that zoomed through my head was how strange it was that Dad never took me on any kind of trip. Not even a medium-sized trip. And now he's taking me on an incredible and impossible journey into the future with a time machine? That didn't square! But this thought was crowded out by so many other thoughts that didn't even have a chance to bubble up to the top.

I wanted to ask him how he built the time machine, but I knew I wouldn't understand it, so that question got pushed out. I asked him if I could bring back a souvenir from the future to show Walt, or at least Mrs. Cummings. I thought maybe Walt would want to play with me again if I had a ray gun, a robot, or even just a shirt from the future that looked like it was made out of tinfoil.

"We'll see what we can round up," he said.

Dad grabbed a key ring from a nail high inside the ironing-board stowaway. I opened the basement door and ran down the stairs. This used to be my playroom. I saw board games and puzzles and some other stuff down there still, probably covered in dust.

I opened the door to the workshop. I felt around for the pullstring for the overhead light and gave it a tug as soon as I had it.

Dad smiled. "Careful there. You're going to pull the string right out of the socket."

Even though he was acting calm, I could tell he was eager to take me to the future, and that made me more impatient. Underneath it all, I was still trying to figure out why he was doing this for me. The only way to know was to go through with it, and then look at all the facts afterwards and see if I could piece together an explanation.

I hurried around the workbench to the second door that goes to the water heater.

"There's a time machine in here behind the water heater?"

"That's right."

"Why didn't you tell me?"

"I wanted it to be a surprise."

"It must have taken forever to build it. How could you keep a secret like that?"

"It wasn't easy."

"How come I never saw you working on it?"

"I tinkered with it while you were at school."

Dad put the key in the door and opened it. The room was small, and the workshop light cast a big diagonal shadow on the water heater.

This is the only room in our house I've never been in. But you could hardly call it a room. It was only big enough for the water heater. It was smaller than a closet. We had to squeeze ourselves around the water heater just to get to it.

"Where are we going? Where's the time machine? It can't be in here."

"Patience, Patrick."

Once we made our way around the heater, I saw there was another door. It looked like part of the wall. I never would have noticed it if we weren't looking for it. It didn't even have a doorknob. It was just a keyhole. Dad put the key in, turned it, and pushed it open. It was dark on the other side.

"You ready, son? I'm going to pop on the light."

Up till now, I didn't know if this was real. How could this even be my dad? This couldn't be my dad. It had to be an alien imposter. Or some other kind of trick. But he seems a lot nicer than my real dad, so I'll take him.

I didn't know what I was going to see when he turned on the light, but I wanted to see some kind of time-travel laboratory, just like in *The Time Machine,* and I steadied myself in case I got my socks knocked off.

"I'm ready," I said.

He flicked a wall switch, and the lights made a sound like a flashbulb going off with an echo. The room was as big as the gymnasium at school, with a ceiling just as high. It was like a cave with smooth walls. The door opened at the top of a black metal staircase, probably twenty steps to the bottom. In the center of the giant room all by itself was an oval-shaped yellow thing that looked like it would fit maybe three people at most. It was floating above some kind of smooth, shallow trench. The trench stretched into a big black circle on the far wall.

"There it is," Dad said.

He was looking at the yellow thing in the center of everything. And I knew without asking that it was the time machine.

I didn't know what to say. All my questions were pulverized by what I was looking at. I never saw anything like it. I wondered if I was dreaming. Or having deja vu. Or remembering a *Weird Fantasy* story. Or all of that at the same time. I couldn't tell if we were already in the future. I felt light in the head. Was this even my house? I might have even asked him some questions, just to try to remember who I was, where I was, or what reality was. But I don't think I knew what I was saying. I was all screwy. I was taking in every detail, and my head was swirling around.

I looked away from the yellow thing and saw the lines on Dad's face as he laughed again and started down the stairs. His footsteps on the metal made loud clanks that bounced off the walls.

We got to the bottom, and the floor was smooth, clean, and looked like stainless steel. I looked up at the ceiling. It was even higher now. I couldn't imagine how Dad built this huge room under our house and kept it secret. I couldn't make sense of this place, that the basement I thought was our basement wasn't even our real basement.

"This is our basement?"

Dad picked up a little black piece of plastic like our Flashmatic and pointed it at the time machine. A curved door on the side of it lifted open like magic. I kept saying "wow" because I didn't know what else to say. I probably said it six hundred times.

We walked to the yellow thing. I stayed close by him.

"You want to go in first?" he asked.

I shook my head. How was I supposed to know this wasn't some kind of trap?

"*You* go first."

He smiled and ducked his head and slid over on the flat, padded seat inside.

"This is the time machine?"

"I call it 'the pod.'"

I nodded and might have said "wow" again a few hundred more times.

"Whenever you're ready, hop in." He patted the space next to him on the seat.

I touched the side of the pod. It was smooth and the outer body was thin, more like curved glass or plastic than like chrome on a car. It seemed like it didn't weigh a lot. I looked under it and saw that it wasn't touching the ground and nothing was holding it up.

"How is it floating?"

"It's not exactly floating."

I wanted to see the pod and look all around it. It was shaped like an egg but with sliding doors in the middle, and it sure looked like it was floating.

"How is it not floating but it looks like it's floating?"

Dad laughed.

"How about we just take it for a spin?"

"It spins?"

"That's just an expression. It means 'go for a ride.'"

"How does it work?"

"That's boring grown-up stuff."

He looked at me and raised his eyebrows, making a face like he was inviting me to get in next to him.

I got into the seat real slow, not sure of anything, touching everything first, sort of like Cleopatra does when she's walking through the rafters in Mrs. Cummings' garage, to make sure she can trust the surface before she puts her weight on it. The pod had a smell that reminded me of when I first got my Freddie Fireplug toy. It was a new plastic smell from something right out of the store.

As soon as I sat down next to him, I felt even smaller than I usually do. I was trying to imagine how he built this machine and how he figured out how to use it. I was starting to believe that he was really going to take me into the future. At that moment, I felt lucky that he was my dad. And I knew now why he always liked to listen to *X Minus One* with me.

The front panel had some futuristic-looking controls that I couldn't make sense of. It was nothing like the dash panel of our car. It was black and smooth, with some small colored lights on it. He pressed one of the lights, and that made the door slide closed by itself. It shut with a seal. The echoes of the big room were gone, and the pod was so silent it felt strange in my ears, like we were inside a cup.

"Fasten your seat belt." His voice sounded like it was coming through a cotton pillow.

I found the belt and buckled it. I looked into the big black circle on the wall in front of us, then I watched Dad push another button on the panel. He put a smaller key from the key ring into a slot under the panel and turned it.

The pod didn't make any noise, but it started to move toward the black circle. Or the black circle was moving toward us. I couldn't tell which.

"What's happening?"

"We're moving. This is how it works."

The black circle moved toward us slow at first but then got faster, and pretty soon we were surrounded by black. I felt like I was being pinned to the backrest. I couldn't tell which way was up and which way was down. I think I might have screamed. I could tell there was a loud whirring sound outside the pod, but it was still quiet inside. It felt like I was on the Tilt-A-Whirl ride from when the carnival came to town.

"Is it working?"

"It's working."

"Are we going to die?"

"Not from this. This is how it works."

I realized this is what it must feel like to be in an atom smasher. I saw a small bright circle of light in front of us.

"What's that?"

"That's part of it."

The circle got bigger and turned into a hoop. Then we went through the hoop. Then another one came. It came faster and got just as big and we went through that one too. Then another. They kept coming, one after the other. We kept going through them. Each one grew and disappeared around us in a split second.

"How long does it go?"

"Not much longer now."

It was like zooming down a hill on my bike, but this was a time machine! I was too nervous to enjoy it or say "whee!" or anything like that. I just had to go blank and take it all in. It was a thrill beyond anything I could ever imagine.

I don't know how long it lasted, but eventually the whirring outside started to get softer and lower, and the hoops of light stopped appearing. It was just black.

"Are we here?"

"Almost."

I could make out a spot of gray ahead that started to get bigger. It felt like we were moving, but slower. We pulled into the big basement room we left from, with the trench in the middle and the metal stairs going up to the door.

"Is this the same room?"

"Well, no, not the same room. It's in another time. It's in the future."

The pod stopped and Dad pressed the panel button. The door to the pod slid open.

"Sixty-three years in the future."

"But are we back where we came from?"

"We're a far cry from where we came from. We're in the year 2020."

I let that sink in for a second. Then, all of a sudden, I felt like I wanted to jump up and down.

"Dad, we went whoosh!" I shot my hand out and made a

whooshing sound.

"We sure did."

"It was amazing! It was incredible!"

I normally don't get too excited about things, especially birthday presents. Not anymore, anyway. But on this occasion, I couldn't help myself. It came busting out of me. I felt like I'd just taken a carnival ride like nobody in the world has ever taken. My whole body felt like it was buzzing with nuclear particles, exploding like a thousand tiny H-bombs inside of me.

Dad got out of the pod on his side and walked to the metal stairs. I got out and stood up but couldn't get my balance at first.

"I'm dizzy."

"Can you walk?"

"I think so."

"Are you ready to see the future?"

"Are we going to see what our house and our neighborhood looks like in the future?"

"Not exactly."

"What do you mean? What are we going to see?"

"Well, a lot has changed. You'll see."

Dad started up the staircase.

When he got to the top and opened the door, I expected to see the small room with the water heater, but the room was bigger and darker. And there was no water heater. Whatever the room was now, it sounded empty when we stepped into it. Dad kept walking. I kept close.

He didn't switch on any light, but some bright overhead lights came on. The room had dark gray walls, and a walkway leading to another door.

"Who turned on the lights?"

He didn't answer. He just looked at me and smiled. I wish he'd stop doing that.

"Where is this? Is this our basement?"

"Not anymore."

Dad stopped at the door and looked at me.

"On the other side of this door is where you're going to see the future," he said. The door had a silver bar in the middle.

I said "okay" and asked him to stay close and protect me from any Morlocks we might run into.

He didn't use a key. He just pushed the bar, and the door opened just enough for me to see in.

5

I stayed behind him but peeked through the opening in the door. It was a big indoor space. It looked like the inside of a building with some glass walls where sunlight shined through, and some shiny, black stone walls. People were walking around. Some were wearing suits. Others were wearing jeans and bright-colored shirts with words on them. A lot of people had cloth covering their mouths and noses. Why did they have to hide their faces?

There was a flat television on the wall. The pictures on it were color like in a movie, but brighter and sharper, more like it was a window than a television screen. It was almost like a moving painting where you could see the brush marks. It had words on it and pictures that kept changing.

Dad wasn't ready to go through the door yet. He closed it and took something out of his pocket. "Patrick, it's important that we wear these."

He had face coverings like the other people were wearing. They had a loop on each side. He knelt down and showed me how to put it on, with the loops going behind each ear.

"Keep your mouth and nose covered." His voice was muffled.

I put mine on, so my voice was muffled too. "Why do we have to wear these?"

"People in the future wear them. For safety."

"You said it was safe. It's not safe?"

"It's safe. Just wear the mask."

"Is it for radiation?"

"No, there's no radiation."

Dad stood up like he was ready to walk through the door.

"Wait, Dad. What are these for?"

"Just trust me and wear it, okay?"

Now regular Dad was coming back out. He didn't want to explain anything. He just wanted me to do what he said. I got a little huffy about it, but I don't think he knew because of my mask. It didn't matter anyway because the "being moody" routine never works on my dad. He'll ignore you before he'll ever play along when you have an attitude.

"You ready?"

The mask kept bunching up in my nose and I tried to pull it out, but I nodded, too in a huff to say anything just yet, especially since I looked like some kind of stagecoach bandit.

He opened the door again, wide this time. He walked out into the space. I kept close by him. The door slammed behind us. We walked through the building.

"What is this place?"

"It's a lobby."

"Is this our building? Is this where we live in the future?"

"Not exactly."

"How big is it?"

"It's big. Tall too."

I'd never been in a building this big before, except maybe my school. But even my school seemed a lot smaller than this.

There was a big man in black clothes by the door behind us. He was wearing a mask, dark glasses, and had a little black clip over his ear. Other big men dressed the same were standing behind a long black desk against the wall. Some of them looked at my dad and nodded like they knew him. After we passed the desk, I looked behind and saw one of them following us and moving his hand toward the other men. And then some of them followed us too.

I wondered if they were some kind of time guards or time enforcers who could see us and knew that we traveled here from the past. I also wondered how they could see us. I wasn't sure if anyone could see us. I wasn't sure why I thought that, but it was something I was confused about. I didn't know if we were actually in the future, or if we teleported here like phantoms who could see everything, but nobody could see us.

"Are we invisible?"

"No, don't be silly."

"Who are those men? They're following us."

"They're here to protect us."

"Are they from the future?"

"Yes. They live in this time."

"Who are they? Are they time enforcers?"

He looked at me and I could tell he was smiling. "Yeah, you could say that."

Dad kept walking through the lobby. We passed more television screens. I noticed a lot of people had clips over their ears. Other people were holding black remote control units like Dad used to control the time machine. Some people were talking into them. Other people were just looking at them and moving their fingers in front of them. I couldn't tell what they were doing, but almost everybody had one.

We passed by what looked like a miniature grocery, a flat space inside a wall where a man with a mask stood behind a counter. There were shelves with candy bars and newspapers. The candy shelf was at my eye level, and it was slanted to make it easy to see. I looked at the candy and recognized a lot of it, but the wrappers were different. They were shinier and brighter.

I saw Snickers bars, Three Musketeer bars, Hershey bars, and Milky Way bars. But they were bigger and longer than I ever saw them at Winneman's. They also had M&Ms, Peanut M&Ms, and Reese's Peanut Butter Cups. There were so many different kinds of Reese's Peanut Butter Cups, I could barely count them all. They had the regular kind, a white chocolate one in a white wrapper, a dark chocolate one with a brown wrapper, thicker ones with extra chocolate for "chocolate lovers," ones with extra peanut butter for "peanut butter lovers," and ones with candy pieces instead of peanut butter. And, like with the other candies, they even had extra long ones called "king sized" with four peanut butter cups in it. Who would eat four Reese's Peanut Butter Cups? A king, I guess.

Next to that were newspapers. They had sharp, clear, bright-colored photographs on the front. The big one in the center showed a giant orange bridge with a big crowd of people walking across it. On top it said, "Enormous protests in Bay Area, nation." Under that it said, "Golden Gate Bridge closed to traffic after marchers spill onto roadway." Other pictures showed crowds of people. There was a man with a shirt that had the words "I can't breathe" on it. At the bottom were numbers printed bright red. It said, "Coronavirus Update." Numbers below that said "cases" and "deaths." A hundred and nine thousand, eight hundred and two was the "dead" number!

People were dying by the thousands in the future. My hand started shaking, and I felt cold thinking of all those people dying.

"Dad, there's a killer virus in the future!"

"It's okay. We're not going to catch it."

"How can you be sure?"

"I'm sure. Don't worry about it."

I asked Dad if I could keep the newspaper.

He said, "Of course," and handed a couple of dollar bills to the counter man.

So there was an alien virus in the future that was going to kill me before I even got home. Dad seemed sure it was harmless, but I had serious doubts. I hugged the newspaper almost like a shield across my chest. I didn't think the newspaper was going to protect me, obviously, but I didn't have anything else besides the newspaper, my dad, and the mask. What else was I supposed to do?

"Do you want a candy bar?"

I shook my head. I couldn't think of eating anything. Besides, what if somebody in the future sneezed on those candy bars? I could get the killer virus from eating diseased future food.

Dad moved toward a big glass wall that had four glass doors with no door frames. People walked in and out of the doors, which made a sound like a mechanical toad when they opened. On the other side of the glass was a sunny street. It was the busiest street I've ever seen that wasn't on television or in a movie. It was packed with people. Some cars were parked on the side of the street. The cars looked different from any cars I ever saw. They were more round and didn't have fins. And most of them weren't very colorful, just black or brown. Everything was brighter and shiner in the future, like the candy wrappers, the clothes, the televisions, and the newspaper pictures. But not the cars. They didn't even look like they could fly.

Dad pushed a glass door open. I put my hand on the glass to feel it while I walked next to him.

"Where are we going?"

"There's a place I want to show you."

We went through the second glass door, and then we were out on the sidewalk. It was hot and loud, and the street was filled with people yelling and chanting and banging on things and holding signs. I couldn't tell what they were saying. Some of them had masks on, some didn't. It was like a parade, but they didn't look like they were celebrating. They seemed angry. They carried signs and banners. I caught a glimpse of them but couldn't get a look at a whole sign. I saw the words, "Black Lives," "Police Brutality," and drawings of rainbows.

There were rows of futuristic soldiers wearing black uniforms on the side of the street, watching the people walk by. They had big powerful-looking ray guns, blast shields in front of their helmets, and big bulging pockets filled with who knows what. I'm guessing ration pills.

I adjusted my mask again. My face was getting hot underneath it real quick.

People in the street were yelling at the soldiers, and one of them, a man with long arms and a checkered handkerchief over his face, walked up to a soldier. He yelled, and the soldier plus two other soldiers pushed him back into the street, and then more people started yelling.

The anger in the crowd was like a heat all around me. I felt like my blood was turning into lava, bubbling and boiling inside my veins. It was going to burst out any minute, and I was going to be an exploding lava monster that burned everybody in a ten-mile circle.

"Is there a war going on?"

Dad didn't answer. I don't think he could hear me.

I stuck close by him. My legs were shaking, but I kept moving even though I wanted to be frozen still so no one would notice me. I counted six of the time enforcers walking around us, protecting us while Dad led the way up the sidewalk.

Some people in the crowd started pointing at us and getting excited about something. They held their little remotes in front of their faces like they were hiding from us. Other people held their remotes above their heads while they looked at them. It was like they wanted us to look at their remotes. Or they thought we were televisions and they could change our channel. Some remotes were black, but others were different colors, like pink or green. Some had tiger and zebra patterns on them.

A lady crouched in front of us and took a picture with a big camera. Someone else got in front of us and took a picture. One of the time enforcers stepped in front and waved the picture-takers aside so Dad and I could keep walking.

"Dad, what's happening?"

He didn't answer again. People were yelling so loud I could barely hear myself.

I looked behind us and saw the picture-takers following us, taking more pictures.

We came up to a big glass building with tall steel beams and a few potted trees in front that all looked the same. Dad turned into the building through another glass door. Four of the time enforcers stayed by the door and blocked people from following us inside. Two others came in with us.

This new building was cold with air-conditioning, but it was quiet. I couldn't hear any fan noise. There were wood tables laid out in a straight line with shelves on a wall behind them under a glass balcony. Above the shelves were more flat television screens with words and pictures on them that kept changing. On the tables, spaced out perfectly, were remotes like people were holding everywhere. But now I could see the front of them. Before now, I only saw the backs. The front was a miniature flat television with words and pictures on it.

I stood at one of the tables in front of one of the remotes. Dad knelt next to me. "Son, in the future, people don't have telephones in their houses. They carry their telephones with them everywhere. Have you seen people walking around with these little things?"

I couldn't imagine why anyone would want to take a phone everywhere, but I just nodded to go along and see if this got interesting.

"These phones also have cameras that can record pictures and movies and sound, so it's like everybody can make their own TV shows all the time."

The year 2020 had me all mixed up. I needed to get some answers before I listened to him anymore. I looked at his face for clues. It was just the lines of his eyes and a mask.

"Why are people looking at us?"

"They've probably never seen people dressed like us before, from the 1950s."

"Why is everybody walking in the street?"

Dad tipped his head to the side like he was trying to figure out how to answer. He was probably thinking up one of his lies to keep me in the dark. "It's one of the ways people tell the government their opinion. It's called a 'protest.' They used to write letters. They don't do that so much anymore."

He turned to the devices on the table. "I want to show you these. They're really something."

Here we go, I thought, another gadget Dad is trying to get me excited about.

Outside, people from the street were pressed up against the glass of the building. Soldiers were trying to move them away. Through the glass I could hear people yelling. Some of them were banging on the glass.

"Go ahead and touch it. Don't pay any attention to the people outside."

I could hardly concentrate on anything with the commotion going on outside, but I touched the screen on the gadget. It had swirly shapes and colors on it. When my finger touched it, the image on it changed, like I made it move. I looked at my dad.

"So it moves when you touch it?"

"It can do a lot more than that. You can ask it any question."

"Is it a robot?"

"Yeah, I guess you could say that."

"What should I say?"

"Just ask it something."

I looked at the screen and asked, "What year is it?"

"Oh, its name is Siri. You have to address it by name."

"Siri, what year is it?"

A robot lady's voice answered from the device. "This is the year 2020."

I think my eyebrows must have gone up because my dad had a good laugh when he looked at me.

"Flip it sideways."

I didn't know what he meant.

He put his hand on it with mine and tipped the device halfway over with the screen still facing me. All the shapes and words on it moved to stay right-side up.

"Pretty nifty, huh?" I could tell he had a big smile under his mask.

It was a nifty device, but my mind was occupied by all the time enforcers, the angry people, and the soldiers outside. I could hardly pay any attention to anything else.

A teenager in a blue shirt and a mask who didn't seem angry at all walked up to my dad and handed him a white square about the size of a shoe box. "Here you are, Mr. Stoodle."

My dad nodded and whispered, "Thank you."

One of the time enforcers leaned into my dad and said, "We'd better get moving."

"It's time to go," Dad said.

Something big hit the glass outside. It sounded like a big rock. The crowd got worked up really good, with lots of yelling and soldiers moving in. Something else hit the glass, and it made a crack like a big spider web.

One way or another, today I was going to die by stoning!

"This way," one of the time enforcers said. He walked fast into the store, through a back hallway and into a quiet passageway that was painted all white. It led to a white door. The time enforcer had a big barrel chest and a bald head. I think he looked at me, but I couldn't see his expression because he was wearing a mask and dark glasses. When he got to the door, he put his hand on the horizontal bar in the center of the door and then lifted his hand up to his ear.

"Everything's going to be okay, Patrick," Dad said.

The enforcer nodded to himself and then pushed the door open. Two other time enforcers were outside the door and waved Dad and me through. And three soldiers were with them.

We came outside into a little space between buildings with a bench and a short row of potted trees that all looked the same.

The men asked us to follow them. I could hear the crowd yelling on the other side of the buildings. I also heard short bursts of an alarm that sounded like a futuristic police siren and somebody making an announcement with a bullhorn.

My mind felt like it was overflowing. It absorbed everything that was happening and it didn't have any more room. I didn't want to think about where to go or what to do, and I was tired of asking questions. I had so much in my brain, I'd be busy for days making sense of it all. For now, I just wanted to do what the time enforcers said. I held my newspaper close to me and kept my head down and followed Dad and the time enforcers.

We came to a door at the back of a black building next to a row of giant metal boxes that smelled like rotting garbage. We were on a thin street that had tall buildings on each side and so much trash all around it that it looked like nobody had cleaned it in sixty-three years.

At the far end of the street, I could see a small section of the bigger street with more people walking on it, chanting. Maybe it was because there were less people, or maybe it was the thin street that was directing the sound like a Dixie Cup in a game of telephone. Whatever it was, I heard what they were saying real clear.

"Black lives matter."

I couldn't imagine what that meant.

The enforcers opened the door and waved us in. Soon enough we were back in the lobby with the shiny black stone and the glass. Dad turned a corner, and we went through the same door we first came out of. Instead of using a key, he flashed his hand in front of it, and a little green light came on. Then the door unlocked by itself.

Dad took his mask off and exhaled. I took mine off too.

I started breathing fast. "I want to go home," I said. "And I don't ever want to come to the year 2020 ever again!"

6

In the time machine on the way back, Dad said, "You okay, sport? You're awful quiet over there."

My brain was swirling around fast. I couldn't think of how to put my words together. I didn't know what to make of everything that just happened. It was nuts! I saw what the world is going to be like in the year 2020, and it was nothing like I could have ever imagined. It was a nightmare. It was hell on Earth. There were mobs of angry people in the street fighting soldiers with ray guns, plus a man-eating virus that left thousands of people dead, according to my newspaper. I counted fifty times more dead people than there were alive people in the whole town of Cordial Falls. It took me a little while to count that up in my head. I got confused because my brain was tired, so I rounded up. The important thing is, it was a lot of dead people. It was too hot, there was trash in the streets, the buildings were too big, and the cars didn't even fly.

"That was a lot," I finally said.

I got that feeling again where somebody gives me a present that they think I'm going to love, but I hate it. I feel bad that Dad worked so hard on this present and I know I should say "thank you," but I don't feel like saying it. It was more of a scary present than a fun present. It was like if the ants in the ant farm escaped and devoured me with a million tiny bites. Why couldn't he just give me a stamp collection or something?

He handed me the white square he got from the teenager. "This is for you."

"What is it?"

"It's a gift. I can show you how to use it."

I said "thank you" and put it in my lap on top of the newspaper.

"Dad, what does 'Black lives matter' mean?"

He let out a big breath and seemed to choose his words carefully. "It means Black people—" He twisted his head a bit. "The word 'Black' isn't the preferred word in 1957. It harkens back to the slave days for a lot of people. The more respectable word in the 1950s is 'Negro.' But in the future, 'Black' is the word most people use. Or 'people of color.' 'Negro' is actually considered a *bad* word in the future. These things tend to change over time. Anyway, in the final analysis, they feel like their lives don't matter."

"Because of the killer virus?"

"No."

"Then why?"

"Well, they feel like they're being treated like they don't matter."

"Like in the states where they can't vote, and have to drink from separate water fountains?"

"Exactly. You know about all that."

"Yeah, from school."

"Of course."

He sat there for a while without saying much, and then he said, "Yeah, some problems we hoped would be fixed in the future are still around. It's not good."

He was giving me his half answers again, trying to tire me out and snuff out any more questions by not telling me the whole story.

As soon as we got home, I collapsed on my bed. I looked up at my poster of the planets on the ceiling.

Why did Dad want to take me to a nightmare future for my birthday? I thought about it and realized he didn't care one way or the other what I thought about it. He just wanted to go himself and show it to me. He did it because *he* wanted to do it, not because I might like it. That's the way he is. Why can't he do something for me instead of himself for a change? Isn't that what dads are supposed to do?

I looked at the white box, the newspaper, and the ant farm box on my floor. I wasn't sure how any of these things were going to help me uncover the truth of my life. Today, things only got stranger and more impossible to figure out.

But I did think of one good thing. If there's a future in 2020, that means the H-bomb didn't wipe everybody out and cause the world to end. Maybe it just killed a few million people, and by 2020 they only had some radiation left around. And maybe that's why they have the virus, why everybody's angry, and why nobody wants to bother picking up trash off the street. They have more important things to worry about, like dying from radiation.

Thinking about that made me remember I was supposed to go to Mrs. Cummings' tonight to let Cleopatra in and take out the garbage. But my legs were worn out, and I didn't want to get up. I felt like my mind was somewhere far away, not inside my skull. It was hard to put myself back in my regular life. I wanted to tell somebody about what happened, and I wanted to try to figure out what it all meant, but I couldn't think of anybody good. I don't have anybody like that anymore.

It was coming up on suppertime, but it was still light out. I heard Dad clinking around in the kitchen. I told him I was heading to Mrs. Cummings', and I went out the back door and cut through the yard to her house.

Cleopatra was meowing and rubbing herself around the back screen door. I let her in and called out a hello for Mrs. Cummings.

"Oh, Patrick. How's my little man?" She said from the front room.

"I'm real swell." I said it like I didn't mean it, but she didn't pick up on that.

She got up from her chair real slow and walked with short little steps over to her wall calendar. She pointed at it and smiled at me. Her bony finger was shaking.

"Calendar says somebody's got a birthday today. Mm-hm."

"You already gave me a present, remember, Mrs. Cummings?"

"Oh, that's right. That's right. Mm-hm."

I took her garbage pail out from under her sink and started to tie up the garbage bag in it.

She turned around to walk back to her chair and kept talking while she walked. "You're the birthday boy. You having a fun birthday?"

"I guess so."

"What did you do, little man? Tell me all about it." She got to her chair and settled in it. She let out a sigh like she just ran around the block.

I was pretty much busting to tell somebody about my adventure. I figured I might as well tell her, even though I didn't know if she would understand.

"I went to the future. My dad built a time machine, and we went to the year 2020."

She didn't seem as surprised as I thought she'd be. "2020. Oh my goodness. That's something. Lordy."

"There were a lot of Negroes in 2020, marching in the streets."

She chuckled at that. "Is that right? Not like Cordial Falls."

"No."

"Marching in the streets. Like Selma."

I didn't know what she meant by that.

She was quiet for a spell. Then she stared out the window. "And boy, we don't say 'Negros' anymore. We say 'Black folks.' 'Brothers and sisters,' you understand?"

"Oh, sorry, Mrs. Cummings." I thought I remembered what Dad said about which word to use, but I must have gotten it wrong.

'Negros.' That's how we said it in the '60s."

I didn't know what "the '60s" was. I wanted to ask her, but sometimes you don't get any more of a straight answer out of Mrs. Cummings than you do out of my dad.

"They marched then too. We had Dr. King. Mm-hm. God rest his soul."

I wondered if she was imagining things. Was Dr. King her doctor?

"In the '70s we had Black power." She was smiling and laughing to herself and looking out the window like I wasn't even there.

"What's that you say, Mrs. Cummings?"

She looked back at me like she forgot I was in her house. "Oh, Patrick." She shook her head like she was trying to jog her memory. "No, it's the 1950s. This is the 1950s. I know that. No, I—" Her lip started to quiver, and she nodded to herself like she was making sure she remembered things right. "He'll take care, now my family's gone. We'll go back to the past."

She was mumbling to herself, and I couldn't make out what she was saying. She looked at me and smiled, then reached out to pat me on the shoulder. I backed away so she wouldn't try to hug me or anything.

"You live in the past, Patrick. You live in," she trailed off. "What's the year now? What does my calendar say?"

I looked at her wall calendar even though I knew what year it was.

"It's 1957."

I had a feeling Mrs. Cummings was getting her daydreams mixed up with reality. Was she talking about the years of the 1960s and the 1970s? I started to get suspicious that she went in the time machine with my dad.

"Did you ever go to the future, Mrs. Cummings?"

She laughed, but it was a nervous laugh. "No, no. I'm just an old woman who gets confused, see. I've never been to the future. It's all good." She said it like she was trying to settle herself. "It's all good."

She leaned back in her chair and nodded to the garbage. "You best finish your chores, boy. You're going to miss your dinner."

I tried to size her up while I finished taking out the garbage. I put some cat food in Cleopatra's bowl and said "see you later" to Mrs. Cummings. She gave me a "goodnight" like everything was normal. But something was definitely not normal.

I started to wonder if we caused a time paradox. Did we mess up people's brain waves here in 1957 by going to 2020? Why was she confused about what year it was? And what did she mean by those other things she said? Did she know the future, or was she just being senile? It seemed like she was keeping something from me. She got nervous like all the other grown-ups in Cordial Falls do. She seemed scared, like she got caught making a mistake, telling me stuff I wasn't supposed to know.

Once I was back in my room, I closed the door and hung my sign on the doorknob. Shirts, comic books, and socks were scattered over the floor. But in the center of the mess, under the white box, was the newspaper from the future. I moved down to the floor and got on my stomach to look closer at it. The pictures were even sharper than on my comic book covers. I looked at the date at the top. Sunday, June 7, 2020.

The newspaper was thick. Twenty times bigger than any Cordial Falls newspaper I ever saw. I flipped it open and started reading. I thought maybe I'd get some clues from it.

On the first page on the inside, it said, "Rallies across globe demand social reform," and next to that was a picture of people wearing masks, holding a big sign that said, "Stop Black deaths in custody" and "Black lives matter" again.

Did the prejudiced people take over in a future war, and Black people lost, so they have to fight for their lives? Is that why they're angry? I read more of the article and it told about the crowds of protestors, just like I saw them. It said people were doing this protesting all over the world, even in Paris, France.

If Mrs. Cummings went into the time machine with my dad, why is she keeping it a secret? Did he make her promise not to tell so she wouldn't ruin my birthday surprise? Why would he make her do that? The way birthday surprises work is you don't have to keep them secret after you get the present. She's in the clear and can tell me all about it now.

Another story on that page was about floods, where it looked like a whole city was under water. Another was about military attacks in Iraq. I didn't know where that was, but they had a colored map on the page that showed it was right next to Africa.

I turned the page and there were so many stories about people getting killed. A bunch of people got killed in something called a "nightclub," two people protesting got killed when a car ran into them. A policeman killed a man by kneeling on his neck while three other policemen watched.

I covered my eyes. I couldn't look anymore. It was too much killing and too much torture. I was feeling my own neck get crunched under somebody's knee. I heard it cracking. I felt the car smash into my back, and my bones cracking. I felt the bullets slicing through my guts.

I opened my eyes again. There was another "Black lives matter" sign in front of a big mountain. It said it was Stone Mountain, in Georgia.

On the next page, soldiers in camouflage uniforms were wearing masks. It said they were helping people with the coronavirus. There was a big traffic jam of people trying to get a test to see if they had the virus. Then there was a big long story about people who didn't have homes. How could people not have homes in the future? If you ever heard *X Minus One*, you'd think all the problems would be solved by 2020. War, hunger, disease. But they're all worse!

I kept flipping through until I saw a big page with the words "Business Report" on the top, and I just about swallowed my own head when I saw what was under that. Right there in the middle of the page was a little color photograph of my dad. He was smiling, standing in a futuristic office. The blood drained out of my face. My elbows got weak, and I didn't think they could hold me up anymore. I changed to cross-legged and studied the picture. It was definitely my dad. Under the photo it said, "Legendary tech entrepreneur Mason Stoodle."

I didn't know what a "legendary tech entrepreneur" was, so I grabbed my dictionary from the nightstand. It didn't have "tech entrepreneur" in it. I looked up "tech" and it said "technology." Okay, I know what that is. Entrepreneur is "someone who organizes, manages, and assumes the risks of a business or enterprise." So, he's the boss. I know that too. I was pretty sure I knew what 'legendary' means, but I looked it up just in case. It means, "something from the distant past that may not be true."

Ah ha!

Now I was onto something.

The first line of the article was, "A fascinating backstory precedes Mason Stoodle's moment of clarity in 2012 as he emerged from a series of lengthy court battles, one a bitter custody battle with his estranged wife, another his fight to acquire Silicon giant Ilumi Industries, which he later subsumed under his mammoth Accel brand." As soon as I read all that, I knew I was going to be spending a lot of time with my dictionary.

About twenty trillion hours later, I got through the whole article. It wasn't that long, just two or three paragraphs, but it gave me some answers. I still had a lot more questions. But I got some excellent clues.

The first thing I learned was that my dad started a company in the future, in the year 2003. He invented something called the "accelerfuge." It makes it so those phones in the future can get tipped over and the screen stays right-side up, just like he showed me. They use this invention in all kinds of things, not just phones. They use it in hospital machines, satellites, and robot body parts in the future. In the year 2020, my dad sells this gadget all over the world and he makes billions of dollars. He's one of the richest people on the entire planet Earth.

How come my dad never told me any of this? How did he do things in the future when he lives here in the present? How long has he been using the time machine to visit the future? He must have lied to me when he said he only went there once to make sure it was safe for me. He must have visited over and over for ages, and he must have changed things and then traveled to different times so he could make money. He was making time paradoxes all over the place and he didn't care! He was messing up time to make money, even though he told me we couldn't go to the Old West because of time paradoxes. He probably has a pet dinosaur.

Another part of the article said, "Having weathered an ongoing controversy regarding his use of wage slaves in Angola to mine rare minerals needed to manufacture the accelerfuge, and in Bangladesh to assemble his computer chips, Stoodle stands triumphant among the multinational CEOs."

Another ninety billion hours later, my dictionary said that means that my dad has slaves. He's a villain! I noticed some of the time enforcers were Black people. Are they his slaves? Are Black people slaves again in the future? How can 2020 get any worse!?

I felt like I was busting this story wide open like Randy Stone. But it wasn't a good, satisfying feeling like on *Night Beat*. It was a horrible, sickening feeling that made my head hurt. My dad's whole life is a lie. He's been keeping terrible secrets. Is everybody in Cordial Falls in on it? They must be. They pretend everything is okay, but meanwhile my dad is a villain as bad as Mortimer Black. Or he's an Egyptian Pharaoh with an evil laugh who commands an army of slaves to build his phone-tipping gadget. Or maybe nobody else in town is in on it. Maybe they're all victims like me. Maybe he's planning to turn all of Cordial Falls into a slave colony. We'll be forced to dig a big mining pit, and we'll chop our pickaxes at the rocks in the scorching sun under the crack of his whip, day after day, every day, until we collapse from heatstroke.

But all these clues and all these little gold nuggets of information were just chicken feed compared to the biggest prize of all. See, the article was a book review, just like I've written a hundred times in school. It was somebody writing what they thought of a book. And you know what book it was? It was called, *Born to Accel*, written by none other than my dad, Mason Stoodle. He wrote a whole book! And I would bet all the gold in Fort Knox that this book has every answer in it. It's a book about his life. And if you wrote a whole book telling all about your life, you'd have to tell every secret.

I had to get my mitts on that book. Then I'd know everything. It's available in bookstores everywhere. That's what the newspaper said. But it's only available in 2020, not here in 1957. I've been to the Cordial Falls library and I've seen the bookshelf at Fawber's. If there are any books from the future here, I'd know about it. Dad wouldn't let me see this book in a million years, because then I'd know his whole plan. The game would be up. If I was Bill Cody, I'd walk up to Dad face-to-face and make him come clean. I'd give him the what-for, man-to-man, and make him spill the beans. But I'm not Bill Cody. I'm Patrick Stoodle, and I'd lose that one. The only way to get that book without him knowing is to sneak back to 2020 in the time machine and somehow find a bookstore and buy that book. That's what I had to do.

My questions and plans and thoughts and brainwaves were shooting out like lasers all over my room. I imagined them shooting out and burning the American flag hanging on my wall. They turned my wooden dresser into splinters. They tore up my bedsheets and my pillow and my bed frame. They smashed the empty aquarium on my shelf and glass exploded everywhere. I put my hands on the side of my head to hold it together. I was pacing and talking to myself, trying to think about how I could plan my escape. I looked out my window. It was dark. My clock said midnight. I don't think I ever stayed up this late.

I don't know when it was, but I tried to lie down. It was no use. I just tossed and turned and twisted up all my covers. My eyes were wide open. They burned. I cried, and then I laughed like a crazy person. And then I cried again, and then I got real still. I kept thinking about what I had to do. And I kept going through the steps of my plan in my mind. It was like I used to do with Myrtle, but this time it was real.

The last thing on Earth I wanted to do was go back to the diseased nightmare of 2020, but I had no choice.

7

THE STARS TWINKLED, and the sky changed from black to bright blue. A robin was singing outside my window like he was making fun of me for not sleeping a wink all night and having an empty feeling in my stomach.

Out my window is our front yard and some houses across the street. The sorry Stars and Stripes at the top of the Garbers' flagpole were just hanging there with no wind to boost them. The dew on the grass was all sparkly until the sun moved up and dried it out.

My eyes felt like they were getting crushed by a nutcracker, and my brain had a lightning storm going on inside it. Termites were crawling all over me and eating my skin. But none of that mattered because I came up with a good plan to escape to the future to get Dad's book.

He'd be busy soon because he's always doing things around the house in the morning. I already heard him getting up and tinkering. I was waiting for him to go outside.

I stuffed some things in my knapsack. I grabbed my cap, my compass, the newspaper, and the white box my dad got me from the future. I brought my dictionary too, in case I saw any new words. The knapsack was stuffed full. I covered my piggybank under my blanket and dumped it onto the bed so it wouldn't make any noise. I separated out the coins from the paper money and counted it. I had eleven dollars and forty-six cents. This was from my allowance and from what Mrs. Cummings gave me, minus candy and comic books and other things I bought that I can't even remember. It was a lot of money, but with luck, it was enough to buy the book.

The back screen door creaked open and slammed shut. I kept watch out my window and the next I saw Dad, he was walking in front of the garage unspooling the hose. I don't know what he was doing. Maybe spraying the driveway. Maybe watering the flowerbed.

I searched around for more stuff to bring. I took a couple of pencils. Why not?

There were a few last burs stuck in my shoelaces. I picked at them while I waited for the right moment to make my escape. It felt like the termites eating my flesh got inside my stomach and were pulling it in like you fold up a tarp, grabbing the edges with their tiny jaws and crinkling it up into a tight ball. My hands were shaking. Trying to pick out the bur pieces kept me from noticing how shaky I was.

Now there were voices outside. Dad was chitchatting with Mr. Ryerson, who was doing little chores around his yard too. It was the regular how-do-you-dos and what-a-nice-days, and then they started trading methods for how to take care of grass. I knew that was my chance.

With my knapsack slung over my shoulder, I turned my door handle nice and slow so you couldn't hear any clicking. I closed my door behind me, made sure my sign was on the doorknob, and tip-toed into the main room, keeping close watch on the front window to make sure Dad was still out there. Even though I couldn't see him, I could still hear him and Mr. Ryerson talking.

I went into the kitchen and threw a slice of cheese between two pieces of bread and shoved it in my knapsack best I could. It got smashed into a ball pretty quick.

The ironing-board stowaway door doesn't have a latch on it, and it doesn't creak either, so I opened it quick and pulled a dining room chair over and stood on it to reach the nail with the key ring on it.

It wasn't there!

This was a critical phase of my plan. It felt like somebody just tossed seven grenades at my feet with all the pins out. I stood there frozen, my plan foiled.

Without moving from where I was standing, I shined my eyes like a spotlight everywhere my neck could reach. I looked in the living room, the dining room, and the kitchen. Then I spotted his billfold and regular keys sitting on the little shelf between the kitchen and the dining room. Under all that was the little time machine key ring. I grabbed it, put the chair back nice and quiet, and then headed to the basement, making sure I stepped in the right places to make as few creaks as I could.

I went through the workshop and then to the water-heater room. There were three keys on the key ring, and I was pretty sure I remembered which ones Dad used. The one I remembered for the water-heater room didn't work, so I flipped it over and it worked upside-down.

Nice trick, Dad!

I ran back, turned off the workshop room light, and closed the water-heater door behind me to cover my tracks.

I think I'd make a good detective who catches jewel thieves. I would see how they tried to cover their tracks, I'd dust for prints, and I'd always catch them no matter how crafty they were. They wouldn't have a chance against me.

I worked my way around the water heater to find my way to the secret door. As soon as I found it, I felt around for the keyhole and tried to get the other key in it. I realized then that I should have brought my flashlight. I shook my head.

I brought pencils but not my flashlight?

It took me a while, but I finally got the key to fit. I took one last listen before I unlocked the door and went into the big room. I didn't hear any footsteps or commotion in the basement. I could only hope Dad was still outside chatting it up with Mr. Ryerson like any old day.

I flipped the light switch, and there was the time machine pod in the middle of the room, just like before. I made my way down the stairs and picked up the remote. It only had a few buttons on it, and I didn't get a good look at Dad when he used it before, so I had to try some things. I pressed a button and the lights to the whole room turned off. Suddenly it was pitch black. I tried to feel my way around the remote to find the same button again. Along the way, I found the door button because I heard the little sound the door makes when it opens. And eventually I got the lights to come back on.

I got in the pod and put my knapsack next to me. By then, I had the remote figured out enough to close the door. Then I found the time machine key, which was the last key on the ring, and put it in the ignition. The dashboard lights came on. I remembered the lights Dad touched on the dashboard before. It was a little green button on the left side. So I touched the same one in the same way I remembered him doing it. It didn't work at first. I tried hitting some other things and lights inside the pod went on and then off. Then the pod rotated, so I was facing the wrong way! I let out a little yelp when that happened. I imagined accidentally backing the time machine into the wall and crashing it like I did with our car and the Garber's garbage cans. Or maybe I'd go back in time and create a paradox that would destroy the world! Eventually I did something that made the pod turn to face the right way.

I kept pressing on the green light, but nothing happened. I tried to press hard and then soft. Finally, I must have hit it just right because the pod started moving, and the black circle got bigger.

As I moved into the black, I looked up at the top of the stairs. The door was still closed, and it seemed like everything was quiet. I started thinking of how much trouble I'd be in if Dad knew what I was doing. I couldn't take getting grounded again, not when I was so close to uncovering some real facts.

As soon as the pod was lost in the black, I got pushed to one side and my knapsack flew right in my face. That's when I realized I forgot the seat belt. I reached all over for it behind me and couldn't find it. Then I got pushed to the other side and bashed my head pretty good, and my knapsack slammed into my arm and I was wishing I hadn't brought the stupid dictionary. I saw the seat belts flapping around. I tried to grab them and pull myself to them and buckle them before I got slammed around more. I got jostled pretty good, but once I got them to click and got hold of my knapsack, I was all set.

I sat and watched the loops of light come towards me and pass over me. I decided I didn't want to starve to death, so I ate some bites of my balled-up cheese sandwich. I sat in there, chewing, and felt like the light loops were hypnotizing me. My eyes got real heavy.

When the pod came to a stop in the future, the sudden quiet jolted me, and I remembered where I was. I looked around for the remote to open the door. I couldn't find it anywhere. It must have bounced somewhere while I was zooming through time, but I didn't see it. I looked for a while. I started to sweat about it.

Where could it be? Am I going to be stuck in this stupid pod in 2020 for the rest of my life?

I thought of my dad and the time-travel detectives discovering my rotting corpse a hundred years from now.

"Too bad," they'd say. "The poor kid tried to travel through time on his own. He was only 12. He never had a chance."

Finally, I found it behind the seat. It was pushed into the

crease between the cushions. And lucky for that. Now this time machine wouldn't be my coffin. I remembered the door button and got out easy, then went up the stairs.

When I got to the final door, I remembered the mask. I stuffed it in my pocket after the first trip, so I grabbed it, put it back on, and opened the door.

Everything looked the same as yesterday. The same futuristic televisions, the same people with their phones. One of the time enforcers saw me come out the door. He looked at me like he was concerned, so I thought quick and made out like Dad was right behind me.

I looked into the door and said, "Just catch up with me when you're ready, Dad. I'm going ahead."

I didn't know if the time enforcers would arrest me and lock me up in time prison if they knew I was here alone. If they're Dad's slaves, I wanted to set them free, but I didn't know how. I was praying they would just let me be, or maybe protect me like they did before, but I didn't know what they would do without my dad here. I should have thought more about that part, but I didn't think about them when I made my plan.

I looked back and saw one of them put his hand to his ear like they do. I walked to the miniature grocery and asked the man behind the counter where I could find a bookstore. He pointed.

"Bookstore, three blocks. Across Market Street."

I nodded and was about to walk out the glass doors when I noticed the next day's edition of the newspaper I got the day before. It had a photograph on the cover that caught my attention. It wasn't the biggest photograph on the page, but I noticed it right away. It was a picture of my dad and me walking down the sidewalk with the time enforcers around us! I picked it up and looked at it. It had big words next to it that said, "Stoodle and son join SF protest." I already decided my dad is famous in the future because he wrote a book, but now I'm famous too because I'm in the newspaper. I wanted to take the newspaper, but I didn't know if I had enough money. I asked the counter man how much the paper was and he saidL

"Two dollars."

I put it back and hoped I'd see it again.

I walked to the glass doors.

"Be careful," the counter man said.

The streets were crowded with the protest like before, with the soldiers lined up. I felt naked without my dad there, but since the soldiers didn't bother us last time, I hoped they'd leave me be. People were chanting and yelling in the street, and the sidewalk was full of people too.

I kept my head down and walked in the direction the counter man pointed to. I looked back to see if there were any time enforcers behind me. There were two, one big Black man and another big White man. They were just close enough to make out with all the people in-between.

I kept moving. I saw a street coming up, so I counted one block. I'd have to count three before I got to the bookstore. The sidewalks were dirty, and some people walking next to me were chanting and moving along with the protestors, some were looking at their phones and crashing into me because they weren't paying attention to where they were going.

The feeling of being surrounded by people and wearing a mask over my face was like being suffocated with a pillow while someone is yelling at you. I kept moving my feet and trying not to think about how hard it was to breathe.

I noticed one person walking next to me. It was a lady with a quick, smooth walk like she was a panther on the hunt. She seemed to be trying to stay close to me while everyone else didn't seem to pay me much mind. She wore tight blue jeans. I noticed a lot of ladies wear that in the future. Almost none of them wear skirts like in 1957. She was wearing a mask and dark glasses just like the time enforcers.

I don't think she was a time enforcer because she wasn't

dressed the same and didn't have the thing in her ear. And they were all big men. Plus, she kept looking back at them like she didn't want them following her, just like me.

She said something and I couldn't tell what it was, but it seemed like she was talking to me. Everything was too loud to hear anything.

I crossed the first street. It was hard to see if any cars were coming because the street was crowded with the protest and the soldiers. I saw a flashing orange light on a big black circle sign that showed a man walking. I wasn't sure what the sign was trying to say, so I just kept walking, trying to stay out of the way of all the people. I felt like I was lost at sea, getting swept here and there by all the people around me. Once I met up with the sidewalk on the other side, I felt like I hit dry land again.

She stayed next to me. I kept my ears open in case she was trying to say something important. She said something again, and this time I heard most of it.

I think she said, "Hi. How are you?"

I said I was fine, but I didn't look at her because I wasn't sure if I should be talking to a stranger, especially in the future. What if she kidnapped me and sold me to space pirates?

"You doing okay? You all by yourself?"

I decided not to answer her again.

Then she said my name. Just my name.

"Patrick."

I looked at her, wondering how she could know who I was.

"Do you know me, Patrick?"

I couldn't see her face behind her dark glasses or her mask. She was a White lady but looked like she was out in the sun a lot. She had dark hair held up on her head with a colorful piece of cloth.

I kept walking and looking straight ahead to stay fixed on where I was going. I saw a second street coming up, and I was getting excited to count two blocks to the bookstore.

"Patrick?"

I didn't look at her again. I just shook my head real quick.

"I don't think I should talk to you."

I walked a little faster.

She kept up.

"I came a long way away to see you."

I didn't know what to make of this lady or how she knew me or what she was saying. Did she know me because I'm in the newspaper and famous in 2020? That was the only way I could explain it. I came up on the second street, looked both ways, and there were more people than cars again.

I started running. I couldn't run very fast because of all the people on the street, but I was getting sweaty, and had to move faster to get to the bookstore if I had any hope of getting back home in time.

The lady ran alongside me. I looked back and saw the time enforcers running too. There were three of them now. I wasn't sure who was going to catch me first or what they were going to do once they caught me, but I kept my mind fixed on getting to the bookstore. I started looking at the stores as I walked by them, to see if any of them had books in the window. I saw a bunch of useless things like fancy pink clothes, picture frames, and more phones.

The people in the street got louder. A bunch of them moved onto the sidewalk really fast and there was smoke coming from the street. People were yelling and screaming. Soldiers were pushing people. I had trouble getting past them. They were squished together thick, blocking the sidewalk. I worked to push through them, but I couldn't. Suddenly my eyes were filled with smoke and started burning, and I had to work extra hard to catch my breath. I started coughing really bad. I panicked and tore off my mask so I could breathe better.

The lady got on a knee next to me and coughed. She lifted up her glasses to wipe her eyes, and I looked at them. They were red, and she looked like she was crying.

She put her hand on my shoulder and looked back at the time enforcers. I looked back at them too. They were pushing people out of their way to get to me. They were set on snatching me up and carrying me back to time jail for sure.

My throat burned, my eyes stung, and I couldn't breathe. I couldn't get the smoke out of me.

She was trying to say something that seemed important to her, but she kept choking and coughing from the smoke like me.

"Patrick—" she coughed. "I'm your mother."

8

My chest was on fire. I kept rubbing my eyes, but it felt like my hands were made of razor blades. I couldn't breathe. I was crying like a baby. It was embarrassing. I didn't know this lady. Did she just say she's my mother!? She picked a swell time to turn screwy, right when I'm dying on the sidewalk from smoke that's probably dissolving my brain.

I searched myself for Bill Cody, Flash Gordon, or anybody to help me get some courage, but they weren't in there. I was getting pushed and tossed around by the riled-up crowd, and I couldn't think straight.

The lady gave up trying to talk. She covered her mouth and nose with her arm and coughed into it.

The time enforcers had different masks on now, like futuristic gas masks with little canisters on them. One of them grabbed my arm.

"Patrick, it's time to go." His voice was low and muffled through his gas mask.

I tried to pull away, but he was too strong. I tried to yell for him to let go of me, but no words came out. I couldn't even catch my breath.

I tried to say, "You don't have to be his slave! Run!"

He grabbed me under my arms, lifted me up, and started to carry me back toward the black building. I forgot I was holding onto my mask, and it fell out of my hand. I watched it fall to the sidewalk. People walked on it, dirtied it up, and scuffed it around until I couldn't see it anymore.

I kicked my legs and tried to scream, but I couldn't catch enough breath. The lady tried to get ahold of my feet to pull me in the other direction. I was crying and screaming from the burning, and now I was crying and screaming from being pulled apart on a stretcher in a Dark Ages torture dungeon. The time enforcer had his arm clamped onto my wrist. It felt like he was peeling the skin clean off. I thought for a second that my knapsack strap might tear, all my things would spill onto the sidewalk, and all my paper money would blow away with the smoke.

Soldiers with gas masks started breaking through the crowd. They were bashing people with big sticks and knocking them out of their way. I couldn't see the soldiers so good after that, but the time enforcer set me down and started talking to the soldiers. They weren't talking so much as yelling, but I couldn't hear what they were saying. Some of the time enforcers opened wallets out and showed them to the soldiers. They were pointing at me and yelling.

I wanted to run but there was nowhere to go with the crowd so thick.

The lady stayed close by me, hanging over me like she was protecting me from everything.

My eyes were burning out of their sockets. Breathing in the tiniest lick of air took all my strength, and the smoke kept coming into my nostrils. I thought for sure I was dying. It wouldn't be the H-bomb after all. It would be this future nerve gas that can kill you even faster than German mustard gas. I never thought I would die on a nightmare future battlefield, especially when I was only 12.

The lady hunched over me and moved us away from the soldiers through a break in the crowd. One of the time enforcers tried to follow her, but a soldier stood in his way. I saw only pieces of all this through the fog with my burning eyes. I could only open them for a second, and then the burning made me want to scream.

I heard a sound like whiz-bangers, and I saw soldiers firing rifles, and people screaming. I was in the middle of a war!

The lady kept holding onto me while we walked through the street to where the smoke wasn't as thick.

"It's going to be okay," she said, coughing. "I got you."

She ran across the street and then kept moving down it. Smoke was still all around us, but only in pockets. I saw people running out of the smoke and then back into it. Some of them had signs. One person had a big black sign made out of cloth as big as a flag but wasn't holding it up anymore. He was just dragging it on the street while he was running.

I lost track of where I was. How would I ever find the bookstore? The smoke started clearing up, but my eyes still hurt, and I was choking on my last breath. My chest felt like it was caved in. People were running around in every direction.

In a clearing where the gas cloud opened up, I saw a Black teenager with baggy pants and no shirt leap on top of a car in two steps. His eyes were wide, like lightning was shooting out of them. He waved a little black flag and yelled as loud as he could.

"Black lives matter!"

It was like he was a Comanche about to die in battle, and this was his last battle cry to the Sky God. I kept hearing his cry afterwards in my head.

The lady stopped in a doorway to a store that was clear of smoke.

A different lady came up to us. She poured water from a wrinkly plastic bottle all over my face. It cooled my eyes down a little.

"Damned police. It ain't right," she said.

The lady holding onto me managed to get a "thank you" out to the other lady.

The other lady just nodded and said, "You going to be okay, little man."

That was good to hear because it was just like something Mrs. Cummings would say. For a second, I was back in Cordial Falls, sitting and having a butterscotch candy in a house that smelled like butter in a pan.

The lady seemed to have somewhere else to go because she ran off in a hurry. The first lady took my hand and walked with me.

"This way, Patrick."

I finally caught a breath. "I need—" My voice burned, and it was hard to get words out. "—to go to the bookstore."

"You want to get to a bookstore? Why do you need to do that, honey?"

"I have to get a book. My dad wrote a book."

"I know."

The more we walked, the more my lungs cleared up.

"How do you know? And how do you know my name?"

"Patrick," she said. She stopped and got down to my level again and looked me in the eye. "I'm your mother."

I guess I wasn't imagining things when she said it before. After she said it again, she cried, and I couldn't tell if it was from the nerve gas or if she was part sad and part happy. It seemed like she meant it. But was she on the level? I had no way to know. I needed more proof before I was going to believe some lady off the street. I had so many questions, and new questions piled on top of those questions. As soon as I thought of a new one, I thought of ten more. And then more questions piled on top of those. I couldn't keep them all straight.

I thought it through, best I could. But my mind was filled with so many other thoughts, all jumbled together in a big mess of burning lungs, war, time travel, a big red mark on my arm where the time enforcer practically twisted it off, and wondering how I would ever get back home.

"Patrick, honey, we need to go this way to get out of here."

She got up and tried to lead me by the hand, but I pulled against her, trying to get my bearings.

"No, I have to find the bookstore."

"It's closed, honey. The stores are all closed today. Because of the protest."

Looking around, I didn't see anything that looked like a bookstore. Where was the third block? Which street was the bookstore on? I was lost!

"We'll find a bookstore, okay? I promise. Come with me, please."

She seemed to know me, so I had to give her that. And she just risked her life to save me, so I had to give her that too. My dad's been lying to me my whole life, so maybe he lied about her too.

I walked with her. "When? I have to get home soon."

I looked at her close. She kind of looked like me. There was something in the shape of her nose that reminded me of me. I had to give her that too. But if she was my mom, how did she get to the future? Why did she leave me when I was little? Why am I seeing her now for the first time? How was I supposed to know she's not a liar just like him?

"How are you my mother?"

She smiled at that one.

"I just am."

"How did you get to the future?"

She shook her head.

"This isn't the future. This is 2020."

"I know. I came here in the time machine."

"There's no such thing as a time machine."

She was talking crazy now. I knew where I came from. At

least, I thought I did. Did I imagine it? Maybe I was so filled up with nerve gas that I couldn't tell real from make-believe anymore.

I stopped. "How did you find me? I didn't tell anybody I was coming here."

She laughed. "It's funny. I've had a Google alert on your name for years. I never see anything, but it popped up yesterday. It said you were in San Francisco with your father. I dropped everything and drove all night to get here. I knew exactly where you'd be, of course. So I waited there, in front of the Accel building, just hoping maybe I'd catch a glimpse of you, you know? I never thought I'd actually get to see you and talk to you. Oh my god, I'm so happy this happened, Patrick. I really can't believe it. It's so great to see you."

She tried to hug me, but I pulled back.

"If you're my mom, what's my favorite ice cream?"

"I have no idea. But I'm eager to learn. Honey, we have to keep moving. Your father's goons will be looking for us."

"The time enforcers?"

"No, the big men in the black clothes. The ones who tried to take you away."

"Yeah, the time enforcers."

"What does that mean?"

"They protect people who travel through time."

"No, honey. Tey're his private security."

"What does that mean? Are they his slaves?"

"What? No!"

"How do you know so much?"

"I'm your mother."

My arm hurt, and my breathing still wasn't back to normal. I walked along with her, and after a few steps, I felt a volcano in my stomach. I stopped and threw up all over the sidewalk. It felt hot and scraped my throat something awful. I think it was the crumbled up sandwich I ate. She used the bottom of her shirt to wipe my chin.

"There, there," she said, just like a mother would.

"You're really my mom?"

"Yes, I am."

She wiped tears off my face.

"How do you know?"

"How do I know? I'd know you anywhere, Patrick. Even though I haven't seen you in so long. You're my baby. But you're so grown up now. Look at you."

"Okay, but I'm not a baby, so don't call me that."

She laughed at that. "Okay, I won't call you that. Deal?"

I nodded. She looked at me like she was sizing me up.

"You've grown up! You're such a handsome young man. Oh my god."

"I have to go home. My dad is going to find out I'm gone."

"He already knows, honey."

"How do you know that?"

"I'm your mother."

My feet felt hot on the ground. I started feeling tears building up. The situation was getting out of control.

"Take me back, please. I don't know you. I have to go home. I have responsibilities. I can't stay in 2020. I have chores. I have to take care of Cleopatra, and Mrs. Cummings, and my dad will miss me."

"Patrick, I'm sorry, but I don't know how to get you home. I'm not taking you back into that protest. We're both going to get killed. Don't worry. Your dad can take care of your chores."

"No. I have to get to the time machine!"

"I don't know what that is, or where it is. If it's in the building, we can't go back there. It's a war zone." She took my hand, and we walked down the sidewalk more.

I thought of what my dad must be feeling right now, if he really knew I was gone. He's probably worried sick that I'm loose in the future, in the war zone without my mask. Maybe he thinks of me more as a pet than a son, but people care about their pets too. I felt his worry. He probably thinks he'll never see me again, or that he has to build a whole new time machine to come after me. That would take him a month! If I had a way to let him know I'm okay, I would. But how can I get a message to 1957? I don't think that's even possible. So if this lady can't get me back to the time machine, I have to stay with her until I figure out how to get back. But what if she's not who she says she is?

We turned onto a new street. Bright colored signs were everywhere—on buildings, in front of shops, and even on the sides of garbage cans.

"Where are you taking me?"

"Right now we just have to get out of here."

She took a phone out of her purse and moved her fingers around on it.

"What are you doing?"

"I'm calling a car. I think we can get one from here. They weren't coming right into the protests, but maybe we're far enough away."

"Calling a car?" I wondered if that's how cars worked in the future, if you just call them on your phone and they come and get you and then give you a ride to wherever you want to go. Maybe robots drive them.

"Yeah." She was concentrating on her phone. I got in close and tried to get a peek at it. There were all kinds of words and colors and what looked like a map on the screen.

"Oh my god. Uber's not working."

"What's Uber?"

"That's the car, honey."

"Your car has a name?"

"It's not my car. It's just a car."

"You should say, 'Oh my *gosh.*' It's a bad word to say, 'Oh my god.'"

She smiled. "Is that right?"

I nodded. I don't know why I decided to say that. It wasn't a cussing rule I cared much about, and I'm not sure why I was coming down on her so hard about it. It popped in my head because I hardly ever heard anybody say it.

"Did you learn that in church?"

"I guess so."

"Well, it's a good rule. We shouldn't take the Lord's name in vain. I apologize, okay?"

I caught a look at her face and she was smiling like she thought this was a funny conversation, but I could tell she meant it when she said she was sorry, so I nodded that it was okay.

Then she got excited looking at her phone. "I got one. There's a car. It says four minutes. I put in an address further up. We have to get there."

I didn't understand why she got so excited. We walked up the street faster.

"Are all cars robot cars?"

She laughed. "You have so much to learn, Patrick."

I didn't know what to say to that, but I thought she was probably right. I didn't know anything about the future.

"Will you let me be the one to teach you? I'd like to."

She was holding my hand while we walked, but she gave it an extra squeeze when she said that.

I wasn't sure how to answer. I didn't want to trust her, but I was lost in this time, and in too deep to get myself out. I had no one else to go to. I thought about it for a few seconds, and then I tried to make a bargain.

"Okay, I'll let you help me figure out 2020. But you have to promise to help convince my dad not to punish me too bad for stealing his time machine and going into the future by myself, and you have to help me get back."

"Of course I'll help you. I'd do anything for you." She stopped and got down next to me and hugged me. I let her do it this time. Somehow I didn't mind it when she did it. "Oh my god, I can't believe it's really you." She held me by the shoulders and looked at me and wiped tears from her face. Then she pulled back and said, "Gosh, I mean! Oh my *gosh*. Sorry."

We got to the address she was aiming for and stood there. There weren't too many cars around. There were some soldiers walking on the other side of the street. There were protesters too, but they were scattered around, not marching or chanting. We were at a crossing. It was two big streets with a traffic light in a big black circle.

I read the signs at the bus stop while we waited for the car. One said, "No matter who you are or where you're from, you're always welcome here. Sftravel.com."

Wherever this place was, it sure had a strange way of welcoming people.

A black car stopped in front of us.

"This is us," she said.

She took my hand, and we got into the car.

The driver was an old man with white hair. He talked to us about the protest and how hard it was to drive today. So the way cars work in 2020 is, you call and have somebody pick you up. It's not robot cars like I thought. What a disappointment!

Mom sat close next to me. She put her arm around me. I guess I'll call her "Mom" now because what else am I going to call her?

"You okay, Patrick?" She talked quiet and slow now. I could finally take a good listen to her voice. It was kind of scratchy, not quiet or dainty like some ladies. She had a short-sleeve white shirt on where you could see some of the skin below her neck. It was tan with a lot of little sunspots. Her arms had them too.

"I'm okay, I guess." That's what I said, but inside my stomach felt like I just ate ten boxes of Hot Tamales at once. My chest felt like a herd of stampeding elephants walked across it. My mouth was dry and hot and filled with the taste of smoke and throw-up, and it was dry as Death Valley from thirst. My head was stuffed from coughing, crying, and questions. My eyes felt like two big dust balls.

My mom found a plastic bottle of water in a little pouch inside the door. She unscrewed the cap and brought it to my lips. I coughed some of the water out at first because I didn't feel like I had enough strength in my throat to make it go down the right tube. She tried again, and I got some to go in. It was like hydrogen peroxide going down at first. It burned, but then my insides went numb and warm and it felt okay.

She put her hand on my back and gave it a pat.

Out the window I could see we were crossing the biggest and longest bridge I ever saw or could ever hope to see. It went on forever. It had tall silver towers in the middle and cables curving down the sides that went on for miles.

The seat of this car was softer than any car seat I ever sat in. My body went limp and sunk into it like quicksand. My eyes felt heavy. Mom held onto me tight and I rested my face on her arm, breathing in her smell. It was a new smell, but it was familiar somehow too, like the smell of my own house, the kind of smell you're so used to that you don't even recognize it.

9

AFTER THE DRIVER LET US OUT, we switched to Mom's car, and she drove us on a big highway. We passed by towns with big stores that had their names in bright-colored lights on top. We saw mountains and crops that went on for miles. Some of the plants I didn't recognize. Others I knew, like tomatoes and lettuce and a lot of just regular old hay. We saw a lot of palm trees, which I never saw in real life before. Some were taller than three houses stacked up.

Her car was more beat up than I imagined a future car would be. It was a small blue car with dents and scratches on the outside. The inside was dirty and the ashtray was crammed full of used-up cigarettes.

My mom is a lot different than my dad. She talks more, for starters. She's almost always talking. And she seems to be interested in what I have to say. With my dad, I would say something, he would say something back, and that would pretty much end the conversation. And lately we haven't been talking much at all. But with my mom, the conversation keeps going. And then other conversations get started inside of the conversations already going, and then new conversations start up inside of those conversations. Sometimes three or four conversations are happening at the same time. She laughs, asks me questions, and then I laugh because she has a funny way of talking. She moves her hands a lot, has a lot of energy, and seems to be having so much fun talking.

I noticed her big smile and white teeth all in a perfect row. Once in a while she took her glasses off and I caught a look at her eyes. They're sparkling bright blue and have little pointy lashes on the top and bottom.

She only smoked once while we drove. She said it wasn't good to smoke around kids, but she couldn't help doing it once.

Sometimes she would look in her little mirror and then look out her back window and say she didn't like the look of a car that was behind us. Then she would slow down and see if the car would go past us.

She kept telling me how much she loves me, how glad she is to see me, and how much she missed me. And she kept touching me—holding my hand, grabbing onto my arm, squeezing my shoulder, running her fingers through my hair, pinching my chin, putting her hand on my back, licking her finger and then rubbing it on my face to clean it, grabbing my knee, resting her hand on my knee, hugging me, pulling me toward her, wrapping her arm around my head and pulling me in, caressing my arm, rubbing my arm, rubbing my head, rubbing my back, and things like that. I could do without the licking of the finger and then rubbing my face to clean it, but everything else felt nice.

She talked a lot about my clothes, my haircut, and my cap, saying all of it was too old-fashioned. I put my cap on because the sun was coming right into my eyes while we were driving at first.

"You look like something out of an old TV show," she said.

I told her that this is how everybody dresses in 1957.

She just shook her head at that and said, "Mason," like it was a big sad disappointment to her.

I asked her why she didn't wear a mask to protect from the killer virus.

She said, "I probably should, but I figure there's already enough to worry about with everything else going on."

I asked her if I should wear a mask.

"I don't see a lot of kids wearing masks, at least not around where I live. Tell you what, if we go someplace and they make us wear masks, we'll get you a mask to be safe, okay?"

I nodded.

We had a lot of conversations about the future. I asked questions about how things worked and what was different and other things that I might need to know. We got into a long conversation about school. She wanted to know what I was learning. I couldn't remember too many details except spelling, math, some film strips we saw about the Soviets and the H-bomb, and how to wash behind your ears. She told me we don't call them the Soviets or the Reds anymore. They're just the Russians. And she said they're not really our enemies, and we don't really worry about them launching an H-bomb at us anymore. I was glad to hear that. Maybe the H-bomb won't kill me after all. I asked her if all the H-bombs got disarmed, and she said she thinks they're all scattered around and pretty much anybody could launch one if they wanted. I wasn't so glad to hear that. I could still be vaporized by an H-bomb any second.

I kept asking her if each building we saw was a bookstore and if we could stop. She told me we needed to keep moving and that we'd get the book later.

She asked about the churches in Cordial Falls, and I told her what I knew about them. I don't know a lot. I said there was a little brown church that the people who call themselves "Lutherans" went to, and a little red church that the people who call themselves "Catholics" went to, and a little white church that I went to with Dad, but I couldn't remember if our church had any kind of name.

"It's just regular church," I said.
"Is it Pentecostal?"
"I don't think so."
"Baptist?"
"No."
"Methodist?"
"I don't think it's that."
"Oh God, not Mormon!?"
"No."
"Presbyterian?"
"That one sounds right."
"Well, that's okay, I guess," she said.

I never thought much about church. I believe in God because somebody had to make the world and everything, but it's not a very fun thing to think about or daydream about. Some people get carried away with it. Like the Seavers. They spend all week talking about church stuff and getting happy about God and talking to people about the Bible. Dad never paid it much mind except saying a little prayer once in a while before dinner that didn't seem to have much thought behind it. Mostly, I just figured maybe it would make more sense to me when I got older. For now, I've just been going along with it. Dad says going to church every Sunday is the right thing to do because we should think about right and wrong and about God, Jesus, the universe, and helping other people. And the reason we should do that is so we're not always thinking about ourselves all the time. That's not exactly how he put it, but it was something like that.

But now I don't want to do anything Dad does. Why would I want to listen to somebody who has slaves, who lies to me, and didn't even tell me he wrote a book? I got thinking about it right there in the car, and I decided I wasn't going to do or think anything anymore just because he wants me to.

And why didn't Dad tell me my mom was living in the future? Why didn't he tell me she was so nice? Why did he make it so hard for her to visit us in Cordial Falls?

Mom talked a lot about her life. She told me she was living in a place called Yuba City and working at a job called "paralegal." I asked what that was. She tried to explain it. It sounded like working for Perry Mason. She told me she's not going into work now because of the virus, but she's getting paid anyway from the government. She told me she had a car accident last year and had to have surgery in the hospital. She said she spends a lot of time with her sister who has two kids.

"You'll meet them. We'll be seeing a lot of them," she said. "They're your cousins."

"I have cousins?" I asked with a big smile.

"Yep." She smiled back.

She said I was going to meet her mother, who lives nearby.

"So you have a new grandmother," she said. "And my brother Jerry. He's been staying with me." I'll meet him too, she said. She told me she had a dog, and that sometimes she volunteers at the nursing home, and that led to a story about delivering Easter eggs to the nursing home, and her dropping a bunch of eggs and having to clean them up. She said some of these things too fast for me to get in there with any questions if I wasn't following along. I was excited about meeting the dog.

The future didn't seem so bad with Mom around. She never mentioned the killer virus or the wars. It looked like a big impossible mess when I first got to 2020, like the end of the world was happening right there. But now it seems a little safer.

I wondered about Dad and his time enforcers. I asked her more about what she said before about them coming after me.

"Well, your father has the legal right to see you. He has custody."

I looked that up before, so I knew what it meant, but I still didn't know the whole story.

"Am I breaking the law by not being with him?"

She kind of laughed at that, but it wasn't a fun laugh. It was a laugh like she was scared.

"You're supposed to be with him, according to the judge."

"I'm not supposed to be with you?"

She took a long time to answer that one.

"We're going to figure it out, Patrick. Everything's going to be okay. I'm not giving you up." She put her hand on my knee and gripped it so tight that I jumped up in my seat. She got a big laugh about that.

"Oh my gosh that's so cute. You're ticklish! Now I know how to get you to do all kinds of chores."

"Hey, that's not fair!"

We were just joking around, but it was funny, and we had a good laugh.

We got off the highway to put gas in her car and pee. Everything in the filling station was colorful and plastic and looked like something out of a Buck Rogers comic, down to every detail. The numbers on the gas pump were lights that lit up and changed instead of regular dials. There was a tiny television right there that you could watch while you filled up your tank. And there were colorful signs and slogans everywhere. The place was huge. There were more pumps at this gas station than all the pumps in Cordial Falls put together.

While we were standing there pumping gas, a boy about my age got out of a car at one of the other pumps and stood there staring at me. At least, I think he was staring at me. He had black glasses on, so I couldn't really tell where he was looking. His hair was shiny and stuck up straight like he just woke up. He had shiny short pants made from a material like a piece of plastic or foil, and shoes that were as bright orange as a piece of candy. His shirt had all kinds of words and pictures on it that sparkled.

I guess I couldn't blame him for staring at me. We looked really different, and I was doing the same to him.

When we finished filling up, we went inside. It was like a grocery store in there, with all kinds of donuts and drinks and candy and newspapers. The only thing that seemed like it hadn't changed or been cleaned since 1957 was the bathroom. It was like an outhouse, but it had its own sink and was built right into the gas station building. They gave me a key attached to a big stick of wood to use it.

I came back to the car and saw Mom coming out of the gas station with a plastic bag. She smiled at me in her dark glasses. She emptied the bag out on the back seat. She got Pepsi and root beer and orange soda in big plastic bottles. And she got a Three Musketeers bar, a Hershey bar, one of those big king-sized Reese's peanut butter cups, and even powdered donuts. My eyes just about popped out of their sockets. I never saw anyone buy so many desserts at one time. She also bought cigarettes.

"I figured we should live it up," she said. "You know why?"

"Why?"

"You know why."

"No, I don't."

"Because it's your birthday, silly."

"How did you know it's my birthday?" As soon as I said it, I realized the answer. "Oh, because you're my mother."

She smiled at that and put her arm around me. "That's right. I gave birth to you."

"Mom, that's disgusting."

"Best day of my life."

I just shook my head at that one.

Once we were back on the highway, we drove a while and listened to music on the radio. Radio music in the future is nothing like radio music in 1957. It's fast and has a lot of electronic-sounding beeps in it so you can't even tell what the instruments are. And most of the singing is fast, loud, and just plain crazy.

Mom got interested in another car that she thought was following us. She slowed down again, but it wouldn't pass.

"I don't like that he's not passing me," she kept saying. She talked so much it was like getting a sports play-by-play of everything she was doing and thinking.

"Come on, whoever you are. I'm no fun to tail. Move along."

Then she looked in the mirror and got upset. Her shoulders dropped like she'd lost whatever game she was playing with the other car.

"Oh no. No, no, no, no, no," she said.

There were red and blue flashing lights all around. I looked back and saw that the light was coming from inside the car behind us. It was a brown car with dark windows.

There was no siren, but I figured out it was a police car. I asked if we were in trouble.

"I don't know. I hope not. Damn it. Don't worry. Everything's going to be okay. God damn it."

My mom cusses a lot. I gave up on the reminders pretty quick.

She slowed down and pulled onto the side of the highway. The other car pulled up behind us and kept flashing its lights. The cars and trucks on the highway zoomed by us fast while we sat there.

I started shaking, remembering what I read in the newspaper. "Wait, Mom, is he going to kneel on our neck and kill us?"

"No, honey."

"But that's what police do in the future!"

"I know, and it's awful. But we're going to be fine, honey. We're White."

"What does that have to do with anything?"

"Shh." She got some papers out of her glove box and flipped her glasses up on top of her head.

"Everything's going to be okay," she said.

A policeman got out of the car and walked toward her window.

My palms were sweating. I felt trapped in the car, and I started breathing too fast. My lungs still didn't feel right after the nerve gas. I couldn't get enough air without my chest hurting. I just wanted to be driving with my mom as fast as we could, and

I wanted to get as far away from everything else and go meet my cousins and her dog, and maybe play in the yard with them.

She pressed a button and her window came down.

"Hello, Officer."

"Ma'am, do you know why I pulled you over you today?" he said.

"No, Officer, honestly, I don't." She laughed like she was nervous.

"Your vehicle and your license plate match an all-points bulletin issued to state troopers and sheriff's departments in the area."

"Uh-oh. What did I do? I don't understand."

She handed him a little card that he looked at.

"Is that your son there? Is that Patrick?"

"Yes, that's my son."

Everybody in the future seemed to know who I was. The policeman must have seen my picture in the newspaper. He looked at me, but he was wearing dark glasses like Mom, so I couldn't get a good look at him. You can't see anyone's eyes in the future.

"Is your name Patrick Stoodle, young man?"

I nodded. I was too nervous to answer in words.

The policeman stood up. I could only see his little round belly in his tight brown uniform. He took a deep breath, and then brought his head back to the window.

"The bulletin advises that you aren't the boy's legal guardian, and your driving with him constitutes a kidnapping offense."

"Okay, wait just a minute," Mom said. Her voice was shaky now.

My body got hot. I couldn't just sit there and let him say my mom was kidnapping me. I said really loud, "Please don't take me back to my dad! Please, just let us go. I want to be with my mom! I promise my mom didn't kidnap me. I promise. I want to be with her."

My mom smiled a shaky smile and patted my chest and said,

"Shh, Patrick. The grown-ups need to talk about this."

Something electronic beeped on the policeman. Then there was a voice on his walkie-talkie that said something I couldn't understand.

"Officer, my son was in danger. His father had left him alone in the middle of a protest in San Francisco, and I saw him and I couldn't just leave him there. That would have been extremely negligent."

The policeman put out his hands like he didn't want to hear my mom's side of the story.

"Ma'am, I'm sure there's a good explanation for why you have your son. And what we're going to do is, we're going to get to the bottom of it with the proper authorities, and make sure that everybody is safe and where they belong. I'm going to ask you to come with me to the county sheriff's station. I'm going to ask you to ride with me in the squad car, and we're going to sort everything out when we get there."

I just about swallowed my own neck. Mom covered her eyes like she was crying. Would he take us to jail? Or would he take me back to Cordial Falls? If he did that, Dad would never let me see my mom again, not even if I had a hundred time machines.

Without looking at us, he stepped back from the window and said, "Step out of the car, please."

10

I MADE FISTS the whole time we rode in the back of the police car.

Mom squeezed them and kept whispering, "Shh," and "Everything's going to be okay."

She was calling people on her phone with her other hand. She called and asked someone about meeting us at the station, talking all serious. And then she had to get the address of the station from the policeman. She called someone else and was more herself. She told the person what happened and how worried and scared she was. I didn't like hearing that because it just made me wonder more if I was going to get sent back home.

Between the front and back seats was a fence like we were in a cage.

When Mom was between phone calls, the policeman looked into his mirror at her and said, "Mason Stoodle is the father, is that correct?"

My mom nodded. "He has official custody. Yes."

"Well, I'm not going to lie to you, Ma'am. When you're dealing with an extremely powerful individual like that, they can hire lawyers to kingdom come."

"Oh, I know all about it." She tucked her hair behind her ear when she talked to the policeman. "I just hope the court is understanding of the situation, you know?"

"You never know how a judge is going to come down on these things," the policeman said.

"No, you don't."

Mom and the policeman kept talking about boring grown-up stuff. I closed my eyes and listened to the beeps and pops and scratchy voices that came on the policeman's radio. And my mind wandered. I imagined the policeman realizing that he should just let us go, take us back to our car, and say "never mind" about the whole thing. He just had a malfunction in his tin brain, is all.

Then my mind went the other way. He doesn't care no matter how much I scream and cry, because he's a robot with no feelings, and he takes me back to my dad and makes me stay in Cordial Falls forever, and every time I try to ride my bike out of town he stands guard and says, "Step back into Cordial Falls, please," in his robot voice.

If they force me to go back to Cordial Falls, it'll be like pulling chewing gum off the bottom of a shoe and trying to chew it again. When I get there, I won't have any flavor anymore, and there'll be bits of rock and sand in me that'll never come out, and it'll taste terrible. I'll be nothing but a chunk of gray goo that turns hard. I'll be a big glob of no-good gum and I'll pick up even more dirt and dust from rolling around from place to place, from my room to the dinner table, and then to school, and everywhere. I won't be able to do my chores or brush my teeth or anything because I'll have no arms. I'll never know what the real world is outside Cordial Falls. I'll only know the world my dad made. I'll eventually get stuck to the floor somewhere, getting stepped on over and over and turning black and getting smashed and flattened out until you can't even tell anything's there.

The police car stopped in front of a building in the middle of a field next to the highway. Lots of other police cars were parked there. We went inside, where a different policeman took my knapsack and helped himself in it like it was his. He took out my phone box, opened it, and looked it over. He tried to put it back in the box just like new but didn't do a very good job. The flaps were hanging open, and the phone was barely in there. He stuffed it in the knapsack along with all my other things and gave it back to me. He looked bored.

We came through a hall to a big counter. Mom stood there talking to more police while they made me sit on a bench against the wall. Some of the police were ladies. Some of them wore masks, but not all of them. Mom looked back at me every now and then and smiled and blew me kisses. I wasn't in the mood for any kisses to get blown at me, but I tried to smile once. I didn't understand what they were saying, and half the day went by. There wasn't much to look at in the station. Things got boring real quick.

Eventually a mostly bald man with a white shirt and tie who was shaped like the clown inside a jack-in-the-box came and shook my mom's hand. She seemed to know him. He had a black briefcase. She introduced us, and he seemed nice enough. He was a lawyer, she said. He worked in her office.

Another man with a briefcase came in the station after that. He didn't seem nice at all. He was wearing a brown business suit and had white hair and a face like a jagged rock that you could never hope to carve a smile into. They all talked, and then they went into a separate room with a big table and talked some more. They opened their briefcases and all sorts of papers were spread on the table. I could see them through a glass wall from where I was sitting. Any minute I expected them to come out and say, "Okay Patrick, time to go home to your dad." And my body felt heavier every second, like I was sinking into the Earth's gravity, deeper into the crust, the pressure getting greater by the minute.

I think I might have dozed off sitting on that bench. But I remember my mom bringing me into the room once. All the people in there, the lawyers and my mom and a policeman, wanted to see all the cuts and marks on me, and they took pictures of them. My cheek scratch from the thorns, the cut on the back of my head from the rock, and the red mark on my arm from the security man.

I also remember Mom sitting next to me on the bench, holding onto me. The nice lawyer, the bald one, was sitting next to her.

He looked at me and said, "Considering all the factors involved, both the social worker and the guardian ad litem assigned to the case decided to issue a temporary ruling allowing you to stay with your mother for a few days. Your feelings were taken into consideration, Patrick, so it's good that you spoke up to the officer. What you said was paraphrased in the officer's report and it went a long way to furthering this outcome, as did the suspicion that you've been mistreated under your father's care." He smiled, nodded, and looked at my mom and me. "There's a court date in a few days. Your mother and father have to appear to hash things out moving forward, but for the intervening period, you're free to go with your mother."

I didn't quite understand everything he said, but I understood the last part. I looked at my mom and she was smiling, and her eyes were red from crying. I lunged at her and hugged her as hard as I could. I didn't have anything to say.

She shook more hands and gathered up our things. She said "thank you" over and over to all the officers and lawyers. She laughed and made a long goodbye out of it. I stayed close by her. We walked out of the police station, and our car was parked out front. I guess the police brought it there.

Once we were in the car, she said a loud "Whew!" and then let out a big laugh. She put her hand on the back of my neck and rubbed it.

"We did it! How are you feeling, honey? Are you doing okay?"

I nodded. I gave thanks to the heavenly angels that we were away from the police.

She asked if I wanted a treat from the bag, and I picked the Hershey bar. She opened the Pepsi, took a sip, and then made a face.

"Aw, it's warm," she said.

I made a face too. I don't like the taste of warm soda either. It's like drinking syrup. I could practically taste it when she made that face.

She put the soda in a little holder between our seats that fit the bottle just right. I had chocolate all over my hands and face from the Hershey bar and I could tell she thought of tackling it with the licked-finger routine, but knew it was too big a job for that.

"You know what I want to do?" she said. "I want to get you some clothes." And before she got back on the highway, she stopped at a big department store that was just down the road from the police station.

I thought my clothes were fine, and the way she was talking, I was afraid she wanted to dress me up like a doll. I'd rather get my brains scooped out and fed to the offspring of alien invaders, but she didn't listen to reason. So we made a bargain. I said she could get me clothes if I could buy my dad's book.

She said, "You've got yourself a deal."

We went in, and the first thing we did was go into the bathroom where I washed chocolate off my face and hands. The bathroom was so bright it hurt my eyes. Then we saw the clothes section because it was right in the front of the store. It was bright in the rest of the store too.

One thing I've noticed about the future is that the lights are a lot brighter—outside the stores, inside the stores, inside buildings. It's like a ray is shooting at you all the time. That's probably why everybody has to wear dark glasses.

There was music playing in the store. At first I couldn't figure out where it was coming from, but then I noticed there were speakers way up on the ceiling.

Mom helped me pick out some pants, some shirts, and some shoes. She wanted to get me clothes that looked more like church clothes than everyday clothes, but I wouldn't hear of it. I never liked dressing up too much. And thanks to the heavenly angels, Mom is more agreeable than Dad ever was. If he wants something, you're best off just going along with it, because getting him to change his plans is like trying to get a mule to ride a bicycle.

The shoes were soft and comfortable. They even had orange ones like the boy at the gas station. I didn't want bright orange shoes, though, so I picked a plain white-and-black pair of sneakers that looked like my regular shoes but were a lot more comfortable. It was like walking on pillows.

I got a new pair of jeans and picked out a few shirts. I saw a lot of shirts like the kind I usually wear, but Mom said she wanted me to look like I belonged in the 21st century. After I ruled out the fancy shirts, she showed me the kinds of shirts kids wear in the summer in 2020. They all had pictures and words on them. I picked some out that I liked. One had a bunch of funny cartoon characters on it that said "Pokemon" with the big and small letters all mixed up. One had a drawing of a fat little peanut-marshmallow-looking monster in overalls that said "One in a Minion." Mom thought that one was funny. My favorite was a blue shirt with a white star in the middle and red and white circles around the star. The shirt was old and faded. I asked Mom if this was a hand-me-down store, and she said these shirts were all new. How does that make any sense? But it's pretty handy that it's already worn in without even having to wear it. I like the shirt because the symbol looks like Captain America's shield. This is funny to me because the future people who made it probably don't even remember the Captain America comic.

A big voice came on a speaker that took over the music. They said something about customer service and register number three. It sounded like an important announcement, but Mom said I didn't have to pay attention to it.

In the book section, we found Dad's book. His picture was on the cover. He was staring into the sun, smiling. I caught a look at my mom turning her eyes up at the book. I felt like I was holding in my hands the secret scroll that had all the answers to my life, that I'd crossed the eons to get my hands on. The whole rest of the world disappeared while I looked at the book and flipped it open and saw the words my dad wrote. I felt like I had a magic key to look inside his brain and figure out all the answers that he was keeping from me. I held the book close like it was a life preserver and I was drowning in a stormy ocean of acid in the middle of the night on a far-away planet—a planet where the night is twelve years long.

My eleven dollars and forty-six cents was plenty. The book was on sale for nine dollars and ninety-nine cents.

I started to read it before we even got back to the car, and I kept reading once we started driving. It wasn't a book for kids. It had a lot of big words in it about technology, but I didn't bother with the dictionary because I was in a hurry to get to the good parts. He wrote about his business at first, and all the things his invention could do. He didn't say anything about living in the past and the future at the same time. Not yet. Then he wrote about his college, how he thought up his gadget, and how he made money at it. So far he was only writing about his life in the future.

Come on, Dad. You'd better spill the beans about your life in the past before this book is over!

My insides were feeling a little woozy from reading in the car. I didn't want to stop, but I had to. I felt like I was going to throw up. By that time Mom said we were almost home.

"You're such a good reader. I've never seen a kid concentrate for so long. Are you learning anything?" Every time Mom gives me a compliment, it feels like I'm sitting in a warm bath eating a piece of chocolate cake.

I shrugged. "Not sure yet."

The sun was going down. We got off the highway and drove down a street that had hundreds of stores. They made the sky white with all their bright lights. Gas stations, department stores, restaurants. In the future they make it so even if you can't read you know what kind of store it is. One of them had a giant hamburger for a sign. The stores kept coming, store after store after store. Some were in big buildings. Others were clumped together with a bunch of different stores in the same building. I couldn't even count them all. Why did people in the future need so many blasted stores?

We turned off that road and drove by houses. They were a lot of different colors besides just the yellow, light blue, and light green of Cordial Falls. Some were dark, some were made of bricks. One was even purple. Who would live in a purple house? But at least they came up with other ideas for how houses could look in the future.

She drove into a driveway of one of the houses. It had brick on the bottom half and dark green on the top. The garage was part of the basement, but she just stopped in the driveway. Stairs went up to the front yard and the door.

"Here we are," she said.

I didn't feel so good. I didn't know if it was from the reading and driving at the same time, or the Hershey bar, or the nerve gas that was still eating away at my insides, or just being in a new place.

We got out of the car, and a big man came out of the house. He wore a black shirt with a big American flag on it, but with black stripes instead of white. He had a little smile right smack in the middle of a pepper-colored beard that covered only his upper lip and chin. The rest of his big face was open. He had dark glasses on, and he wasn't wearing a mask.

He said, "Hey, you two" in a loud gravelly voice.

"This is my brother, Jerry, who I told you about," Mom said. "He's your uncle."

Mom gave him a hug, but she kind of leaned into it so their bodies didn't touch, only their arms and shoulders. Jerry didn't lean into it at all. He just reached around with one arm, smiling at me with his little mouth.

She said to him, "Look who I picked up!"

"Well, if it isn't the man himself! How are you doing, Patrick? I've heard so much about you." He just kind of stood there with his big stomach hanging out, smiling. "Big, strong-looking boy. Don't say much, but that's okay." He laughed.

"Oh, he's just nervous," Mom said.

I don't know why she had to embarrass me like that in front of a new person. I wanted to make a stink about it, but I was too tired. Also, I didn't want Jerry to think I was a brat.

"I made spaghetti. You two want to eat?"

"Is it spicy? He's a kid, Jer. He can't handle your crazy sauce. I can barely handle it."

"Well, it's got to have a little kick to it," his little smiling mouth said.

She took my hand and knelt next to me. "You hungry, sweetie? Maybe I can make you a peanut butter sandwich."

I shrugged.

"We should eat something." She looked at Jerry. "Oh my god, it has been such a day."

"I'll bet. You go up to the Gay Area, you never know what you're going to see."

She looked at him like she was annoyed. "Jer!"

"Ain't nothing but the truth."

She looked at me with a concerned face. "Are you feeling okay, hon?"

"Not really." I didn't want to talk anymore. I just wanted to sit somewhere and read my book.

She put her hand on my forehead. "Hm. You do feel a little hot."

Jerry said, "Hey, it's okay if nobody's hungry. You come on in and take a load off. We'll eat later."

Mom walked me inside. The house smelled like cigarette smoke and tomato sauce. A fluffy light-brown dog came trotting towards me with his tongue flapping out and his tail wagging. Mom said his name was Buster.

"You make yourself real comfy, Patrick," Jerry said.

I sat on the couch for a while and read my book. I got through more of the things Dad made that go inside computers. Mom and Jerry talked and smoked cigarettes in the kitchen, and they smelled terrible. Then they sat at the table and invited me over after a while. I was kind of hungry, so I got up. I was surprised by how tired my legs were. I could barely walk to the table. Mom must have seen me hunched over because she asked if I was going to make it.

When I sat, I saw a sandwich and a couple of orange things on my plate that looked like carrots carved into little round tubes.

Jerry put his hands together before we ate. "Lord, we know you're watching over us tonight. We thank you for bringing young Patrick to us. We ask that you watch over him, and America, and guide the leaders of this great nation to do your will. Amen." Then he served the spaghetti and sauce to himself out of two big separate bowls.

Mom had a little bowl of lettuce and tomatoes.

"How was the protest? You were really in the thick of it, huh?"

Buster was sitting and looking at me. I fed him one of my carrot tubes. He ate it, but then walked away. I guess he doesn't like vegetables.

"Oh my god, were we ever. Right, Patrick? Sorry—oh my *gosh*! I keep forgetting," she smiled at me. "We got tear gassed."

"No kidding?"

"Mm-hm, and almost got taken away by the riot police."

"Couple of lawbreakers!"

I didn't feel like I had anything good to add to the conversation, but I wanted to be a part of it, so I said I heard people chanting "Black lives matter."

Jerry shook his head and said, "Don't you listen to that, Patrick. All lives matter."

"That's racist, Jerry," Mom said.

"If you think one color of people matters more than another," Jerry said, "that's what racism is, right there. God loves everybody the same, and so should we. We're not supposed to see color." He took a big bite of his spaghetti.

I wondered why the Black people I saw were so upset. Especially the teenager I saw on the car. Were they trying to say they were more important than White people? I must have said this thought out loud because Jerry shook his head again.

"That's a good question, Patrick." His mouth was full of spaghetti. "It really is. Because, fact is, more innocent White people are killed by police than Black people. A lot more. And the Blacks, they're the ones killing each other, but you never hear them complaining about that." He raised his eyebrows.

"You're watching *Fox News* too much," Mom said. "All they want to talk about is Black-on-Black crime."

"What? That's the facts."

It sounded like a lot of people were getting killed by police in 2020. I started thinking about all of those dead people and I didn't feel like eating anymore. I kept thinking about the soldiers on the street hitting people with those sticks. Mom called them "riot police." Maybe they weren't soldiers at all. Maybe that's what some police wear in the future. I wonder if they were trying to kill those protestors. Were they going to kill us? My body got tense and sweaty, and I felt lucky that we got out of the police station alive. I wondered if it was because we were White people, like Mom said.

"What ticks me off is that they've ruined sports now too. I can't watch football. I can't watch basketball. They're saying 'Black lives matter' in college sports now. Everybody has to be a social justice warrior. I just want to enjoy a game. Is that asking too much?"

"That's your White privilege talking right there," Mom said.

"It's a free country. I'm entitled to watch a game and not hear about that crap," Jerry said.

I started feeling the nerve gas in my chest. It was bubbling up. I started coughing again. It hurt everywhere, and it swirled around with the Hershey bar, the smell of spaghetti, the car reading, the cigarette smoke, Jerry's loud voice, and everything else, and I had to ask where the bathroom was. Mom dropped her fork and rushed me into the bathroom where I threw up in the toilet. It tore up my throat, made me yell, and was so embarrassing with Jerry there. My whole body was shivering.

Mom wiped my mouth with some toilet paper she ran under the water.

"Poor thing," she said.

Jerry stood in the bathroom doorway. "Looks like the little guy has the flu."

The Punchline

11

I didn't get better. I faded in and out of sleep for the next few days. It seemed like all my body could do was sleep and suffer. My coughs were tearing out the inside of my neck, and my stomach felt like it swallowed the planet Jupiter and was trying to digest it. Mom took care of me, made me soup, and fed me crackers, but I didn't keep much of it down. I spent most of my time on the couch in a little room Mom calls the TV room. It has a futuristic television and a couch. Sometimes Buster would come up to me and lick my hand or sit next to me, and that was nice. It was like having my own dog.

I read my book when I could, but my eyes got tired fast. It's rough going through it because it's mostly about computers. I wanted to skip ahead to see if there's anything in there about me or about Dad's life in the past, but I didn't want to miss anything important, so I'm reading every bit of it in the right order, trying to be patient to get to the good parts.

I didn't meet my new cousins yet because Mom says their mom doesn't want them to catch whatever I have. Jerry doesn't seem to be worried about getting sick because he would come in and try to talk to me all chummy. I was never sure what to say to him.

Another person who didn't seem to care about catching my sickness is my new grandma. She came over the second day I was there and she was so happy to meet me she pinched my ear and laughed out loud right in my face. She's shaped like a big pear and waddles when she walks. She has a voice like a nursery rhyme and a big belly laugh that bounces through the house. She wears glasses that she took off to look at me.

"Let me get a good look at this boy. Oh my word," she kept saying. "Oh my word, he's a nice-looking boy."

Grandma stayed over for a couple of days because she wanted to get to know me. But she didn't ask after me much, not like Mom does. She mostly sits, eats her arthritis pills, and sometimes does word-search puzzles from a booklet she has. When it comes to me, she tells me what I should be doing, or asks my mom if I'm doing certain things.

"Where does he go to Sunday school? Is he baptized? What does that man feed him? He's thin as a beanpole. Is the boy saved? Does he have a Bible? You have to get him a Bible, Marion." That's when I learned my mom's name is Marion.

I got the news real quick that Grandma is one of those religious people who talks about church stuff all the time. But she's nice enough and fun to have around because she's always in a good mood. She talks to me a fair amount, but if I ever try to say anything back, she just keeps talking at the same time about whatever she wants to talk about.

She gave me a bag of orange-slice candies for my birthday, but I was too sick to even think about eating them.

One night, when I was sitting on the couch coughing and feeling like I couldn't even get up, Grandma sat by me and held my hand and finally asked me some questions instead of my mom.

"Patrick, I want to talk to you about the Rapture."

I wasn't sure what she meant by that one, but I knew she would explain it because she just kept talking.

"Do you know Jesus Christ?"

Of course I knew of Jesus, and I started to say so, but she talked right over me.

"That's good. But do you really know him? Do you know he loves you? That he died to save you from sin? That's what it means to be saved, see."

I shrugged. I'm usually a little embarrassed to talk about religious stuff.

"Patrick, God loves you so much that he sent his own son to suffer and die on the cross for you. Did you know that?"

I felt like I was the one suffering and dying right now, not Jesus.

"His blood washes away our sins," she said.

She's usually laying it on pretty thick with the religion, but that night she got really carried away. She started talking about the future. She looked different while she talked. She put on a serious face, and I pictured her as a witch with spells and curses.

"We're in the last days, Patrick. The end of the world. The prophets in the Bible foretold it. The Lord gave us the signs and all of them are coming true. Praise his name. Someday—any day now—Jesus will come back and there's going to be a great tribulation." She waved her arms up on that word. "The angels will trumpet! And you want to be on Jesus's good side when that happens, I can tell you that."

I looked at her to try to figure her out. She was all worked up. I asked what it meant to be on Jesus's good side, and she started answering before I finished.

"You have to give your life to him."

I didn't want to give my life to anybody. I wanted it for myself. But I was too weak to argue, and I think she would have talked over me anyway.

"You have to pray. You have to say, 'Dear Jesus, I have sinned, and I accept you, Jesus. I accept you into my heart as my personal savior.' Say it along with me, Patrick. That's what you have to do."

"What happens if I do that?"

"You'll go to heaven when you die instead of hell."

The idea of heaven sure sounded better to me than hell. I didn't want to burn in fire forever, so I did the sensible thing and went along with her.

"In heaven, you'll be surrounded by God's love. I'll be there. Your mother will be there. It'll be—" Her eyes sparkled for a second. "Well, it'll be heavenly!" She laughed big at her joke.

She held my hand so tight it kind of squashed it, and she said the words and made me repeat along with her. But she was saying it with a lot more energy than me because I was barely alive.

"Jesus, I ask for your forgiveness for my sins and I accept you into my heart as my personal savior. Because I know you are the way, the truth, and the light." That's what we said together.

She relaxed and was very happy after we said it. "Amen and thank you, Lord Jesus. That's all there is to it! Now my grandson will be there with me in heaven."

She looked around the room. "Now, I had some pamphlets that they gave me at church that I need to give you. They tell you all about your new life in Christ. You'll read those."

She didn't see them in the TV room, so with a lot of effort she stood herself up and waddled into the next room. When she came back, she sat back down on the couch by me and gave me some colorful little booklets. They said, "Your new life in Jesus," and "What to do now that you've accepted Christ," and things like that.

"You'll read these up, Patrick."

She patted me on the head and got up again with a big groan and walked away.

"You get rest now," she said after she left the room. "I'm praying for you to get better."

As soon as Grandma left, I felt like I had a little more energy. Maybe she gave me some heavenly spirit or something. But I didn't want to read her pamphlets. I picked up Dad's book again. I read a lot of it in one go.

I read a long chapter about how Dad started a company to build rockets that can go to Venus. He wants to dig for minerals there and have robots be the miners.

What's the big idea, Dad, you don't want to use your slaves on Venus?

After a while I finally got to a chapter called "Looking to the past." This is the part of the book I was waiting for. He wrote about a big piece of land in Nevada he bought that he called "a land of yesteryear." What it seemed like is that he figured out a way to make time stand still in this one part of the world using some kind of science that he was going to explain.

He wrote about how expensive the project was. He spent billions of dollars on it. Of course, that's peanuts to him because he has hundreds of billions of dollars. He wrote that everyone thought he was crazy for doing it, but that he wanted to do it anyway. It was fun for him. He wasn't doing it to try to make money. That sounded just like the Dad I know. He built the whole town, he said. He brought in trucks and diggers and made Humboldt Creek bigger and raised up the land to make a waterfall. He brought in soil and planted trees in the desert and watered them with machines. He planted crops like apples and corn using special seeds that were old and that he said had more vitamins in them than new seeds. He invited people to live in his town and made them all sign what's called a "non-disclosure" agreement that said they would promise to live like it was sixty years in the past.

I got my dictionary out for that one. It means they promised they wouldn't tell anyone. They had to keep it all secret.

Anyone who lived in his town had to dress old-fashioned, talk old-fashioned, and act old-fashioned. He made his own radio and television and played old shows and printed up old newspapers so that nothing new, nothing from 2020, could ever get into the town.

He started building the town in 2010.

I set the book down in my lap and just stared into the empty room for a moment and let everything settle into my infected head. It was like he poured hydrogen peroxide on it. I didn't know what to think. I didn't know what was real and what was imaginary. Did I not even travel through time? My life and everything I ever knew was pretend. It was just dreamt up in my dad's imagination. He was playing a big joke on me the whole time, trying to make me think it was real. He tried to pretend my mom wasn't even alive too.

Why? I kept asking myself over and over. *Why?*

And what about the time machine? How did he make that work? I read through more of the chapter and there it was. He started writing about a special underground magnetic train he built that would take him from Cordial Falls to San Francisco in less than an hour.

It was just a stupid train.

I didn't know what to feel. I had no feeling left for my dad. I started thinking of some of the nice times we had, like the couple of times we hiked to the falls. When he took me to the carnival when it came to town and got me cotton candy. When he taught me how to ride my bike. When he showed me how to shoot my BB gun. The baseball game. Heck, even when he took me to the future in his time machine. All those fun times are ruined now. They were all lies. I hate them all, and I hate him.

I crumpled the pages and tore them and threw the book into the corner of the room, and my face and arms got even hotter with my fever. I didn't want to cry, but I could feel the tears coming.

I kept saying to myself, *Why?*

I woke up one night hearing voices and smelling cigarette smoke. I sat up and listened. It was pitch dark in my room.

"You don't want me to spend time with my own nephew?"

"I didn't say that. He's a kid. Just try not to be so heavy all the time. He's going through a lot and he's already got so many dark thoughts."

A dish clinked like somebody was washing dishes.

"It's not like you've had the greatest luck finding father figures for him."

"I can't believe you just said that."

"What? That son of a bitch didn't leave you a penny. You screwed the pooch bad on that one."

"Okay, rub it in." I could tell my mom was talking with her teeth clenched.

"Son of a bitch. And he takes the boy on top of it."

"Just stop, Jerry. You're not helping."

"And that other 'person,' I don't even know what to call him. Them? It?"

"You use their name. It's Rene."

"Whatever."

"Are you trying to make me kick you out? Is that what you're trying to do?"

"Hey, come on. We're having a spirited conversation. Nothing wrong with that."

There was more clinking, and they didn't say anything for a while.

"I have to figure out what to do about him."

"He's got the flu. It's not like he's going to die on you."

"Shh. He might hear."

They got real quiet after that, but I could still hear.

"What if it's not the flu?"

"Don't tell me you buy into the hype now. President says it's a hoax. He wouldn't lie about something like that."

"Jerry, you can't be serious."

"It's the Plandemic."

"Why do I bother with you? My god, I can't afford to see a

doctor. I don't even know how I'm going to pay the mortgage this month."

"I'm going to help. Should get my next unemployment check Friday."

"Yeah, I need that. Or you can go stay with Ma."

"Okay, now you're getting nasty."

"I'm just stressed out." Mom let out a big breath. "If it is the virus, I just hope he can get tested."

The virus. Mom thinks I got the killer virus. I felt like a burlap sack of rocks was pulling me to the bottom of a swamp. I lost my breath for a second, and my head was so light it felt like it popped off my body. I didn't feel like I had a killer virus. But what if I did? How long would it be before I died?

"You can't even believe the test, I heard."

"You're not helping, Jerry."

There was a long pause, and then Jerry talked again.

"When's that court date?"

"Less than a week. Monday. I have to go back to San Francisco. Can you watch him?"

"Of course."

"If I had to bet, I'd say he gets what he wants again. The man has more money than God almighty."

"Can you just, like, stop. Please?"

"Hey, it's a bad situation, that's all I'm saying."

They were quiet after that. I drifted back to sleep and I'm not sure if what I heard was a dream. It seemed real, but everything was getting mixed up.

My cough was extra bad that night. I could hardly sleep. And the worst part is, I wasn't coughing up anything. It just scraped my throat and made me feel like somebody was punching me in the chest. And then I couldn't catch my breath. It's not like when I catch a cold and get a stuffed-up nose. It's more like the nerve gas. There was bad smoke in my lungs, and I couldn't push it out to get any air in. It took all my strength sometimes just to fill up my lungs.

Jerry sat in the TV room with me one day and watched a baseball game on the television. He talked a lot during it, and we tossed a pink rubber baseball back and forth. Well, I did my best to toss it back, but I was pretty tired out.

During a slow part of the baseball game, Jerry said, "Hey, you want to see something cool?"

I shrugged. "Okay."

He held up his finger and then went in the other room. He came back with a thick, gray case with ridges on the outside. It was smaller than a briefcase but bigger than a lunchbox.

He sat down next to me and put the case on his lap.

"You ready for this?"

"I guess so."

I started imagining what kind of futuristic gadget he was going to show me in this case. Maybe there was still some amazing thing like a teleporting blaster or disintegrator ray that I didn't get to see yet.

He took a key out of his pocket and used it to unlock the case. He opened it, and inside, around a bunch of soft gray ridges, was a gun from the future.

"She's a beaut, isn't she?"

"Is that a real gun?"

"You know it. It's the Taurus G2 nine millimeter."

This gun was shaped like the Dick Tracy cap gun Walt used to have, but it was real. It looked heavier and had more details on it like fancy grips on the handle, and it had silver steel on top. It was a lot fancier than my BB gun, which seemed pretty old-fashioned to me all of a sudden.

"It gives you twelve rounds, so it's ideal for home defense. See, I keep it locked and loaded right by my bed to protect this house in case anybody ever breaks in. Any federal agents ever try to bust in here and sneak up on you, I've got your back."

"You would shoot somebody and kill them?"

"To protect myself or my family, you're damned right I would."

I imagined Jerry shooting people in this house, with dead bodies full of bullet holes, and smoke coming out of the holes. They were slumped over by the door and in the windows where they tried to sneak through. It gave me the willies.

"Why does everybody want to kill everybody in the future?"

"Hey, I don't want to kill anybody. But I'll do it if I have to."

I hoped he would never have to.

"You want to hold it?"

I nodded, reached over to the case, and picked up the gun by the handle with my thumb and pointer finger.

"Careful now."

It was heavier than I thought it would be. I imagined the loud gunshots, felt the bullets going through the skin and bones, and I saw the blood squirt out and the people screaming. I let go of it and let it fall back in the case.

Jerry laughed and said, "Whoa," while he tried to make sure it didn't fall out of the case. "Quite the weapon, isn't it?"

He closed the case, and we finished watching the game. He left after.

That night, I wondered if Grandma put me in good enough with God and Jesus so they'd listen extra careful to my prayers from now on. On the off chance that was true, I closed my eyes and put my hands together and asked God to protect Mom's house from burglars so nobody would try to hurt us, or steal from us, and so Jerry wouldn't have to shoot anybody with his gun. I asked him why so many people had to die in 2020. Maybe he could ease up on that a little bit. I asked him to make me feel better so I wouldn't die just yet. I said I wanted to feel at least good enough to go to court with Mom. I asked him to free all my dad's slaves and anybody else's slaves. And I asked him to explain to me why my dad tried to fool me my whole life.

I said the whole prayer in my head. It would be too much

to say stuff like that out loud. I said "amen" at the end because that's how people always end prayers. That was in my head too, of course. I think saying "amen" helps it get to heaven, so God has a better chance of hearing it.

The next day, bright light was coming through the window when I woke up. Mom was sitting next to me with her hand on my forehead.

"You're so hot," she whispered.

"Mom?"

"Yeah, honey?"

"Am I dying?"

"Of course you're not dying, silly." She said it sad, though, not like she was being funny.

"Is the doctor going to come?"

"No, but we're going to go see him."

"You can't afford it. I heard you talking. How much does it cost?"

"Doctors are expensive, but you have to go."

"I have money left over from what I brought to buy my book."

"Shh. We're not going to use your money. I got in touch with your father. And when he found out you were sick, he said he would cover it, thank God."

I turned my head away. I didn't like the idea of Dad trying to help me with anything. And I didn't like that she talked to him either.

"What's the matter, sweetie?" She looked at me like her face was asking the question. Then she looked around the couch and then in the corner. I could tell she saw Dad's book laying with pages all crumpled up and sticking out. "Did you figure some things out about him?"

I nodded.

"I'm so sorry, Patrick. I wish I could have come to visit you when you lived with him. I couldn't. They wouldn't let me. I wish I could have shown you all the wonderful things in the past twelve years that have happened in my life, and in our family, and in the whole world."

"The world isn't wonderful. It's horrible."

"Aw, don't say that."

"Why did he do it? Why did he keep me there? Why didn't he let me see you?"

"I have no idea. He's a strange man. I don't know if anybody knows why he does the things he does. I don't even know if he knows."

She rubbed her hand in a slow circle on my chest. "Hey, but you're here now. We have our whole lives ahead of us. Things are going to be different."

I'm glad my mom is here. But the only thing that seems different to me now compared to when I lived in Cordial Falls is that I'm going to die by a killer virus instead of an H-bomb.

12

Mom drove me to a doctor. Almost everybody at the doctor's office was wearing a mask. I was starting to feel like I was the only one who lost his mask in 2020. And look where it got me. I'm pretty much just a walking dead person. I wish I never took it off. The lady behind the desk had a mask and a blast shield over her face. She wasn't kidding around. After we came in, she gave mom and me masks. She also made us squirt some goop on our hands and rub it in before we sat down to wait. It smelled like chemicals and stung my nostrils.

The doctor was a short man with almost no hair. Mom talked to him while I was sitting on the table. She asked him if I should get tested.

He said, "I don't think that's necessary, not the way he's breathing. With his kind of viral infection, I advise you admit him from here."

Mom put her hand over her mouth. She seemed to know what he was talking about, but she asked what he meant anyway. He explained that he wanted me to go to the hospital.

I never went to a hospital before. The worst accident I ever had was when I was running in the back yard with some of the kids from the block and didn't notice a little hole. I stepped right into it and twisted my ankle. It hurt so bad I cried, and my whole ankle swelled up. I couldn't walk for a long time, but Dad put ice on it and then it got better on its own even though I limped for quite a while after.

I imagined the hospital in the future would look like an alien spaceship, with people's heads inside glass domes and lots of wires and machines with blinking lights like the dash panel in the time machine. Would they even need to prick my finger or give me shots? Maybe it was all done with rays. I crossed my fingers.

Before we left, Mom got into an argument with the lady at the big desk. The lady didn't want to let us leave, but Mom was trying to tell her we needed to get to the hospital. The lady was being stubborn about it, even though the doctor told us to go.

Mom talked on her phone and said, "It hasn't come through. I gave him my PayPal." She was acting like she wanted to be angry and yell at everybody, but she was trying to keep her cool and be polite.

I was sitting in a chair in the waiting room looking at some fish in a tank. They were swimming about like they didn't have a care in the world. They didn't know anything about killer viruses or H-bombs or the end of the world.

Out of the corner of my eye, I noticed Mom trying to wave me over while she was on the phone. It was a lot of work for me to stand up and walk, but I got up and made my way to her. She put her arm around me while she talked on the phone some more, and then talked to the lady behind the desk some more. Eventually, the lady was satisfied with things and let us go. My mom gave her a "thank you," but said it like she was more mad than thankful.

The hospital wasn't that far from the doctor. Mom helped me out of the car and held onto me so I didn't have to work so hard to walk. I coughed through my new mask. We walked past some people walking through the big glass doors that opened by themselves. They were wearing masks, but they looked scared and tried to get away from me, fast. I felt like a skunk, a dying skunk that everybody knew would explode as soon as it died so you'd better stay clear. The coughing kept scraping my throat. It hurt like dragging your fingers on a concrete sidewalk until they bled down to nothing. And every breath shook my whole body. Everything was hard. Walking, breathing, talking, even thinking. Every second, it felt more like I was curdling up and dying like bad milk.

Mom had to stop to talk to another lady at the hospital, and then she had to get on her phone again. She kept saying, "I don't have insurance. I'm going to pay out of pocket." She dug in her purse for cards and papers she had to show to the lady. My legs hardly worked anymore, and the waiting room chairs were too far away, so I just sat down on the floor next to her and hung off her pant leg.

The hospital was a busy place, with people walking around and voices on a speaker. I saw a lot of doctors and nurses and some kind of policeman. I imagined asking him to please shoot me and put me out of my misery. I saw a man with a bandage on his head get wheeled out in a wheelchair. The sounds of the hospital echoed around me like I was under water. I imagined that I was at Cordial Falls, listening to the water. But then I remembered that Dad built those falls, and I didn't want to think of them anymore. I tried to think of something that would take me away from where I was, but I didn't have any memory I could go to that was real. I heard the baseball crowd from the radio. I heard the static on the television in the morning before the first show comes on. But those were all sounds Dad played for me as part of his big trick. I thought of the wind on a nice breezy day, and maybe some rain. Dad didn't control those things, I don't think. I closed my eyes and listened.

Pretty soon I was in a different room, and Mom wasn't there

anymore. It was only doctors and nurses. They all wore masks, plastic gloves, and suits that made them look like space travelers. I was on a bed and they put a bowl over my mouth connected to a tube. It felt like it was pushing in the bones of my face, but I think it helped me breathe better. They poked my arm with a needle and it zinged me even worse than a finger prick. It was just another way 2020 is no better than 1957. I tried not to cry, but the tears came anyway. The crying made my throat tighten up, made me cough more, and snot was coming out of my nose so much they had to lift off the plastic bowl and give my whole face a wipe down. It was like I was melting.

I prayed to God again in my head. I asked him to just make it all stop.

Maybe this could just be the end. Let the policeman come back and execute me. I just want it all to go away.

I think I went to sleep after that.

When I was awake, which wasn't very often, I felt like I was going crazy from the boredom. But most of the time I've been asleep, I think. It hurts so much to be awake. They have a tube down my mouth, to feed me, they said. I have another one attached to my weenie that takes the pee into a bucket somewhere. It hurts and makes me feel like I have to pee all the time. I wish they could take it out, except I think that would hurt even worse. And, anyway, I don't have enough strength to get up and go to the bathroom. They have to help me. I'm like a wrinkled, helpless old man who doesn't even have the strength to keep living.

One time I woke up in the middle of the night after a bad dream. I dreamt that Mom went to San Francisco on Monday and they decided I had to go back to Cordial Falls, where nobody cared about me, Tommy Haddigan kicked my teeth in every day, and Dad ignored me and kept the prank going. It seemed real, and then I realized it was a dream. But then it seemed real again because I heard her say she had to go to San Francisco, and the lawyer said the court was going to decide. That Monday must have gone by already, but I had no way to know.

They don't let me see my mom. Not face-to-face anyway. I see her through a big window on the other side of the room once in a while. She's wearing a mask, so I don't even get a good look at her face. I miss her touching me and squeezing me all the time.

One time she held up my knapsack so I could see it, and she took out the white box my dad gave me with the phone in it that the policeman didn't pack up very well. She pointed to it and was trying to say something to me about it with her hands, but I couldn't tell what.

The next day she came back and gave something to a nurse. The nurse brought it in a room and I saw that it was the phone in a plastic bag. The nurse and another nurse took it out with their gloves and wiped it down with a spray bottle and a rag and made it all wet and shiny. They let it set for a bit, and then they gave it to me. Mom lifted up her phone and pointed to it. I heard a funny little music sound and noticed the viewing screen on the phone changed. It said "Mom" at the top, and had a red button and a green button on the bottom. She kept pointing to her phone. I saw her use her phone enough before that I think I knew what was happening. She was calling me. I touched the green button.

"Hello?"

"Patrick, hi!"

"Hi." I sounded like a robot with a dead battery, talking through the plastic bowl on my face.

"We're talking on the phone!"

"Yeah."

"Did you ever talk on a phone before?"

"I didn't come from the stone age, Mom."

She laughed at that.

"Baby, now we can talk. When you have the energy. They said it would be okay. They said you're doing great."

"I am? I don't feel great."

"You're doing great."

"Mom, did you go to the court on Monday?"

"No, sweetie, the court date got postponed because of you getting sick."

"So I don't have to go live with Dad?"

"For now, you have to be here."

We have conversations on the phone every now and then. Sometimes about serious stuff, sometimes not so serious. She tells me a lot of things that are happening, like that she's supposed to be going back to work soon and they want her to wear a mask to work. She told me Buster got away from her on a walk and tried to catch a squirrel, but he was too slow. She said she's been noticing Jerry coughing.

"But I'm sure he'll be fine," she said.

She also said Jerry was planning to go to a rally to see the president. I asked who that was.

She said, "The president of the United States, silly."

I just said, "oh." I figured the president of the United States was Dwight D. Eisenhower, because no matter how much money my Dad had to pull off his big hoax, there was no way he could change who the president of the United States was.

She explained more about how to use my phone so I could do things on it and not be so bored all the time. She showed me how to do "texting." Now I can write messages to her. It's like writing a letter, but she gets it right away, and she can send a letter back right away. My phone makes a little beep when a new message comes in. And when I'm sitting in the bed, bored, and can't sleep, sometimes we have a conversation with texting.

She told me in a message the next day that Jerry came back from the rally and was having a hard time breathing. She said he was trying to sleep it off at Grandma's house, so she hasn't seen him for a couple of days. I worried that I made him sick. I prayed really quick and asked God to make sure Jerry didn't get as sick as me. I imagined him coughing and hurting like I did, and I felt it twice as bad.

"When is he going to get better?"

"We don't know. I hope soon. He refuses to go see a doctor."

If Grandma really did give me the power of Jesus, maybe that means God will answer my prayers. Mom said I was doing great, so maybe I'm getting better. I felt strong just thinking about it, like when I imagine punching out bad guys. I wondered if I'd have that kind of power in real life after I got better. It might seem impossible, but so many impossible things have been happening to me lately, I'll believe anything. I prayed again and asked God to make me super strong, and to make sure Jerry wouldn't get the virus.

One day they moved me to a different room. The new room had a TV and less machines than the other room. But the most important new thing was that I wasn't wearing the plastic bowl on my face, and the other tubes were gone too. I just had a regular mask on. And the window where I saw Mom was closer to my bed than in the other room. We talked on the phone.

"I'm in a new room."

"I know. You're feeling better, they said."

I was starting to feel better. I didn't feel so hot all the time.

"Do you think they're ever going to let me out?"

"Any day now, I'm sure of it. I can't wait to see you."

"I'm excited to see you too, Mom."

"I love you so much, Patrick."

I think when somebody says "I love you," you're supposed to say it back. I wanted to. I love my mom. But somehow I couldn't bring myself to say it. It was too embarrassing. It felt a little like praying out loud. Someday I'll do it.

Later that day, when Mom wasn't there anymore, Nurse Sarah was checking my tubes and changing my bag and stuff. She's a Black lady with big brown eyes and strong arms. I asked her about "Black lives matter" because I was confused after what Jerry said. She was real interested in it and had a lot to say about it.

"Patrick, thank you so much for asking about that," she said. "People are marching and saying 'Black Lives Matter' because they're tired of Black people being picked on by the police."

"The police pick on them?"

"Yes, they do. I don't believe they mean to, but it's just something that always seems to happen."

"Because some people are prejudiced?"

"That's right."

"But Jerry said police kill White people more."

She made a funny sound with her lips. "I don't know who Jerry is, but if that's really happening, is he out marching in the streets to save White people? I don't think so." She laughed. "You ask any Black person, and they'll tell you they've been pulled over by the police, hassled by police. It happens all the time. And they get beat up by the police. They get sent to jail. That's just the way it is. White people don't have that problem."

I thought of when Mom and I got pulled over by the police. Even though he was mean, at least he didn't beat us up.

"Jerry said Black people are the ones killing Black people."

"Patrick, it's a sorrowful thing when anybody kills anybody. Black people, we've got a lot of problems that go a long way back. What should not be our problem is the police. They're supposed to look out for everybody, and when they're not doing that, that's something people want to change. That's why they're marching."

After that conversation, Nurse Sarah was extra nice to me, staying to chat with me sometimes even when she didn't have work to do on me.

After a few days in the new room, they brought me out in a wheelchair and handed me over to my mom. I was free. I was going home from the hospital. I wanted to jump up and down and get excited, but I was just feeling lucky, and only wanted to get out of there as fast as I could.

Mom brought balloons, and she wore a mask and gloves.

I wore a mask too. She hugged me, but with the gloves. The doctors told her to make sure I always wear a mask when I go out, and they said to practice "social distancing," which means I should stay six feet away from everybody except my family. That sounded like a good idea to me because I didn't want to get crushed by any more big crowds.

God was doing his best to kill me, but I cheated death again. Tommy Haddigan didn't get me. I managed to avoid the H-bomb, so far. I escaped the police nerve gas in the war zone. And now, somehow, I got through the killer virus. With the rest of my life ahead of me, I felt like I had a second chance. I knew I had to keep working to uncover what the world was about. There were still secrets and mysteries all around me, and I was going to crack them wide open.

Grandma was waiting in the car. She laughed and hugged me.

"There's my boy," she said when she saw me. "Oh my goodness gracious, he's even skinnier." She wasn't wearing a mask.

"Grandma, you have to wear a mask," I said. "You could get sick."

Grandma just flapped away the idea with her hand.

"Jesus is my mask." She laughed, but I could tell she meant it.

Somehow I couldn't picture Jesus giving up on all his other duties to hold his hands over Grandma's mouth and nose all day.

In the car, Mom said, "I'm so proud of you, Patrick. You fought this thing and you made it out. You had me so scared. I love you so much and I just don't know what I'd do without you."

My face definitely turned red when she said that, but it still felt like a warm bath and a piece of cake.

That night Mom took me out to a restaurant to eat. Grandma doesn't like restaurants, so she stayed home. I was fed up with the bread, soup, and jello at the hospital, so it was a nice treat to have some good food. I got a hamburger. It felt strange going down my throat, like my whole insides were an open sore. Mom sat next to me in a booth. It was a fancy place where somebody comes and brings food to the table. Some people in the restaurant were wearing masks, but not everybody.

"Why doesn't everybody wear a mask?"

"Some people just don't want to wear them."

"But why? The doctors said to always wear it."

"They don't want other people to tell them what to do. Or they're just stubborn."

"But what if they get sick and die?"

"Well, if somebody doesn't wear a mask and they get sick and die, then they get sick and die."

"Why would you want to get sick and die?"

"Well, some people don't like to listen to doctors."

"Why?"

"They don't believe them, I guess."

"Why would you not believe doctors? Are they lying?"

"Doctors don't lie, honey."

"You should wear a mask more."

"I know. You're right. I should. And I'm going to. This was a real wake-up call for me. Thank you for that. I didn't take it that seriously until you got sick. I just got lazy, I guess. It's terrible. Figured it could never happen to me, you know."

While we sat there, I thought about everything that's happened in 2020, and how it seems like the world is going to end any day like Grandma said. With all the floods, wars, virus, and H-bombs just lying around for anyone to use, the end is even closer than it was in 1957. The human race is running out of time.

"Mom, when do you think the world is going to end?"

"Honey, why do you even think about that?"

"What else is there to think about?"

"I don't know. School? Friends? Having fun?"

I almost never think about things like that. I just shook my head at her. She laughed.

"Remember how you said you were going to help me figure out 2020?"

"Yep. What do you want to know?"

"What's going on? Is 2020 really happening? Or is it just a nightmare I'm having? It's got to be the worst year ever."

"Well, it's hard to argue with you there."

"Why is that? How did the future get so bad?"

"I don't know, honey. Sometimes it feels like," she tapped her straw into her glass while she was thinking, "2020 is just throwing everything at us, with no warning. It's so unpredictable, and it's just too much. The virus. Wham! It starts killing a lot of people. And then you can't go to work. Wham! You get laid off. Wham! The government is going to take away your unemployment. Wham! You have no money. You can't pay your mortgage. Then a wildfire burns your house down, a drought, a race riot. Wham! Wham! Wham!" She started to get all worked up.

She settled herself before she kept going. "That's what 2020 feels like. And if you ever watch the news, there's always something new and terrible happening every day, so I just don't watch anymore. It's like you can't predict what new, awful thing is going to happen next, but you know it's right around the corner, and it's probably going to turn your entire life upside-down."

I tried to imagine what the next terrible thing would be. I imagined I was Randy Stone getting the goods, thinking of what story I'd write in *The Chicago Star* about the year 2020.

Mom's phone lit up.

"Uh-oh. That was a bad segue," she laughed. But as soon as she looked at her phone, she burst out crying and covered her face.

"Mom, what is it?" I didn't know what happened, but I started crying too, just because she was crying. And then, exactly like she was saying, the next "Wham!" came.

"Jerry."

13

Why Jerry? He treated me like a real dad would. Maybe God was too busy planning Grandma's end of the world that he didn't hear me praying, asking to please not let Jerry get killed by the virus. Maybe I should have said it louder.

My whole body turned into spoiled meat, squishing around all green and smelly, knowing he got sick because of me. My green, coughing, oozing face grew into a monster that swallowed him up. Now he's not here to smile his little smile, make his spaghetti that was too spicy, watch his ball games that he said got ruined by people talking about how Black lives matter, and run his mouth with all those opinions that made Mom crazy.

"It's not your fault," Mom kept saying. "He was the one who decided not to wear a mask." She said it over and over.

It made me feel a little better for a minute or two, but then I'd go right back to being spoiled meat. My whole body went cold, like the monster breathed its cold breath at me and gave me prickly goose bumps. I felt lucky that the monster decided not to eat me, that it feasted on Jerry instead, and then I felt like a dirty rotten heel for feeling lucky. I kept thinking of Jerry showing me his gun, telling me how he knew it would protect him in case somebody ever snuck up on him.

The morning of the funeral, Grandma was holding her black veil over her head while she painted her lips bright red in front of the bathroom mirror. She was doing a good job holding herself together. She wasn't as cheerful as normal, but I didn't see her burst out bawling yet. She kept telling me she was happy I was there, that I was a blessing to her now, and things like that. But when she looked at me from the bathroom while she was putting the lipstick on, something must have hit her. I just finished getting dressed in the suit and tie my mom managed to wrangle from one of the cousins, and Grandma looked at me and cried. She came out of the bathroom and gave me a hug.

"My poor little Jerry," she said. "I know you're in heaven now. Momma will be joining you soon. Hold on. We'll grieve you in this world. My beautiful boy." She looked right at me with tears in her eyes and her red lip shaking.

"I love you so very much, Patrick. You're a comfort to me."

She went back to her lipstick project after that.

"I'll make a mess of my makeup today, but I guess there's no avoiding that."

Mom was wearing shoes with pointed heels and a black dress that fit tight to her hips. I never saw her wear a dress before. All she needed was a cape, and she'd be a superhero Lois Lane.

Before we left, I was doing the exercises the doctors gave me to get my strength back. I have to do them twice every day— once in the morning, once at night. Mom helps me. I lay down on my back and she bends my knee against my chest and I have to try to push against it. There's another one where I have to get on the floor and kick my legs in the air like I'm on a bike. I wish I brought my bike to 2020. Then I could just go for a ride instead of kicking my legs in the air like a dying bug.

Buster likes to sit next to me when I do the exercises. His long fur is nice to run your fingers through. He looked at me with his shiny little black nose and floppy ears that hang down past his neck. He's just the right size for a dog, if you ask me. He comes up just a little past my knee, and I can lift him. But I only did that once. He didn't like it, so I don't torture him with that anymore.

While she was pushing on my leg, Mom said, "I haven't had a chance to talk to you. Things have been so crazy. I've got some news for you."

"What is it?"

"Do you want to guess?"

"I get to meet my cousins?"

"Yes. They're going to be at the funeral. But that's not the news."

"We're having pizza tonight?"

"No, but that's a good idea."

"We're going to the moon?"

"No, silly."

"I know. Impossible." And that was all my guesses. "Okay, I give up. What is it?"

"Well, there's some good news. I think. And some not-so-good news. Which one do you want first?"

"Hm. Good news first."

"Remember that court date that got postponed?"

"Yeah."

"They decided that they didn't have to wait for you to get out of the hospital, after you were out of ICU and recovering. So they scheduled the date. And your father and I went. And the judge made a decision."

I practically jumped out of my pants. This news was going to decide my fate for the rest of my life! I tried to get up, but she kept holding my knee down.

"What did he say? What did he say?"

"Well, first of all, your father seems to have had quite a change of heart about a lot of things. He's confused, I guess you'd say, about how you reacted to his big time-travel stunt. And he wants a clean slate. He seems to understand where you're at now, and he's opening his mind to thinking about a lot of things differently."

"But what did the judge say? Where am I going to live?"

"I told you it was good news, didn't I?" She smiled.

"I get to stay with you?"

"All the way, baby."

She let go of my knee and I hopped up and hugged her.

"The judge listened to all the lawyers, and your father's lawyers were very fancy, and there were a lot of them, but the judge heard all about what your father did, sending you into San Francisco on your own, not to mention the whole keeping you in a make-believe 1950s fantasyland. Plus, they took your testimony into account, even though you couldn't be there. The lawyer you met at the police station and the officer that wrote down what you said in the car, they all convinced the judge that your father had abused his privileges and didn't deserve to keep you, and they said you should stay with me."

I was so happy I hugged her again and bounced up and down at the same time.

"Now the not-so-good news."

I stopped hugging her.

"You father wants to see you."

"No. I don't want to see him ever again."

"Patrick. It was part of the deal, and we all agreed to it."

"I didn't agree."

"No, I did. Okay? It was either that or maybe you have to see him even more. Do you want that?"

"No."

"All right then. Look, honey, it was very difficult for me to trust your father during all this, so I understand that it's hard for you too. We just have to take a leap of faith with him that this is all going to work out."

I pushed out a big breath and asked her how long I would

have to see him. She said it wouldn't have to be long. I asked her when. She said it would be this morning.

"This morning!?" I yelled.

"He's coming to the funeral. So, I'll be there. Grandma will be there. You just have to see him today, and he wants to talk to you. That's all. If you want to see him down the road, that's up to you."

"I don't and I won't."

"I know you're angry with him now, Patrick, but someday you might want to see your father again, you know? And you need to know you have the right to do that if you want."

"Okay, whatever. I never will."

We finished doing my exercises and then Mom made peanut butter and banana toast for breakfast. It's my new favorite. I like to let Buster lick the peanut butter off my fingers when I'm done. Mom sat next to me and drank her coffee. Grandma said she wanted to keep her mind busy, so she sat on the couch doing word puzzles.

I tried to imagine my mom and my dad together. They seemed like they belonged in two different solar systems.

"Mom, why didn't you live with me and Dad?"

"Oh, I wanted to live with you. I wanted to live with you so bad. But sometimes grown-ups think they're going to get along, and then they don't. And we split up. We couldn't live together."

"How old was I?"

"You were 3."

"Why did I have to live with him and not you?"

"I wanted to live with you. When they cut you out of my life, that was the worst torture I could imagine."

"But why couldn't you? I wanted you there."

"Me too, honey. But I couldn't."

"Why?"

"When I met your father, we were both in college. After that, after I had you, he started his company and made a lot of money. And he got it in his head that he wanted you to live with him. And he could afford a lot more lawyers than me, a lot better lawyers, and they convinced a judge that I wasn't good enough to see you. They made up things about me. They dug up things that made me look bad. It was so unfair and so ugly. Some of it wasn't even true. But that ass of a judge decided that I shouldn't see you."

"He wouldn't even let you visit me?"

"It's what your father wanted too."

"Why?"

"I don't know. I hated him for it. He just wanted me out. I could never understand it. It was cruel and selfish, and—"

She wiped her eye and then smiled. "But I'm glad you're here now, Patrick. It doesn't do any good to dwell on all that. It's water under the bridge."

"Not for me it isn't."

Grandma spoke up from the couch. "We're all so glad you're here with us, Patrick. You're such a blessing, and we love you so very much."

Mom rubbed my head and hugged me some more. I lowered my head and probably turned as red as Grandma's lips.

After another bite or two of toast and some finger cleaning from Buster, Mom said it was time to go.

I never went to a funeral before. When my other grandma died, Dad said I was too young to go, so I had a babysitter. Now that I was older, I wanted to see what it's about. I wondered if I'd make any discoveries about dying, and if that will help me understand 2020.

In the car on the way there, I thought about how Jerry was here and talking to me just a few days ago, and now he's dead and gone. Grandma said he's in heaven, and I guess he is. I tried to put myself in his skin. I imagined living, and then not living. I tried to think of what it would feel like to not feel anything—no touch, no sound, no taste, no sight. Nothing. It wasn't easy.

I closed my eyes, but I kept hearing the car motor, feeling the car moving, smelling Grandma's perfume, and tasting the last traces of peanut butter on the roof of my mouth. I even saw black and orange shapes with my eyes closed. It was impossible to feel dead.

After we got there, there was a part of the funeral that was a lot like church, except in a smaller room. In the front was a big coffin that looked like it was made out of the same chrome as a car. It had flowers on top and flowers in vases on the side, and a picture of Jerry next to it.

Grandma had to wear a mask even though she didn't want to. The place said she couldn't come in without it.

Mom pointed to the coffin, and whispered to me and Grandma, "Thank goodness it's closed."

"Why would they open the coffin?" I asked.

Grandma patted me on the back. "We would never do an open casket funeral." She said it like it was the most obvious thing in the world.

The preacher wore a mask, and the chairs were set up six feet apart so everybody was separate. Grandma and Mom and I sat together, but almost everybody else had to be apart. The preacher talked about Jerry. Grandma cried a little during that part. And then we prayed.

I kept wondering when I would see my dad. I looked around the room and didn't see him anywhere. I saw two kids, a girl and a boy. They were a little younger than me. Maybe third or fourth graders, if I had to guess. They were wearing masks and sticking close to their mom, looking at me. At least, I guessed it was their mom. Either that or an alien who kidnapped their mom and twisted its body to look exactly like her so the kids would never know.

After the church part of the funeral, everybody left the building and went back into their cars. While they walked, Mom was talking to a Black man who stood up very straight. She told me his name was Rene, but she said, "*Their* name is Rene."

Rene looked at me and said, "Hello, Patrick. Great job defeating the virus. I commend you highly." It was nice how he made it out like I accomplished something even though I almost died. He had a voice like a big-band crooner on the radio. It was an even sound that cut through the air, clear as a note of music. He had big shoulders and wore a white button shirt just like mine, but with no tie.

The girl cousin, who had curly brown hair and chubby cheeks that were popping out the side of her mask, said, "You're our cousin."

"You're *my* cousins," I said. I guess I didn't have anything more clever to say just then.

The girl got shy after that. The boy with her just looked at me and didn't say anything.

Mom, Grandma, and I followed the other cars and drove a little while to a graveyard. The cars stopped on a little road inside the graveyard, and everybody walked to an open grave. The clouds were dark and moving around a lot. Sometimes it was bright and sunny and then all of a sudden it would get gray.

That's where I saw Dad. He got out of a big black car and walked toward the grave. His head was down, shoulders slumped over, like usual. Strands of his hair were waving in the breeze. He was wearing a mask. He was dressed in a black tie and jacket. I noticed one of his security people get out of the car too, one of the time enforcers I recognized. He stayed back by the car while Dad walked to the open grave where the other people were. He saw me and waved, but he was too far away to say anything. We stood in different places around the grave when they put Jerry's coffin in. The preacher said more stuff there, led more prayers, and sprinkled some dirt on the coffin.

My cousins started to play peek-a-boo with me behind their mom. I was on the other side of Grandma, so I played along, but just with my eyes. I knew it wouldn't be polite to play like a kid now. It was a silly and childish thing to do, but it was fun to do it a little since everybody was supposed to be quiet and serious.

When the preacher was done, some people left the graveyard, but a few stayed and chitchatted in little groups, with everybody staying apart six feet.

The cousins and I ran around. I found out Liam, the boy, was in second grade. I thought he was older but he's just big for his age. He has the same chubby cheeks as his sister and was always sucking his mask inside his mouth. Emily is in fourth grade, just like I thought. She laughs a lot and her curls bounce all around when she runs.

Dad was talking to the preacher and another man. They were listening to Dad like he's important, like people always do.

Mom was standing and talking to Grandma and her sister and Rene. I would run by them sometimes. Mom would catch me and say, "Say hello to your Aunt Margie," and I would say hello and then run back with the cousins. Sometimes I would hear a longer slice of conversation.

"You're looking good too," Rene said. "I want to say five or six years? I was up here for a lecture, I believe."

"What kind of things are you working on now?"

"Well, the stuff that I can talk about—"

"Ooh secrets!" Mom said.

Rene chuckled at that. "That's all going well. Working on some robotics projects. Some government contracts are always in the offing."

"That sounds so interesting." Mom looked at me. "Honey, Rene builds real robots."

I said, "Gee whiz! Real robots?"

Rene looked at me and nodded. "That's right. Real robots."

And then I ran back to the cousins.

The grass and trees were losing their color as the sun went further down. But the sky looked like a planet exploded in it. It had big bursts of orange and red and purple. It was easy to forget we were in a cemetery because it was just like a park with all the trees and grass. We played six-feet tag for a while, where you tag people with a stick. Then Emily tried to make it more interesting by inventing new rules, like if you accidentally got closer than six feet, you couldn't move beyond the area between the big tree and the big pink-and-gray tombstone that said, "Markham" on it. I think Liam wanted to be like her because he tried to invent some rules too, but they made the game too complicated. Emily and I couldn't understand most of his rules, so we only used one or two just so he wouldn't feel left out.

They both kept trying to take off their masks. They said they didn't have to wear them at home, and they were tired of wearing them. I sat them down in the grass like I was a schoolteacher.

I told them, "You have to wear your masks when you're with other people. Otherwise you could get them sick or you could get sick yourself. And you don't want to get sick. It is no fun. I know because I almost died from the virus. Anyway, it's doctor's orders."

They called me "Doctor Patrick" after that and did a good job keeping their masks on.

When I came up to Mom and heard part of the grown-up conversation again, part of me wanted to be standing with them, talking, and another part of me wanted to run off and keep playing with the cousins. I was stuck in the middle.

I was all sweaty under my suit from playing. I took my jacket off and hung it over a tombstone.

Mom said, "Don't forget that, Patrick. We have to give it back."

I promised I wouldn't forget it.

My dad pulled himself out of the group with the preacher and stepped over to me.

"Hey, kiddo."

I felt like he somehow caught me in a freezing beam.

"Hi."

Mom gave me a look like I should go talk to him.

Emily and Liam ran away to a tree on the other side of the grave where they circled it, trying to catch each other.

I walked away from the grave to where there weren't as many people. Dad made his way closer to me. He got about six feet, but I moved away.

"Social distance." I said.

He put out his hands like he was remembering to keep his distance. "Of course, yes. It's great to see you, Patrick."

I didn't say anything. I wasn't trying to be rude. I just couldn't think of what to say.

"I'm glad you're getting your sea legs. We were all worried about you. I heard about what happened."

I wanted to give him a piece of my mind, and tell him I only got the virus because he wasn't straight with me and I had to escape into the future to find out the truth, but that seemed like too much to start off a conversation.

"Patrick, I understand you're ticked off with me. About the time machine and all that."

"It was a stupid train. There's no such thing as a time machine."

"Okay, fair point." He seemed to be trying to think of how to say something. It took him a while.

He took a deep breath. "I want to explain everything to you."

14

"When you were just a little sprout, it was about 2009, we had the Internet. We had iPhones. Hope and change won the White House. It seemed kind of like the future was here, and it was bright. That kind of future was something I worked my whole life to help bring about. It was an exciting time. So I had this big idea. I thought, wouldn't it be amazing to visit this future, from the past, and see all these changes like a time traveler? I started by thinking of my dad, who grew up in the 1950s. What would he think if he were somehow transported to this future? I was captivated by this idea. Obsessed, really. I knew I couldn't give an experience like that to my dad, obviously. And I couldn't give it to myself. But there was someone I could give it to. You. I hatched this idea that if I could raise you in the 1950s, as much of a real, bona fide 1950s as I could create, then you'd get treated to the surprise of a lifetime. And I went all out. Money was no object."

"I know. I read your dumb book."

"Oh. Okay. You read that. Well, I wanted it to be the most real time-travel adventure imaginable. Like the best carnival ride in the world. I wanted to capture the wonder of time travel and have it be as real as—"

"But it wasn't real. It was all a big lie."

"It wasn't so much a lie as it was one of those little white lies you tell when you give someone a birthday present, but you don't tell them where you're hiding it. That's how I saw it."

"You can't tell one of those types of lies for somebody's whole life. You wouldn't even let me see my mom."

"That was unfortunate. She wasn't onboard with the whole 1950s thing. I couldn't risk her tainting the project. I wish that could have worked out differently."

"I wish you didn't do it at all."

"I know you feel that way. But that's not the whole story. The worst part of it is, I always planned to take you on the trip when you turned 12. It was the perfect age. And I couldn't delay that because I was afraid you were starting to figure things out. If that happened, it would all be for nothing. Then, four years ago, we got a new president. He was a bully and a con man, and a throwback to all the worst things about the 1950s."

I didn't realize my dad hated Dwight D. Eisenhower so much.

"And in the years after that, it started to feel like the whole world was coming to a crashing end, with race riots, the pandemic, climate change, bees going extinct. Suddenly, the future seemed awful, and scary, and not exciting or fun at all. When I started all this, I couldn't have imagined the future would be so bleak. That was just terrible timing."

I didn't say anything to that. I just stood there, breathing steam through my nose and trying not to look at him.

And what did he say about bees!?

"Patrick, I hope one day you can appreciate on some level what I tried to give to you, how much I devoted my life to creating this singular experience that I had every reason to believe would be pure magic for you. You got to experience what it would be like to travel into the future! Nobody's ever gotten to do that before. I never considered the possibility that you wouldn't like it. I was so convinced I'd constructed everything so perfectly. That's what I do. I make the future. I'm good at it."

I tried to listen to him, but mostly I was imagining giving him a piece of my mind, like Sam Spade with a nervous and sobbing client who won't talk straight. I wanted to grab him by the collar and shake him. He didn't seem to get it. All he thought about was his project. He never cared about me. I was just a way for him to get his kicks. He didn't care that he was playing me for a fool my entire life.

"Was everybody else in on it but me? Did Mrs. Cummings know?"

"Well, everybody had to sign an agreement before they came to live in Cordial Falls. Everybody except the kids, of course. A lot of people thought it was a quaint, romantic idea to go back and live in a simpler time. Except your mother. She never understood the concept. But in the end, all it was about was to give you this amazing experience. I did it all for you, Patrick."

I felt like my breath was boiling hot steam now, coming out of my eyes, ears, mouth, and nose. And for the first time ever, I imagined punching my dad instead of Tommy Haddigan. I wanted to punch him so hard he'd fly into outer space and bonk into every satellite that had his stupid acceler-whatever in it.

"You're worse than Tommy Haddigan because you put him in Cordial Falls. Why did you have to do that?"

"Tommy Haddigan? A kid from school?"

"A terrible person from school."

"Oh, I see. Well, those relationships were for you to navigate. You needed that. The kids grew up same as you, blissfully unaware there was anything awry. I just wanted you to have a picture-perfect 1950s childhood. The jig is up now, of course. You seem to be happy with your mother. And that's fine. I did what I could. I did my best. I tried. This was my way of showing fatherly affection. Maybe it was a little screwy. Maybe the project was a bit of a misfire. But I'm built to make the future for people. Maybe not built so much for being a dad."

At that moment I didn't see him as my dad. He wasn't standing in my way anymore. I got the truth out of him, like Randy Stone. And at least the first part of the puzzle was solved. I was after bigger fish now. The rest of the story for *The Chicago Star* was this terrible future that he put me in. And he wasn't going to stop me from finding out what 2020 would throw at me next, and what's waiting for me at the end of the world.

He got up and seemed like he was going to reach out his hand for a handshake but decided not to. I wouldn't have shook it anyway because of the six feet. He just tipped his chin to me and walked away. The security man opened the back door of the car to let him in.

"You shouldn't have slaves!" I yelled at him. He looked back at me like he was confused. Or maybe he didn't hear me.

I felt a little less like a pet after that, but not much. Sure, he played me for a sucker, but I didn't care anymore. All he really did was give me a rotten birthday present. And who cares? I'm used to that feeling. It was a present so rotten it turned me inside out and made all the other birthday presents before it, and every day of my life up till that day, just as rotten. Grandma's bag of orange slices was a better present because at least it was real.

While I was standing there, I felt a stick poke me in the back. Emily giggled and ran away, saying, "You're it!" Liam ran next to her.

I looked on the ground for the stick I was playing with before. As soon as I found it, I picked it up and ran after them. They squealed.

While I raced through tombstones with my cousins, I tried not to think about my road to the truth. I wanted to close the book on the past.

Emily turned and darted off to one side. I stuck with Liam because he was easier to catch. I caught up to him with my stick and tapped him on the shoulder. He fell over and rolled in the grass. He had a giggle like Woody Woodpecker. Emily had a funny way of saying "Whoa" when I turned to her with my tag stick.

When I needed a breather from running, I went up to the group Mom was in to see what they were talking about. They were mostly just chitchatting.

Rene said to me, "Patrick, I understand you're experiencing 2020 for the first time now? What an experience that must be."

I nodded. I wasn't sure what to say.

Mom said, "Oof," and Aunt Margie said, "Tell me about it."

"What are your favorite things about 2020?" Rene asked.

I tried to think of all the things. "Texting. Comfortable shoes. The different kinds of Reese's peanut butter cups." That was the stuff I could think of.

A couple of the grown-ups laughed at my list, but I didn't see what was so funny about it.

Grandma said, "Patrick, you didn't mention the very best thing about 2020."

"What?"

"Our little talk the other day?"

Then I remembered, but Grandma kept talking before I could say anything.

"Patrick and I prayed, and he accepted Jesus Christ into his heart."

Why do grown-ups always have to tell each other my private business and make me embarrassed?

"It was a moment you'll never forget as long as you live," Grandma said. "Isn't that right, Patrick?"

"I guess so." I decided to be polite.

"That's sweet, Ma. You're looking out for his spiritual life. Better you than me," Mom laughed.

Grandma reached out her arm toward Rene and said, "Now if we can just get this fellow to accept Jesus, we'll have accomplished something!"

Rene tried to laugh about that. "That would be quite a trick to pull on a lost-cause scientist."

"You know what the Bible says about science, don't you?" Grandma said. "The Bible says it's foolishness. So you have to be careful, Patrick. Man's foolishness will try to deceive you."

"Well, as someone who has a PhD in foolishness," Rene said, "I have to say it's not all bad."

Grandma did that thing where she flaps her hand down like Rene didn't deserve to be spoken to anymore. But I wanted to hear them talk more about science. I remember from church the preacher said the Bible explained things that science couldn't, and that you had to have faith to believe the Bible.

Mom said, "Patrick, I was thinking of the other best thing that happened in 2020 that you didn't mention. You thought of Reese's peanut butter cups but not me?" She pretended to be upset. "I'm crushed. I feel so rejected." She was kidding and laughing about it, but I felt embarrassed that I didn't mention meeting her as one of the good things about 2020. I should have thought of it.

"That's one of the best things," I said.

Mom's eyes smiled, and she knelt down and hugged me.

I razzed her a little and said, "I guess."

Then she laughed and play-hit me in the shoulder. "You meanie!"

Grandma said, "Oh, isn't that the sweetest thing!"

Mom rubbed my head.

"You have to find a good church down in Pasadena, Rene," Grandma said.

"I understand that's important to you, Gail."

That's when I learned Grandma's name is Gail.

"It's important to everyone."

"Well, we can just agree to disagree on that one."

"Ma, leave Rene alone, huh?"

Aunt Margie said something to Mom about her necklace, and after that it seemed like they were going to stop talking about the interesting stuff, so I ran off with my cousins.

After we played six-feet tag and the other games for a while, Emily sat on a headstone across from me while Liam poked his stick on the ground along the edge of the tombstone, saying he was hunting for treasure.

"It's boring at our house," Emily said. "I want to go back to school, but Mom says it might be closed because a boy got the virus at camp, and everybody had to stay home."

She told me her favorite thing to do at home is watch *Ashley Garcia, Genius in Love*, and *Alexa and Katie*. "All the best stuff is on Netflix," she said.

Liam was using his tag stick to dig a hole in the middle of the grass now. His mother had to keep asking him to stop, but he was determined.

I got up and told Liam and Emily that we needed to do some exploring in the dark. I went further into the cemetery, and they followed. I told them we were going to go to the ends of the Earth, the point where the world ended.

I found a big flat tombstone that reminded me of a ship, and I got at the helm of it.

"Captain Patrick Stoodle is commanding the U.S.S. *Maine*. We will take this battleship to the edge of time, and we will not stop until we discover what horrors await us there. Will it be sea monsters? Killer mermaids? A black hole? We do not know." I looked very serious at the others. "Some of us may not return."

Emily wanted to go diving and meet dolphins. I told her that could be dangerous in these waters.

"The dolphins on the edge of the world are a hundred feet long, and they have sharp teeth and claws on their fins. They'll claw your head open and eat your brains so they get smarter."

"There's no such thing as a dolphin like that," she said.

"But you've never been to the end of the world before, have you, young lady?" I asked.

Liam asked what he should do, and I said, "You need to swab

the deck, mate."

"What does that mean?"

"It just means you mop it."

"But I want to explore!"

"We can't very well go exploring if our deck isn't swabbed, can we?"

"No fair."

He started using his stick as a mop, scraping the tombstone. And then he went right back to digging holes in the grass.

They started calling me "Captain Patrick" after that. Liam kept seeing rainbows ahead and wanted to search for buried treasure, which was turning the end of the world into something with a happy ending. But Emily understood we were on a serious mission to map the edge of the Earth.

"Will we die at the end of the world?" she asked.

"Yes. Everybody's going to die a horrible death."

"But then at least we'll go to heaven."

"But what if heaven is a big hoax?"

"That's impossible," she said. "I know heaven is real because my grandpa is there."

When it got too dark to see, except for a few lampposts here and there, Aunt Margie called the cousins over like it was time to go home. I followed them back to where the grown-ups were, but the grown-ups didn't leave. They stayed there talking for a while.

I decided to stand with the grown-ups some more and be a part of their conversation.

"I said what I liked about 2020 before," I said. "Now here's what I don't like. The killer virus, of course. How everybody has to wear masks. How there's still H-bombs but nobody even knows where they are so they could get blown up by just anybody who finds them lying around. How the police are more like soldiers, and they kill people, especially Black people, and how nobody has any money except my dad."

"Oh, heavens!" Grandma said.

Aunt Margie and Mom looked at each other and raised their eyebrows. Mom said to her, "He thinks about this stuff," and then laughed. Why was I so funny to them?

"That's quite an impressive list, Patrick." Rene said. "You forgot climate change and all its self-fulfilling feedback loops, floods, wildfires, the acidification of the oceans, the poisoning of our habitat, the rise of fascism around the world, the rejection of science and the rampant spread of ignorance, propaganda masquerading as news. I could go on if anybody wants."

I wasn't sure what too much of that meant, but I got the idea pretty well that I wasn't the only one who thought 2020 was the pits.

"And the bees going extinct," I said, because I wanted to sound smart like Rene.

He nodded at me, "Absolutely. Our poisoning of bees and other insects is a terrible problem."

"These are signs that the Lord is coming back," Grandma said. "You can't argue with that, Rene. It's in the Bible."

Rene raised his hands. "If that gives you comfort, Gail, I think that's wonderful."

"No, it's not a comfort. It's just the truth. The end times aren't going to be a picnic. The antichrist will reign. Jesus and his angels will gather all the faithful to his kingdom, and all the rest will burn in a lake of fire. It'll be a terrible, terrible day." She said all that like a serious warning. Then she said, "If you're not saved!" and laughed.

Rene didn't say anything.

Mom looked at him and said, "You don't have anything to say to that?"

"It's your beliefs, Gail. I don't take any issue with that."

Mom helped him out. "It's okay, Rene. We don't mind a spirited discussion in our family."

"Yes, I can remember some doozies," Rene said.

Grandma laughed. "It's true. You can't offend us. I might argue with you and your lifestyle, but I'll still love you, Rene."

"I'll stick with peer-reviewed journals to find truth, thank you very much," Rene said. He was calm and sure in how he figured out the truth of things, same as Grandma. I'm excited to be a grown-up so I can be sure of things like that someday.

"You can't accept God's word unless you open your mind to it," Grandma said. "You have to have faith. Faith is the virtue."

"Yeah, the preacher says you just have to have faith," I said.

Rene had a lot of thoughts about this subject.

"In science, faith is against the rules. You can't just accept things on faith. You need evidence. Where does it end if we have no kind of criteria for distinguishing myth from reality? People don't listen to the doctors and scientists. They put their faith in someone like the president instead, and they don't wear masks, and they get sick. Faith doesn't pan out so well for those people."

"That's Jerry right there, God rest him," Mom said.

"Oh my god. I'm sorry. I didn't realize—" Rene said.

"Oh, no. How could you? Please. None of us were careful enough. It could have been any one of us." She put her arm around me. "Thank God Patrick got through it."

"Yes, thank God," Aunt Margie said.

"Amen to that," Grandma said. "But faith in the Lord is something entirely different."

That was about when Mom said, "Well, it's getting late," and everybody got in their cars to go home. I said goodbye to the cousins. They wanted to hug me, but Mom said we had to stay six feet apart. Aunt Margie said, "We'll see a lot more of your cousin Patrick. I promise."

In the car on the way home, I asked Mom, "Who is Rene?"

"An old friend."

It was a short drive. Grandma and Mom seemed all talked out, because they mostly just sat quiet.

When we got home I was surprised to see Rene getting out of his car too.

"Is he staying the night, Mom?"

"Yeah. They drove a long way. This will save them the hotel."

"Why do you call him 'they'?"

"That's a long story."

Rene laughed, "Oh, it doesn't matter, Marion. 'He' is perfectly fine."

Once we got inside, Grandma started into Rene like she was thinking about it in the car on the way home and couldn't wait to spring it on him. "Rene, if Jesus himself came back to gather the faithful, would you believe then? Would that be enough proof for you?"

Rene said, "Boy, you don't give up, do you, Gail?"

Grandma laughed. "I like to give people a good challenge."

"I think we should all start winding down, don't you think?"

"Just answer me that," Grandma said. "It's important."

I was eager to hear Rene's answer. I rubbed Buster's head while I listened.

Rene sighed. "Ordinary claims only need ordinary evidence. If you told me you had cereal for breakfast this morning, I'd believe you. That's likely. But extraordinary claims require extraordinary evidence. If you're telling me the Christian savior is going to come back in the clouds and save humanity tomorrow, I'd need a lot more evidence. If I saw Jesus come back, maybe I'd believe it. But until then, I remain a skeptic."

"Okay, he's open to it," Grandma said with one of her big belly laughs. "There's hope for him yet!"

We said our goodnights pretty quick after that. I hugged Mom, hugged Grandma, and got a "nice to meet you" from Rene. Mom set up Rene on the couch in the living room.

"I'd give you Jerry's room, but that would be weird," she said.

In the TV room, Mom kissed me after I settled into my couch. She wished me goodnight, and I told her I liked Rene.

"Mom, is Rene right, or Grandma? Where do you come down on it?"

"Oh, honey, I'm somewhere in the middle. I believe in God with all my heart, but I have my doubts sometimes."

"Don't you want to know the truth?"

"Sure. But maybe we'll never know. We have to be okay with that."

It wasn't okay with me. I wanted all the answers. And I was about to get a big one. It was mighty strange that we were talking about these things that day, because the next day everything in the world changed. It changed even more than when I came from 1957 to 2020.

The Switcheroo

15

I woke up kind of halfway to Grandma saying "Praise his name" and "Hallelujah" in the other room. I heard my mom talking, but I couldn't hear what she was saying. I could tell she was running around collecting things like she was in a hurry. She normally wasn't so busy in the morning. She usually sits and drinks her coffee and moves a little more slow. I didn't hear Rene.

Mom came in my room and shook me to wake me up. I told her I was already awake.

She said, "Come on, honey, we're going." She seemed riled up but not upset.

"Huh?" I was too sleepy to know what to say.

I came out of my room and saw Mom on her phone and packing a suitcase at the same time.

"Where are we going?" I asked.

Grandma was standing in the middle of the living room with her hands up and a big smile on her face, spinning around best she could, singing, "Praise the Lord" and "Praise be to his name." She was laughing at Mom, saying, "You don't need to pack a suitcase, Marion."

Mom kept packing and said, "Ma, we're getting on a flight.

There are things we need for the plane."

Rene was looking at the TV with his arms crossed like he was thinking really hard. He was still wearing his mask.

As soon as Grandma saw me, she hugged me and said, "The day has arrived, Patrick. The day has arrived!" I looked at her close and she had tears in her eyes.

A lady's voice was talking on the TV, and I went to look at it. That's when I got my first clue about what was going on. It looked like a scene from *The Ten Commandments*, which played at the Cordial Falls movie house last winter, except there were moving words and red boxes all around the picture. In the main picture was a big blast of sunbeams coming through the clouds, and a giant staircase going into the clouds. A giant crowd of people was moving toward the staircase and up the stairs. The image was shaky, like someone was holding onto the movie camera. Then it moved in closer to the top of the staircase. There was someone there who was wearing a robe and had his arms outstretched.

The lady talking on the TV said, "And there is Jesus Christ at the top of the staircase welcoming his flock as they ascend. This is the most inspiring and moving image that I think we've ever seen on this Earth, and certainly on this network. It's the most incredible thing I've ever seen. I'm in shock. I'm speechless. Everyone in the studio is tearing up."

And then a man started talking on the TV like he was having a conversation with the first lady. "I think we can all relate to what Jill is saying. It's time for all of us to ask ourselves how we've lived our lives. To ask if we've accepted Jesus."

And then a third voice said, "What I'm thinking about, Jill and Peter, is all the Muslims, and the Jewish people seeing this, and the non-believers especially. This is confirmation that the Christian faith is the one true faith, and what a beautiful moment of—well, I want to say reckoning, but I don't mean it like that."

And then the lady's voice came back. "A moment of decision. A moment of clarity, I'm sure, for many."

"Yes," the man said. "Clarity. And people from all over the world, I expect, are seeing this and are moved now for maybe the first time in their lives, to give their hearts to Jesus at this hour, those who have not already been saved."

"Friday, July 24th, 2020," the other man said. "This is the day Jesus has returned to the Earth, and the world will never be the same."

The lady said, "We're bringing you this special coverage live without commercial interruption. No, wait, I'm being told we do need to take a commercial break for just a moment, everyone, and then when we come back we'll have more from Israel and we'll be joined by Dr. Dupre Zachary, who is on his way to join his fellow believers to meet Jesus Christ today and become part of his heavenly kingdom, but he graciously agreed to talk with us for a little bit this morning about everything that's happening. We'll be right back."

And then a commercial came on.

I looked over at Grandma and Rene. "Is this a movie?"

Grandma wrapped her arms around me again and said, "It's real, Patrick. It's real! Jesus is here."

"It's on all the news networks," Rene said.

"Everything I told you about," Grandma said, "Everything in the Bible is true, just like I told you. This is the end times. The last days. No more suffering on this Earth!"

I was confused. The end of the world was here all of a sudden? And Grandma was happy about it? I got a cold feeling in my arms and legs. I asked Mom what we were going to do.

"Honey, we're going. Jesus came back. It's all real. It's time to go up to heaven. Everything's going to be okay, honey."

But this didn't sound like an okay thing to me at all. People went to heaven when they died. I wasn't ready to die. I just cheated death. More than once! And now I have to die on purpose?

"I don't want to die!"

"You're not going to die, sweetheart," Grandma said with a laugh. "The furthest from it. This is life. A new life in Christ. We're all going to live forever with him in heaven."

Rene took a deep breath and didn't budge from where he was standing, fixed on the TV.

Mom came up to him and said, "Are you sure you're not coming?"

Rene didn't seem to know what to say at first, but then he said, "For now I need to get back to Pasadena. There's no signal. There are some people I need to talk to."

"Rene, open your heart," Grandma said like she was begging. "It's right in front of your eyes. All you have to do is open them."

"I just need some time to think. This is quite extraordinary."

Mom held her phone out to him. "I'll be in touch. If cell service comes back, I want you to let us know if you change your mind, okay? Texting, at least iPhone to iPhone, still seems to work, thank goodness."

"Wait," I said, "Where are we going, Mom?"

"We're going to try to get to Israel. That's where it's happening."

"Where is that? What is it? How far?"

"It's a long flight," Mom said.

"It's God's holy land," Grandma said. "It's another country."

"Probably about a fourteen-hour flight, I think," Rene said.

"And Rene's not coming?"

"No, I don't think he wants to come, honey. Not yet."

"Oh, he'll come around. I have faith." Grandma laughed.

"But I want him to come," I said.

Rene was being serious, but I noticed a little smile poke through his eyes when I said that. "I appreciate you saying that, Patrick." But he was mostly looking at the TV.

He used the remote to change to a different station where there was another picture of the staircase and the clouds and

Jesus. This one showed it from above, like it was taken from a plane. The stairs looked like a giant tower of blocks that reached into the clouds, and big rays of sunshine lit up the stairs and the giant crowd of people moving up them, bunching up around the first step on the ground. Words on the bottom of the screen said, "Drone footage of the Second Coming."

The whole thing was making my insides flip. It was all happening too fast. *The end of the world? Jesus? Go to another country and give up my life?* This was too big of a "Wham!" I wanted to ride my bike, explore more woods, read more books, and make more friends. I wanted to grow up, get a job, be a grown-up, and maybe have kids of my own someday. I wanted a horse. Heaven doesn't have any of that stuff, as far as I ever heard. It's just sitting around and playing harps, I'm pretty sure, and being loved by Jesus all day. I was starting to have some serious second thoughts about my promise to God and Jesus and Grandma.

"I don't want to go."

Grandma was saying her Hallelujahs and Mom was running through the house going through things she was trying to remember. She mentioned turning off the water, stopping the cable bill, calling the electric company, calling her sister, and things like that. Rene was looking hard at the TV. It seemed like no one heard me. I felt like I was in the center of a tornado and everything was too loud, and sound didn't work anymore.

I said it again, louder. "I don't want to go!"

"Of course you're going, Patrick," Grandma said. "Don't be silly."

"I want to live. I want to grow up. I don't want to go to heaven and die!" Now I had tears. Why do they always come when they're not supposed to?

Mom stood behind me and hugged me with her hands on my chest, saying, "Shh, shh. I know this is big stuff, Patrick. All of us are in shock right now. But it's really a wonderful thing. It's Jesus. He's come back. It's a miracle. We have to go."

"Patrick, do you know what happens if you don't go?" Grandma said.

I shook my head, but Grandma barely paid me any mind. She just kept talking.

"What happens is you'll be cast down." She pushed both her hands down. "You'll suffer the tribulation. It'll be the most terrible time in the history of the world. You'll be thrown into the pit of fire, and the antichrist will—"

"Ma! You're going to scare him to death."

I caught a look at Rene, and he didn't seem scared.

"But Rene's staying."

"Rene has to make his own decisions and live with that, honey," Mom said. "You're my son and I want you to come with me. Grandma makes a good point. When everybody goes, who's going to take care of you? Where would you go?"

"I'll live here." As soon as I said it, I knew it would never work. I might survive a few days, but then what? Would I try to steal cans of food from the grocery store? I don't even know where the can opener is in this house.

Then the thought of Mom and Grandma going, leaving me here by myself, hit me like a sock in the nose. I felt a big flood of tears coming, but I tried to hold them back. "Don't leave me alone, Mom! Don't leave me behind!"

She turned around and hugged me tight. "Then come with. It's going to be okay. Jesus isn't going to let anything bad happen to you. I promise. Heaven is whatever you want it to be. If you want to grow up and live, you can do that, I'm sure of it. The only difference is Jesus will be there."

"We'll be at peace in his heavenly kingdom," Grandma said. "Hallelujah!"

I settled down after Mom kept hugging me. She wiped my tears, and I was hoping Rene was paying closer attention to the TV than to me so he wouldn't see me crying.

"This is really a wonderful opportunity, honey. You get to be alive when Jesus comes back. People have been waiting for this for thousands of years."

I knew I had no choice, but I had to take a stand at least. I sat on the couch and crossed my arms.

"Okay, I'll go. But I'm going to wait and decide whether I go up the stairs once I get there."

"Okay," Mom said. "That's good enough for now." She got up and kept going through her list. She mentioned calling to cancel the newspaper delivery, calling her boss at work, and putting food in the dog bowl.

"Mom!" I sat up. "We can't just go to another country and leave Buster! He'll just have food for a day or two and then he'll starve to death!"

"Patrick, honey, we can't take him with us. I don't think dogs go to heaven."

"No, dogs go to heaven. That's well established," Rene said.

"Then we can bring him!"

Mom sighed big. "Okay. Fine. We'll bring him. But you're in charge of him. I don't know how we get him on the plane, but I can't worry about that right now. Oh, no, we have a carrier." Mom was just mumbling about everything now, going from one subject to the next. "I have to call the bank. And my credit card."

Grandma reached her hands out to Mom. "Marion, settle down. Settle down now." She hugged her, and my mom went limp in her arms. I thought for a moment about how my mom used to be a kid like me, and Grandma was her mom, and she hugged her like Mom hugs me and calms me down. "It's time to let go of the material world, sweetheart. Those things don't matter anymore."

"I'm just trying to be practical," Mom said. "Thanks, Ma."

Mom tore herself away from Grandma and went right back to being busy. She gathered her suitcase and my knapsack. She packed clothes, toiletries, snacks, and water bottles she wanted us to have for the plane. She brought the dog carrier and went through her purse to make sure she had everything she needed.

When it seemed like she and Grandma were ready to leave, Rene turned away from the TV and they talked about how they were going to get places. Rene said he would drive south. He promised to keep in touch with us. He turned to me and said it was nice to meet me. I said it back to him and I felt like a genuine grown-up doing it.

"Mom, I want to text with Rene."

Mom thought for a second and then said, "Sure, I don't see why not."

"Rene, would you text with me? You seem like you'd be a good person to text with."

Rene took out his phone and smiled. "Of course, Patrick. I'd be honored." We traded phone numbers. I had mine memorized already. And then we sent a text to each other, and I put his name and even took a picture of him for my phone like Mom taught me.

We said our goodbyes, and Rene got in his car. The rest of us got in Mom's. It was a hot day, but thankfully Mom's car has air conditioning.

Once we got to the highway, the road was packed with cars. They were barely going any faster than a turtle could walk. Then we saw people getting out of their cars and walking on the side of the highway.

"Oh my god, they're just walking to the airport?" Mom said. "That's got to be a five-hour walk."

"It's an army of the faithful," Grandma said. "Just look at them."

Mom curved around cars best she could. A lot of cars were honking. She kept trying to move around the cars on the road and drive on the grass next to the road, but there was a railing there and she couldn't get through. When she found an opening with no railing, she got on the grass, but even the grass was full of cars, some of them driving and some of them just sitting there with no people inside and with the doors hanging open. One of the cars I saw like that was a police car.

Grandma switched on the car radio and turned it to a station where a man was talking about Jesus.

"No man knows the day or hour, not even the angels in heaven. That's from Matthew 24:36. But friends, the Rapture is here. It is upon us."

"Blessed be your name, Jesus," Grandma said. "We're coming to you, Lord."

The man on the radio said, "We who are saved have already listened to his word, and we have seen the signs of his coming. We have seen the prophecies coming true all around us. We have seen the nation of Israel established. We have seen Europe become unified under a single governing body. We have seen war all over the world—in Yemen, in Syria, in Iraq, and in Afghanistan. We have seen so much biblical prophecy come to pass. What we have not seen and what we do not know is, who is the antichrist? Who is the powerful, evil ruler, this most powerful of all rulers on the Earth, the one who utterly lacks morality, who exalts himself above God, who mocks the word of God? This we do not know. We who are saved need not fear him because we are saved, and the Lord protects us. But this terrifying figure is among us. There is no doubt of that. Be ever watchful. Be ever vigilant. He could be anywhere."

While we drove, my mind wandered. I imagined the scary antichrist like a ghost or a Dracula lurking around with a cape, biting people as they walked along the highway to get to the airport. I watched all the other cars making their way through, and I watched the clouds in the sky. The world seemed like it wasn't real. All of 2020 felt like a bad dream. I was glad Buster was in the seat next to me. I was glad Mom was there. I couldn't imagine what would happen next, but I was glad I wasn't alone.

Another man came on the radio and talked to the first one. He asked, "Doctor, where are the dead believers who Jesus will resurrect? This is an important part of the biblical prophecy, and we haven't seen it yet."

And the first man said, "Oh, I believe we have already seen it. But not with our eyes. With our hearts. Jesus is raising the dead all over the world, but they are of the spirit. They are not visible to us. Their spirits are perfect, and that is what Jesus Christ is lifting out of the graves to meet the Lord now. He will make them flesh and blood. He will make them live again. That's what I believe."

"Glory be to our savior Christ Jesus," the other man said.

"Praise his name," Grandma said.

The end of the world keeps getting stranger.

From the backseat, I texted Rene, "People are leaving their cars and walking to the airport. And there are zombies now."

Rene texted back. "Not surprised. I took Highway 65 to bypass Sacramento. Looping around Folsom Lake. Not as much traffic."

16

The airport seemed like it was a trillion miles away. The abandoned cars on the highway were like stones on a creek. A giant could walk on cars to the airport and never let his feet touch the street. We drove on the grass next to the highway to avoid them when we could, and that was like driving through Mrs. Cummings' garden. Sometimes high weeds would slap against the windows, other times we had to go over bumpy dirt holes. Sometimes we waited for an hour while people honked and sat still. People were walking on the highway and on the grass, and the closer we got to the airport, the more people were walking. Almost none of them were wearing masks. I guess they figured Jesus wouldn't mind.

"Mom, are the cousins meeting us there?"

"I couldn't get in touch with my sister. I wanted to carpool. I'm sure we'll see them there."

"What does 'carpool' mean?"

"It means all take the same car."

"We can't do that. How would we social distance?"

"Does that even matter anymore?"

"Yes, it matters, Mom! Remember what the doctor said?"

"Right. Of course, honey."

Jesus was making everybody's brain go soft, including Mom's. He may have come back, but everybody going up to heaven was going to die of the virus before they got there.

Mom kept saying she wished we could get out and walk. She didn't say so, but I knew she meant that Grandma wouldn't get very far with her arthritis.

One time there was no way to get past a line of cars. They were blocking the whole road. Mom and some other drivers got out and talked over how to get through. They looked inside all the cars that were blocking the way and found one with the key still in it, so somebody drove the car off to the side, and that made a small passageway where the other cars could make it through. I heard some people outside clapping when that happened, and drivers rolled down their windows and said "God bless you" to my mom and the other people after they moved the car.

But even after that, Mom had to make her way around a lot of cars that people left on the highway. She and Grandma kept talking about how close she came to hitting some of them. But Mom is a good driver because she didn't hit a single car the whole way. Some other cars didn't care. They slammed into other cars like it was the bumper cars at the carnival. One flat black car zoomed by us, screeching his tires and curving around everybody, knocking into cars and almost running over people that were walking. After he went by, everybody yelled at him to be careful and to slow down.

Grandma shook her head. "He's not going to make it to heaven driving like that."

Finally, we got close enough where we could see big blue signs for the airport. There were more people on the road than cars now. Some of them were carrying suitcases. Some had little kids on their backs. Women carried babies. I saw a lot of cat and dog carriers, so I was glad I wasn't the only one who brought a dog. Some people weren't carrying anything. We saw one group of people that was completely naked. I thought it was funny, but Mom and Grandma thought it was foolish.

"How do they think they're going to get let on the plane?" Mom said.

I passed a lot of the time watching the little blue dot on my phone that showed where we were on the map. I stretched it out and looked at the whole world map, and I found where Israel is. It's on the other side of the world.

Grandma stopped playing the preacher on the radio and found some choir music instead. That helped me concentrate, and I decided to text with Rene. I got into some good conversations with him. I told him about the strange things we were seeing on the road and he thought some of it was funny, I could tell.

I told him about the radio show Grandma was listening to and he said, "Sounds very educational."

I asked him, "Do you believe in God?"

He answered, "No."

I wasn't sure what to say to that at first. I was trying to think if I ever met anyone before who didn't believe in God. I thought everybody did. God is everywhere, after all. And now there's proof. So how could anyone not believe in him?

"Why?"

It took him a while to answer back. And when he did, it was a big message. He said he had a lot of reasons. He said if there was a being more powerful than us, they would probably want to either study us or conquer us. Why would they want to be worshiped? Then he said the thing from the night before, about how "extraordinary claims require extraordinary evidence."

I asked him what he thought of the evidence of Jesus coming back, because that seemed pretty good to me and everybody else.

He said he's been thinking about it a lot. Then he asked how close we were to the airport.

I told him we could see the signs for it, so maybe we were close.

That's when Mom stopped the car and said we were going to walk.

"You're just going to leave the car like the other people?" I asked.

"We don't need it anymore."

Grandma agreed. "You don't need a car to go to heaven."

I thought of saying, "but I guess you need a plane," but I knew they would call me a smart aleck for that, so I didn't.

Mom and Grandma said they talked about it, and they decided the airport was only a half a mile away, and Grandma thought she could make it. I had my doubts. The last thing I wanted to do was leave Grandma for the buzzards.

"Grandma, you're not going to make it," I said. "Don't try it!"

"Don't worry about me, Patrick. Jesus will help me walk. I have faith."

"No!"

But when she sets her mind to something, Grandma can't be stopped. And she got out and started waddling down the highway. I let Buster out of his carrier and put his leash on him. Mom carried the suitcase. I carried my knapsack. Grandma didn't carry anything. There were no clouds, so the sun was hitting us straight on. It was like walking in an oven.

We walked along the grass and followed the rest of the people. Most of them were smiley, trading "God bless yous" and "Praise the Lords" with Mom and Grandma. Mom seemed a little more embarrassed than Grandma to say those things to people, but she was getting into the spirit of it.

Grandma was waddling best she could, but I could tell she was getting tired. I felt her feet hitting the ground and her knee bones knocking into each other with every step. I imagined what it must feel like, a hammer of pain shooting up your leg every time your foot lands.

Mom kept asking, "Are you doing okay, Ma?"

"I can make it," she said. "Nothing's going to keep me from Jesus."

I was worried about Buster not getting enough water. He has a fur coat, after all. I fished out one of the water bottles Mom put in my knapsack and poured some by his mouth. He lapped his tongue at it and tried to get as much as he could.

Grandma lost her balance for a moment, but then righted herself. Mom and I tried to steady her.

A big man came up to Grandma and asked if she needed some help.

She said, "Oh thank you. God bless you."

The man put his arm around her and helped hold her up while she walked. Grandma is pretty big, so I was impressed that the man could help her at all. Then, after a while, another man got on the other side of her and they both helped her. Grandma laughed. "Oh thank you, boys, so much. You're a blessing to me. Jesus loves you both. You'll get your reward."

And that was Grandma's faith working out for her after all. It was like Jesus himself brought those two men to her.

I dug my face mask out of my knapsack and put it on because I didn't want the men to get sick.

Once, we had to make our way over a highway railing. They're taller than they look from the road. It was easy for me to climb over, but Grandma and her helpers had a challenge on their hands. Another lady came and helped lift Grandma's legs over the metal part, one by one. I saw her leg scrape on the thin metal edge of it as she was coming down, and it started bleeding. I told Grandma, but she didn't seem to mind. She kept walking. The blood was running pretty good down her leg after that.

There was no shade anywhere. I knew Buster's feet were probably getting burned on the hot pavement so I poured water on them. It didn't really help because the water evaporated fast.

I tried to carry him for a little, but I didn't get far. And he still didn't like it. I begged Mom to carry him in the carrier, but she said she had enough on her hands with the suitcase. I could feel the burning in my feet for Buster and kept telling him I was sorry that he was too much to carry.

"Are you hanging in there, honey?" Mom asked me every now and then. I would always say, "I'm okay." I was thinking it was Grandma and Buster she should be worried about, not me, but I didn't want to hurt Grandma's feelings by pointing that out. She was still sweating and working really hard, even with her helpers.

When we finally saw the airport, I thanked the heavenly angels for Grandma's sake. It was a big fancy glass building. There was a big crowd of people outside, and just a parking lot to get through before we got there. I couldn't see over the crowd. The men holding up Grandma said there were police by the doors, and they weren't letting people in.

When we got closer to the airport, the crowd got thicker. The sun was even stuffier in the heat of all the bodies, and it smelled like everybody's hot sweat. We came about a stone's throw from the airport and the crowd stopped moving. People were yelling at the police. The police were just standing in front of the airport. I hoped they weren't going to start killing us. I sat down by Buster and let him rest his feet on my folded legs. I pulled my shirt over my head to shield me from the sun, but that just made me hotter.

Grandma also sat down. She was breathing real loud and sweating. She looked at me and smiled.

"We did good, Patrick. We made it. Jesus brought me here, and he won't let us down. He'll make sure we get there. I know it."

People in the crowd were talking to each other. Mom was part of a couple of conversations. I didn't hear all of it, but I picked up that they were trying to convince the police to let us in.

They started chanting, "Let us in! Let us in!"

I tried to stand and look up and see what was happening, but there was no way I could see anything in any direction. It was just a thick forest of muggy human bodies all around me. If only I had a dad who could put me on his shoulders. I saw some little kids up there like that. This was one of those times in life when you wish you either had a dad or a periscope.

A siren came blaring from behind us and I heard a car pull up. It might have been more than one car. A voice on a loudspeaker came from the same direction.

"Step away from the doors. Step away from the doors," the voice said.

People in the crowd booed and yelled at the voice. Some of the people around us said they thought the police were being stupid and didn't understand that we had a higher calling than some dumb police rules.

"We're here to meet Jesus, not play footsie with a bunch of airport cops," one man said.

The crowd started moving. At first, people cheered, but pretty soon I heard people screaming. I felt people coming up behind me, but the people in front of me didn't move. It was like a big wall pushing me in and crushing me. I stood up and tried to help Grandma up, but everybody pressed against us, and they wouldn't stop pushing. It happened so fast, changing in just a few seconds from hot boredom to a fight for our lives in a real-life atom smasher. Before I knew it, I was one of the people screaming.

"Stop! You're stepping on my grandma!" I yelled.

Mom was pulling on my shirt and yelling. She was hitting against people. People stepped on Grandma's legs and just kept coming

"Stop!" I screamed. Buster barked with me.

I was getting crushed to death in a crowd of people again, with Mom and Grandma this time too! I didn't see any way out of it. They were squeezing the breath out of me.

"Back away from the doors." The voice said again. I couldn't figure out why they were saying the same thing again when the last time they said it they made everything worse because that's when everybody started cramming into us.

I tried to pull Grandma, but I couldn't move her. I was suffocating between somebody's fat, sticky back and somebody else's fat, squishy stomach.

Grandma started praying out loud. "As I walk through the shadow of the valley of death, I will fear no evil!"

Pretty soon I heard more cheers from the front. The crowd moved toward the airport, and some of the pressure eased off Mom and Grandma and me. I couldn't move as fast as the crowd moved, not with Grandma sitting down. I pulled her by her shirt, but I don't think I moved her much. Mom pulled too. Then one of Grandma's helper men grabbed onto her arms and dragged her on the pavement like a sack of dirt while people around us moved with him. I kept pulling her too. Mom was crying and asking Grandma to get up, but Grandma was just mumbling to herself. I don't think she was saying anything important. Just prayers. Buster stayed by us, barking and whimpering.

I bumped into some kind of beam behind me. I looked up and saw it was a door to the airport. I felt a blast of cold air. We were going inside. I saw police standing in there, watching the people come in. They had face masks on and just stood there with their arms behind their backs.

We got inside, and the man propped Grandma up against the glass of the front wall. It was like a big window and the sun was shining right through it. There was dainty music tinkling, echoing all around. He knelt and asked if she was going to be okay. Grandma was breathing so heavy and sweating so bad, I didn't think she would be able to talk. But she managed to say, "God bless you. Good man."

The man got up and left. He reminded me of Bill Cody. He came in like a hero and then went off, probably to help other people, and he didn't even ask for anything in return. He was the kind of hero who'd say, "Just doing my job, Ma'am."

Mom took out a tissue from her bag and dabbed Grandma's face.

"Don't fuss over me, Marion," Grandma said. "The spirit is all that matters now. Not this worldly body."

When she said that, I got a little spooked, like Grandma was saying she was ready to die.

I put my hand on her and said, "You're going to be okay, Grandma."

Mom looked Grandma over and saw all the blood on her leg. She lifted the back of Grandma's shirt and we saw more blood on her back. It made me shudder. Her skin was torn up from being dragged, like somebody took a cheese grater to it. It had tiny bits of gravel all over it. Mom tried to dab it with her tissue, but it got used up pretty quick. She found a shirt from the suitcase and wrapped it around, tying the sleeves in front.

Grandma whispered to me that she wanted water, and I gave her the bottle I fed to Buster from my knapsack. She took a long drink and emptied it.

"We need to get more water," Mom said. "Also we need to see about flights. I don't know what we're going to be able to find. I feel like we're on the early side, but there's no telling. The lines at the ticket counters are unreal. I can't even see where they start."

She looked at me. "Patrick, stay here with Grandma and Buster. Watch them while I get some water and try to get some information, okay?"

I was a little unsure about being here myself in case Mom got lost, but something inside me made me nod and say "okay" like it would be fine, especially after that Bill Cody hero helped Grandma.

Mom smiled, rubbed my hair, and walked off.

I hugged Grandma, hoping that would make her feel better.

"Oh, you sweet child," she said. She reached one of her arms around me to hug me back.

Buster stood by us and wagged his tail. I think he was happy to be out of the sun and the hot crowd. I'm sure the air-conditioning in the airport felt just as nice for him as for me. There were plenty of people running around inside, but at least they weren't all bunched together. Every once in a while a big voice would come on a speaker that filled the whole airport, but it didn't sound like the police. It was calmer, usually announcing that a flight was leaving, or where you could get on a flight. I've figured out that you don't have to pay attention to any big voice on a speaker in 2020.

Mom came back after a while and said she talked to someone who worked at the airport. She looked tired.

"A lot of the airlines are diverting all their flights to Israel, but they're booked. Every one of them. Booked for days. All we can do is wait. They don't know how long police are going to let people just camp out at the airport, but they don't think they can control this many people either. It's a mess. And there's more people coming. They can't keep anything staffed. Police, airport people, everybody—they all want to go to Israel."

"We need a miracle," Grandma said with a little laugh. "Jesus is going to send me a miracle. I know he will."

I figured Grandma would turn out to be right about that because she's been right about everything else so far.

17

I HAD TO DECIDE if I was going up the big staircase to Jesus when we got to Israel. I was trying not to think about it, but it was all I thought about. My mind went in a circle. Would I figure out more things if went, or if I stayed back? Mom is set to go. Grandma is excited to go. Do I really need someone to take care of me if I'm on my own? I couldn't bear to lose my mom. I'd have to convince her to stay back with me. If I stayed, would 2020 swallow me? If I went, would it open up a new life for me where I get all the answers? I can't imagine Grandma making it up those stairs. They'll have to wrap a chain around her and pull her up with a pickup truck.

I've been trying to focus on each chore we have to get done before then. Right now it's waiting at the airport. We waited a long time. Mom stood in a lot of lines at the airline counters and finally got our names on a waiting list. Grandma slept for a lot of that time, resting up against the glass wall. Buster was hungry and thirsty. I fed him some of the snacks Mom brought, a candy bar that she said was supposed to be healthy, and some popcorn. I found a cardboard box in one of the trash cans that I filled with water for him, after clearing out some leftover food from it.

On one of her runs to wait in line, Mom tried to get more water but said none of the airport stores had any left. She was able to get some warm orange juice though. Grandma drank most of it. I figured Buster wouldn't like orange juice, so I didn't even try feeding it to him.

More people came into the airport all the time. I couldn't see if the police were still standing there because there were so many people.

The sun was still out, but it was starting to get lower in the sky. It got so bright sitting right in front of the window wall, it was like Grandma and Buster and our little camp were glowing orange.

Some people started camping out around us. Right next to us was a big family of people speaking German. I decided it was German because they sounded like the Nazi bad guys from a radio show I heard once. I don't remember the name. They were teenagers. They didn't talk to us, even though we were right next to them. That was okay by me because I wasn't sure what I would say to them. I didn't know if the Germans were still our enemies after the war. I figured they weren't because none of them tried to stab me with a bayonet. Then Buster made friends with them, and they asked if they could take a picture with him. They were friendly after that. I felt silly that I ever thought they would stab me.

I checked my phone to see if Rene texted. He did.

He wrote, "Get some tinfoil."

I texted back, "Tinfoil?"

"Just get it."

That's when I noticed the Germans got up and ran off. I looked around the airport and it looked like a lot of people were leaving the airport in a hurry. Everybody seemed like they were either confused or had a better idea all of a sudden. A moment ago we were all dying to get inside the airport, now they were racing to get out.

Mom was on one of her runs, so I just stayed put with Grandma and Buster. I sat there and watched as people poured out of the doors. I started wondering if we were missing out on something.

I texted Mom, "Everybody's running out."

She didn't text back right away. She normally does.

I sat snug against Grandma and held onto Buster. I was bursting inside to know what was happening and why Mom wasn't texting back.

A big voice came on the airport speakers. I thought it was going to explain what was happening, but it was just another regular announcement. "Final boarding call for flight 9287 to Tel Aviv."

Then I wondered if we were missing our plane. I saw Tel Aviv on my map of Israel, so I figured that's where everybody was trying to go. I didn't think Mom would ever leave us, but the thought crossed my mind that she just decided we were too much trouble, and she got scared she'd miss the plane, so she got on without us.

"To heck with Patrick and Grandma. They'll be fine."

I don't know why I was thinking this, but I couldn't stop it from coming into my head, and it was getting me all worked up.

Then I saw her coming toward us, pushing a big blue wheelchair.

"Look what I got!" she said. "They were fighting over them and I had to give up some cash, but I got it. It's worth it. We're getting out of here. We're leaving the airport."

"Why? Where are we going?"

"Just get Grandma up and get your stuff and let's get going. I'll explain. Hurry."

I nudged Grandma awake.

She opened her eyes and said, "Oh, Jerry."

"It's Patrick, Grandma."

"Oh, Patrick."

"You have to get up now."

I felt the red flush into my face when she got me confused for Jerry. I imagined her getting lost in a dream and didn't know if this was now or when Jerry was my age. She pretended like she wasn't sleeping and tried to get up on her own but didn't have much luck.

She saw the wheelchair and said, "Oh thank you, my dear. There's my miracle." And she tried to laugh, even though she was working really hard just to stand up and get in the wheelchair.

Mom figured out how to lock the wheelchair so it wouldn't roll, and eventually with all of us working together, we got Grandma in the seat. If only we had pulleys it would have been easier. I hung the empty dog carrier on the back. Mom pushed Grandma in the wheelchair and walked fast out of the airport with the other people, and I ran to keep up with her. I had Buster by the leash and my knapsack over my shoulder. Everybody ran outside. A lot of them just kept running away from the airport. Some of them stopped and looked up in the sky. Mom just wheeled Grandma and kept looking back to make sure I was keeping up.

"Is there a plane on the tarmac?" Grandma asked.

"No, no plane," Mom said.

We crossed a street and then went through another parking lot, and then an airplane parking lot. The sun was lower, and the sky was turning light purple. It was still hot but not as bad as before. I thanked the heavenly angels for that because I felt like I practically melted on the way there. We walked by a bunch of planes parked that were purple, orange, and white that said "FedEx." I figured that was the name of one of the airline companies. There were so many planes just sitting there. They didn't seem to be in a hurry to get anybody to Israel. I decided they must be the laziest airplane company of them all.

We walked on a big flat road that seemed to go on forever. I looked down one of them and saw an airplane turning to face us.

"Mom, I don't think this is a sidewalk."

"I know, honey. It's okay."

People were walking in every direction away from the airport. The ground was flat everywhere you could see, just dry sand and rocks with little dead shrubs here and there. There were mountains off in the distance. The wheelchair was too hard to push on the ground, so Mom stayed on the pavement. A lot of the people were walking into the fields.

I asked Mom why we left the airport and where we were going. She kept saying she just needed to focus on getting clear of the airport and that she didn't trust her sense of direction. She had to keep looking at the map on her phone and wheeling Grandma this way and that. I stayed on her tail.

Grandma wasn't being her usual self. She wasn't saying much and seemed like she lost a lot of her energy. But she managed to get out some words.

"Marion, where on Earth are we headed?"

We got off the pavement and Mom had to get Grandma across a short stretch of bumpy ground to get us through a chain-link fence that some other people tore up from the bottom so you could lift it and pass under. We could have used more men to get through that, but we managed with me holding up the fence and Mom pushing her through. I felt like a World War II commander ordering his men to clear a path through the French countryside to get Grandma through.

We came to some kind of back road with no cars on it. It had old pavement in the middle and gravel on the sides. The other people wandered in different directions, but we stayed on the road because of the wheelchair.

Mom looked at her phone and said we were in a good position. She took a deep breath and explained why we came out here. She said she heard people talking in the airport, and then she saw on the airport TVs that people didn't have to get on planes anymore. She said Jesus was sending angels to gather people and bring them to him.

"Angels!?" Grandma said. "Praise Jesus. That's my miracle. Not the chair. Though I am very grateful for the chair."

Mom said she listened close to make sure she had it right. They said it over and over on the TV, she said. And then she watched more TV on her phone. I didn't know you could get TV on your phone, so I asked her to show us.

I was just as surprised as Grandma, and couldn't wait to see these angels on the phone TV. It was like at the house, with the words and colored boxes all over the screen, only smaller. It had different movies of floating angels with long robes, glowing white and yellow with big wings. They had light all around them and shooting out of them. They were moving across fields and over little towns.

Mom said the angels started appearing in Israel around Jesus, but people were seeing them all over the world now.

One announcer said, "You're looking at some cell-phone footage of Christ's angels here from a variety of places. We believe they are gathering people and taking them to Jesus. It seems they are appearing mostly in open spaces, like fields, parking lots, and over small towns and villages."

Grandma grabbed the phone and took in the angels like they were a drink of water. She looked like she was going to cry.

"They're lovely."

"Watch more, Ma. I don't need it for a while."

Grandma kept watching the phone, and every once in a while I would hear a voice giving out more clues about Jesus and the angels. I heard that the angels were blaring a loud tone to call to people. They played the tone, and it sounded a bit like a horn but also a siren.

They showed a man in front of a house pointing up and saying, "I saw that angel pick her up, and he just lifted her away. I never saw anything like it. God is real. He's here."

"Jesus, thank you for sending your angels for me," Grandma said.

Every once in a while Grandma would repeat something she heard or got excited about.

"One million souls brought to Christ. From all over the world."

"The angels come with fire and smite the nonbelievers!"

"They're lifting travel restrictions. Borders are opening so people can come to Jesus."

"Muslims are coming. Hindus. Nonbelievers. Praise the Lord."

I fixed my mind on the part about the angels smiting nonbelievers with fire. Would the angels know I believed? Or would they see inside me and know that I wasn't as convinced as Grandma? Would I pass their test? I held tight to Buster's leash and stayed close to Mom, but I couldn't get the angels' fire out of my head. Now, instead of an H-bomb, I was going to get burned by an angel? There were too many crazy new ways this world was going to kill me. I couldn't keep up.

"Are you doing okay, honey?"

"I don't know."

"This is pretty wild, isn't it?"

"I guess so. Are we going to get picked up by one of those angels?"

"I think so. They said to go to an open area. That's where people see them. And they said they were everywhere. We should see them."

"When?"

"I don't know, honey. They're angels. They can be here whenever they want, I guess."

"Do you think they'll help us, or are they going to burn us with their fire?"

"Of course they're going to help us, honey. Why would they burn us?"

"Do they know Grandma helped me get saved?"

"I'm sure they do, honey."

"Do they know what I'm thinking?"

"I don't know if angels can read minds. I'm sure God can, and they work for God, so—"

"What's going to happen when they find us?"

"I don't know, honey. Let's have faith, okay? If there was ever a time for faith, it's now."

The sun started to disappear. This was partly good because at least it got cooler. This was partly not good because pretty soon we couldn't see where we were going. There were some woods coming up on the side of the road that looked like a big black blob. Except for the phone TV, our feet on the road, and a tiny squeak in Grandma's wheels, you couldn't hear anything in the night. It was like we were the only people in the world.

I asked Mom more questions about the angels, like how big did she think they would be, would they be boys or girls, did they talk, and lots of other questions, but mostly I couldn't get my mind off whether they would kill me or not.

I heard the same man we heard on the car radio before on Mom's phone. Grandma must have found him in there.

"Matthew 24:31 prophesied that Jesus will send his angels out with a loud trumpet call and he will gather his elect from the four winds. Luke 21 prophesied the roaring of the seas and the waves, and it prophesied people fainting with fear and foreboding."

The sky started rumbling, and little flashes of lightning were popping up around.

Just then the man said, "For as the lightning comes from the east and shines as far as the west, so will be the coming of the Son of Man."

Mom said she thought there was a house coming up and wanted to stop to see if they'd let us in. She asked Grandma to turn her phone off when we turned off the road.

The gravel driveway led to a big two-story house with a porch. There were no lights on in the house or outside. I could tell it was a white house because pretty much everything else was pitch black except the house.

We heard a dog barking. He had a low bark and sounded like he was a big, mean dog. Buster barked back. I asked him to hush, but he kept barking. I got the shivers when I imagined the dog running out and chomping onto my leg, knocking me down, and then chewing me up and eating me like he was a hound from hell with red eyes. The bark sounded like it was coming from the house.

Mom borrowed her phone from Grandma and flashed the screen around so we could see around us. There was a big barn across from the house. She gave the phone back to Grandma and walked up to the house. I tied Buster's leash to Grandma's chair and went with her.

She knocked. No one answered. She cupped her hands to look in the windows and then knocked again.

"I don't think anybody's home," she said.

"They probably left to go to Israel like everybody else."

The dog was barking like crazy now.

Mom thought about it for a moment and then said, "I could just try the door, don't you think? If they didn't lock it, then they don't mind if people come in, right?"

I liked that Mom was asking my opinion about things and not just leaving me out of decisions like Dad always did. Now that we were by the door, I could tell the big dog was outside, behind the house, and I figured he must be tied up because otherwise, why wasn't he attacking us? I was nervous about what would happen if we opened the door, but with Mom there I felt safe, so I shrugged.

"Okay, I guess," I said like I wasn't scared at all.

She tried the door. It was locked.

She looked back at Grandma, who didn't seem to be paying

attention to much of anything except the TV.

Mom whispered, "Let's see if they have a back door."

We went around to the side and found a door. She tried it, and it was open. She looked at me and smiled. She poked her head in.

"Hello? Is anybody home? Hello?"

Nobody answered. The big dog stopped barking and started whining.

Mom whispered in my ear, "Now Patrick, it's wrong to steal."

"I know."

"But we've eaten up all our snacks. And if these people are gone, if they've gone to Jesus, which I think you're probably right about, it's not really stealing. They'd *want* us to—" She froze like she couldn't think of the words.

"Steal from them?" I said.

"Yeah, I guess that's what I mean."

We went inside, and I was about to say I wish we brought a flashlight when Mom asked if she could borrow my phone. I dug it out, and she pressed a control that made it into a flashlight. I didn't know it could do that.

The kitchen was up a couple of stairs from the back door. Mom opened the fridge and found some bread, cheese, and oranges.

Then we heard Grandma's voice from outside.

"Marion!" she said. "Are you in the house!?"

Mom ran out and whisper-yelled back to Grandma, "Yeah, we're just trying to—"

"Get out of there! That's not your house! Jesus has come back and you're disobeying one of his ten commandments? I'm surprised at you!"

Mom let out a big breath and came back in the kitchen and asked me to turn around. She loaded my knapsack with the food from the fridge.

"Okay, fine. Coming, Ma!" she yelled. She looked at me. "I'll never stop hearing about this if I don't back out now."

I pictured Grandma spending all of eternity in heaven yelling at Mom for stealing food from this house.

The dog who lived here started barking again. I don't think he liked Mom and Grandma yelling.

Mom grabbed a couple of cans of beans and chili off a shelf and loaded those too. She whispered for me to look in a drawer for a can opener. After a few tries in a few different drawers, I found one. I also saw a roll of tinfoil and remembered what Rene said, so I took that too.

We came back out and felt rain starting to come down. Mom held her shirt over her head and ran to Grandma.

"Of all the foolish things to do," Grandma said. "Don't sin on the day he comes back. Jesus can see you! I don't understand you sometimes."

"You'll be glad when you're eating a cheese sandwich, Ma."

"I will not eat a stolen cheese sandwich!"

Mom pushed Grandma toward the barn. The doors weren't locked. I helped slide them open. I really felt like I was one of the Army men now. Inside it was warm, stuffy, and smelled like straw. Mom left the door open to at least let moonlight in so we could see a little. Straw bales were stacked up high on one side. A big go-cart vehicle was on the other side. If this wasn't the actual end of the world, I'd be thinking of how I could take that go-cart for a ride.

"Make yourselves comfortable, everybody. We might be sleeping here tonight," Mom said.

Buster loved being in the barn. I think the straw smelled good to him. I was excited to feed him some bread and cheese and maybe some chili.

Mom got us set up in a little circle in the center of the barn and asked everybody if they were all right.

That's about when Grandma went crazy.

It happened without any warning bells. She held Mom's

phone above her head and then threw it at the floor.

"Ma, what are you doing? You're going to break my phone!"

Grandma brought her head back and screamed. I went cold and felt like I couldn't move. It was so loud it hurt. It was like she just went bonkers out of the blue. The big dog started barking again. Buster barked too.

"The antichrist! The antichrist!" she yelled.

Mom tried to grab onto her and settle her down.

"Ma, what is it? What happened?"

I stood back. I never saw anybody go crazy like this. She was screaming her head off like that lady in *Cat Women of the Moon* who got poisoned by the giant alien spider and then turned evil. What next? Was she going to spit out her new twenty-foot-long tongue and wrap it around our necks and strangle us? I held onto Buster and stayed back.

"My daughter has his mark! My flesh and blood! Patrick has his mark! It must be a mistake! It can't be happening!" She was crying and twisting like she was trying to get Mom away from her. She tried to get out of the wheelchair but couldn't lift herself.

"What are you talking about, mother? What is going on? You're scaring the shit out of everybody!"

I never saw Mom lose her cool like this before.

Grandma shook and blathered about the antichrist and didn't make any sense.

Mom picked up the phone and looked at it for a few seconds. Then her shoulders went limp. "Oh, no."

18

Mom thought Grandma might be upset because she didn't take her medicine today. I got it out of the suitcase, and Mom tried to give it to her with the last of our water, but Grandma wouldn't eat it.

Mom knelt in front of the wheelchair and held onto Grandma's arms. Mom's wet hair was hanging in front of her face and kind of sticking to it. I asked her what was happening, and she told me Grandma saw something on the phone that upset her.

"What did she see?"

"Please, just help me get her to take her medicine."

I moved toward Grandma nice and slow. I put my hand on her shoulder from behind. I was waiting for her to snap her head around and beam laser eyes at me and scream at me with her new alien voice, but she was just breathing and shivering. I think she was worn out. I could feel her worries like I was alone outside in the rain, like the dog who lived here.

I said, "It's okay, Grandma. Don't worry." I don't know how, but my voice came out sounding calm.

Grandma was whispering and muttering. I only heard some of it.

"It's the antichrist. The great deceiver is here."

"Ma, you're listening to crazy people on the Internet. Please, just put it out of your mind."

"What did she see?"

Mom tried to blow a clump of wet hair out of her face and look at me.

A big clap of thunder shook the whole barn. And lightning lit everything up for a split second. It made me jump.

"Somebody on the Internet had a stupid theory of who the antichrist is. They figure one of the richest people in the world, has a lot of power—"

"My dad!?"

"It's not true, honey. It's some crazy person's idea. And it must have really upset your grandma."

When she first said it, it kind of made me laugh inside. It would have been funnier if Grandma didn't believe it and wasn't acting so creepy.

"Your dad is not the antichrist."

"He is," Grandma whispered. "He is the evil one. He has signs and wonders. His money rules the world."

"Ma, you're being ridiculous."

"Pastor Zachary said. It's prophecy. The phones are his mark, the mark of the beast. Everyone has one. That's what he said." Then Grandma looked up at Mom. "And Marion, my sweet Marion, you've known him. And Patrick, my sweet little boy Patrick, the spawn of—"

Mom snapped at Grandma fast, "Don't you say that, Ma! Don't even think about saying what you're about to say."

Grandma burst out crying. She cried worse than I did before. Like a big old baby.

"No," she kept saying. "No. Jesus, please no." She said it over and over, shaking her head.

I felt how heavy things were for Grandma and it made me cry too.

"Ma, it's okay. Calm down." Mom looked at me and said, "We have to get her to take her medicine. She needs to take a sleeping pill too."

I looked in the suitcase for Grandma's other pills. I noticed the dogs were settled down. Maybe the thunder helped. Buster was sitting with his head up on a straw bale next to us.

Grandma was talking to herself. "The boy is saved. Patrick is saved now. He's with Jesus. He's saved."

Mom finally convinced Grandma to take her medicine, or maybe she was just too tired to fight anymore. I stood there a long time, just petting Grandma's shoulder. When Mom felt like she could leave Grandma alone, I helped make some sandwiches and open a can for Buster. Mom even sent me back into the house by myself to fill up our bottles with water. She wanted me to find some cloth in the house so she could make Grandma's bandages better, but I was too scared to go upstairs and look through dressers in any bedrooms. So I stayed with Grandma while she was still half awake, and Mom went in and found some pillowcases and also some blankets so we could sleep. After that, Grandma finally went to sleep in the chair, but she seemed to be having bad dreams.

"What if Grandma's right?"

"Oh, Patrick. Your dad is not the devil."

"But what if he is?"

"Well, then I guess we're safe because he's not going to hurt us. Your father would never hurt anybody."

"He has slaves."

"He has what?"

"Slaves. They make his phone things."

"No, honey, he pays people."

"The newspaper called them 'wage slaves.' It said they hardly get paid at all. They dig his chemicals in Africa, and they work in Sir Lanka."

"I think it's '*Sri* Lanka,' honey, but yes, I guess maybe he does have that." She said it like it was okay or something.

"Mom, that is not okay. You can't have slaves! It's wrong."

"Okay, you're right. Yes, he should pay people and take care of them if they work for him. But that doesn't make him the devil. A lot of people use cheap labor in other countries. I think everybody does."

"Do you have slaves!?"

Mom laughed. "No. I mean everybody who owns a big company. I don't own any companies, silly."

I had so many thoughts and feelings and daydreams floating around in my head. I felt like I was going to burst open. The rain was tapping on the roof of the barn and that seemed to rustle all of it up like a drum at the head of a revolutionary war party marching into battle with the Redcoats. It stirred up my brain and made a big storm of ideas that I didn't know what to do with. What if my dad was the antichrist? What did that make me? Was I evil? Or maybe it's Grandma. Maybe she's possessed by a demon or an alien. What kind of world is 2020 when slavery is back, everybody has slaves, and even my own mom thinks it's normal? Are the angels going to free all the slaves? Are the angels going to protect Black people from killer policemen? What will the angels do when they find us? Will they burn me because my dad is the son of the devil? Are they ever going to find us at all? Am I protected because I'm saved? Or is everyone else in the world going to go to heaven except me? Are the angels just going to leave us here like vultures to live off moldy food we find in people's dusty cupboards?

I thought again about that one. I don't think we'll have to eat like that. We could go into any store and take as many candy bars as we wanted, and no one would make us pay for them. Except Grandma. She'd probably make us put money on the counter when we left.

What if the angels take us to Jesus? What will heaven be like? Will everybody be happy then? Will all the problems go away?

Will Buster get to go? Will Dad? What about Rene? I never slept in a barn before. I wondered if the dog who lives here was okay outside in the rain. I wondered if my body would ever heal since I haven't been doing the exercises the doctor gave me. I think Mom forgot all about them. I guess it doesn't matter since I'll be dead in heaven soon.

"You're tired, honey. You should rest. We're all tired."

Mom was right. My brain was marching along, but my eyes felt heavy. I got down on the straw between Mom and Buster, but I couldn't close my eyes. Mom was looking at her phone.

I picked up mine and saw a bunch of texts from Rene.

"I made it back home to my friends."

"How are you?"

"Did you make it onto a plane?"

"Hope you're okay."

"Did you hear about the angels?"

"Are you and your mother and grandmother still together?"

"I hope you are all doing okay."

"I'm hearing not very good things on the news."

"Let me know you're okay when you can."

I felt bad that I didn't look at my phone for so long. It seemed like he was worried about us.

I texted back, "Got tinfoil."

I saw the little dots come on the screen. He was right there to write back. I liked that.

"Patrick! I'm glad to hear from you."

Then he sent another text. "How is everybody? Where are you?"

"We're in a barn. Grandma kind of went crazy. She thinks my dad is the devil."

"Ha. I heard about that. He's not. Don't worry."

"I know. Mom said so too."

"Patrick, can I call?"

I asked Mom if we could talk to Rene.

"Oh, are you texting? I got some too."

"He's nice."

"Yeah. Very nice person."

She thought about it for a second and then said, "Okay, we can try to talk for a bit, but then we should rest."

I texted him, "Yes."

The phone rang and I put it on the speaker. We traded hellos, and Rene said he was surprised we could talk because a lot of the phones weren't working. His voice got cut off here and there, but we could mostly tell what he was saying. He asked where we were and we told him about our adventures today. He told us he was at his work and with his friends there.

Mom asked, "I suppose you have some theories about what's happening?"

"I do," he said. "My colleagues and I are trying to verify some things."

"Can you tell us anything about it?"

"It's not quite ready for prime time."

"I thought you'd say that."

"But I did ask Patrick to get some tinfoil. It was a hunch I had earlier. But it's looking more and more likely—" We couldn't hear what he said after that. His voice came back for just the end of a sentence: "—wrap yourselves in tinfoil."

Mom scrunched up her face. "What?"

"Just wrap it around you, and seal it if you can, with tape or something."

"Rene, that is literally the craziest thing I've heard all day, and I've heard some seriously crazy things today, believe me."

"I know, I know. I'm sure it seems completely ridiculous, but just do it. It could protect you."

"From what?"

"I don't know yet. I can't say for sure. It's just a precaution."

"Rene, I will not be wrapping myself in tinfoil, thank you very much."

I liked the idea of protecting myself, and I didn't think it sounded as crazy as Mom did, so I said, "I want to do it."

Mom shrugged and said, "Honey, you can do it if you want. Of course."

"Should I wrap Buster too?"

"Wrap anybody you can," Rene said. He said more things, but his voice was starting to get cut off.

Mom said, "Rene, we're losing you. We didn't hear that."

"Okay, we can text. Be safe," he said. "And be careful. There's a lot of crazy stuff happening out there."

"Yeah, I've been looking at the news," Mom said. "You be safe too, okay? Stay in touch. We'll try to do a better job. It's been quite the day."

"I'll keep you posted."

"Have a good night, Rene. Thanks for giving us a call," Mom said. "We really appreciate it."

We said our goodbyes and hung up.

I asked Mom why she thought he wanted us to wrap ourselves in tinfoil.

"I have absolutely no idea." She said it like she thought Rene was crazier than Grandma.

I went back to the house and looked through the kitchen drawers for tape. The dog barked a little more when I went over. I looked out the kitchen window to see if I could see him. I couldn't. I didn't see any tape in the kitchen. I used my phone flashlight to look around the house. I felt more brave somehow after talking to Rene. He was calm and seemed to know things, and he made me feel less like a little kid and more like a grown-up. I felt like I had armor around me.

I found a desk with some pens in a cup on top and drawers under it. There was a roll of tape in one of them.

Back in the barn, I wrapped tinfoil around Buster but he kept wriggling out of it. I was worried I was wasting all the tinfoil on him, so I gave up. I wrapped some around Grandma and taped it to the back of her wheelchair. I asked Mom if she was sure she didn't want any tinfoil on her. She said she was sure. I wrapped it around my arms and legs and then the rest of me, but not my head. I looked like the tin man. I made a crinkly sound whenever I moved. Mom laughed at me, and I thought it was funny too, so I laughed.

"I love you so much, Patrick," she said.

I gave her a hug. She hugged back a little too tight, and I was worried she was tearing up my tinfoil, so I asked her to go easy.

"Okay, you crazy little man. Go to sleep now."

I settled back down on my spot between her and Buster and pulled a blanket over me. This time I think the rain on the roof helped me drift off to sleep.

I don't know how long I slept, or if I slept at all, but I woke up when I heard a wail like an elephant. Just like the one I heard on the phone. A chill went through me like I touched an electric horse fence. I sat right up.

"Mom!"

It was still dark, but the wind was strong and whistling through the barn. The rain was gushing down and blowing inside. I saw lights flashing outside. It wasn't as blue as lightning. It looked like sun sparkling on water. It was shining off the house and then the ground. It moved around fast. I could see it pass by the open barn door. The dog started barking again. The elephant sound happened again and it was a lot louder this time. I had to put my hands over my ears.

"Jesus! I'm here!" I heard Grandma yell. Then I saw the light bouncing off her wheelchair. She was wheeling herself closer to the doors.

Mom sat up. I hid behind her and held my blanket over me.

The barn doors were knocking against the walls in the wind, and bits of straw and dust were flying around everywhere mixed with the rain.

"Are the angels here, Mom?"

"I don't know."

Mom held onto me. Buster got in front of Mom and me and looked at the opening between the doors, barking at the outside.

The lights flickered by again. They moved like fireflies, but they were the size of horses.

Grandma waved her arms and tried to get through the opening between the sliding doors. Scraps of tinfoil blew off her as she made her way through. She moved around too much and tore them off.

"Take me, Jesus!"

One of the lights got close to the doorway. A strong gust of wind blew Grandma backwards a little. The barn doors rattled faster, and then all of a sudden they tore away. Both doors blew off and flew outside into a million splinters like they were in an explosion. I screamed and held onto Mom. I think she screamed too. The elephant sound came blaring again and echoed through the barn. It sounded like a freight train chugging straight inside my ear. I felt like my eardrum was going to burst, even with my ears covered. Buster was howling.

Grandma reached her hands out to the light, and it dimmed down. I could see it was like the ghost of a lady with long hair and robes. She had big white wings behind her. They were like a bird's, and twice the size of her. I thought I must be dreaming. I never saw a real angel before, but I knew that's what this was.

She stretched out her arm and said, "Come," with a voice like a loud bell.

"Take me now. I'm ready." Grandma started moving up out of her wheelchair and floated in the air toward the angel. Then the angel took her in her arms, backed away, and flew off with her.

Another light came up behind her. This light did the same thing, getting dimmer so it looked less like a moving blob of light and more like a shining person. It came right inside the barn. Buster didn't seem to know if he should howl, whine, or bark. This angel was a man with long waving hair and a long beard. His big white wings barely fit inside the barn.

Since these are angels, I figured I was supposed to feel love and happiness, but I have to admit I was scared of them. I think my mom was scared too because she kind of pushed backwards when the angel came in the barn.

The angel got low, right in front of Mom's face.

"Come." He had a booming voice that seemed to vibrate in every plank and beam of the barn.

Mom hugged me and said to the angel, "I don't know if we're ready."

The angel stretched out his arms at her, just like the first angel did to Grandma.

"We might need a little more time to think about it," Mom said with her voice all shaky.

That's when I felt Mom lifting away from me. The angel didn't look like he was listening to her. He didn't look very understanding. He just had one face. Her hands slipped off my blanket and tried to grab my hands while she was lifted up and floated away from me. She pulled the blanket with her and then her wet fingers tried to grab onto mine, but they were slippery and couldn't hold on.

"Stay with me, Patrick!" She looked in my eyes and I could see she was afraid.

"Mom, don't go! Don't leave me here!"

Mom started crying.

The angel carried her and rose up and floated out of the barn. Mom tried to wrestle her way loose.

"Not without my baby!" She screamed and twisted herself to try to get out of his arms, but he was so strong he held her tight like it took him no effort at all.

"Patrick!"

"Mom, wait!" I ran after her and tried to grab her feet, but she moved too high and too fast.

She screamed as loud as she could and then sobbed like there was nothing she could do.

"Patrick!"

The angel turned into a ball of light like the other one and flew away. I ran outside and saw the two lights moving off high into the sky until they disappeared.

I stood there in the dark and just let the rain pour on me.

19

I don't know how long I stood there in the cold, dark rain. I was shivering from the cold, but I didn't feel anything, not even the cold or the rain. My mind was empty. I didn't feel afraid. I just felt like I was standing in the middle of nothing, like I was floating in outer space, and this is how it was going to end. There was blackness all around me and I was going to drift forever until I ran out of air and died alone.

It was the end of the world, and I was alone in the middle of nowhere.

Then my empty mind filled up with the screams and the loud elephant trumpet, and I could smell the straw in the air, and I could feel the sharp raindrops on my face and the touch of her skin on my fingers trying to grab hold. I put my hands over my ears. It was too loud. Why was I standing outside?

I tried to change the pictures in my head, so I stood up to the angels and scared them off because I had to protect my mom. I played the new idea over and over. I had to keep my brain busy so it wouldn't get sucked into outer space.

The rain died down some. The sky started to turn from black to dark blue on the horizon. Then a lighter blue. Then a little slice of yellow. Buster came up next to me and sat down. The light of day helped clear my mind. I remembered what happened, and I knew what was a dream and what was real. Mom and Grandma weren't here anymore. They got me this far, but from here on out, I was on my own.

Standing there for so long, I felt like something important happened to me. I wasn't sure what to think of it, but the best I can describe it is, I felt like I became a man. I didn't cry. Well, not much anyway. I went through everything that happened in my mind, and I felt like I had it all straightened out. I understood what it meant. And I accepted what I had to do. I knew what my mission was. I knew the angels must have picked people up all over the world, just like the phone TV said. That meant everybody got picked up by an angel and got carried away to Jesus and went to heaven. Everybody except me.

I was the last person on the Earth.

My mission was to survive. By myself. I had to figure out a way to carry on the human race now that I was the one left behind. And even though I didn't know how yet, I thought I could do it. I felt like I was up to the challenge. I didn't know if I would die, but I knew that I would try my hardest to stay alive. Maybe there would be bands of devil-worshiping outlaws that survived, and I would have to fight them. And I didn't know if I would lose, or get killed, or get beat up, or maybe even get taken as their slave, but I knew I would fight for my life when the time came. I'll never give up, and I'll always remember my mom, my grandma, and my life before this. No one was ever going to take those things away from me.

I knew there was plenty of food on the Earth. I could go into every house and every store and take every can and box of food or Reese's peanut butter cup that I wanted. I could camp out anywhere. Sleep anywhere. I could even explore. Maybe I'd even discover new things no one else ever discovered.

The sun poked through and the rain stopped falling. I heard

birds, but nothing else. There was no sound of people anywhere.

I looked down at Buster, and he looked up at me. He wagged his tail.

"You're a good dog, Buster."

We went back into the barn and I collected anything I thought was important from the suitcase and put it in my knapsack. I took a water bottle. My phone wouldn't turn on. Maybe the battery died. Or maybe it got wet. I brought it anyway.

"Okay Buster, there's something important we need to do now. Follow me."

My sneakers made a squeaking sound on the wet grass. I walked with Buster around to the back of the house, and that's where we saw the other dog. His collar was tied to a rope on a post. He perked up his ears when he saw us and didn't bark. He kind of moved back and forth and wagged his tail. He was a nice-looking big black dog with slick hair. I felt bad for him. He got left all alone by whoever lived in this house, and his rope was twisted up around the post a good amount so he only had a few feet to move around. They went off to be with Jesus and just forgot about him tied up back here. I knew he must feel sad and lonely without his family. If God put me in charge, I'd never let those people into heaven after leaving their dog like this. I'd make them go to hell and get tied up to a post by the devil so they'd learn their lesson.

Buster and I walked up to the dog. They smelled each other's butts and spun around a little bit. I put out my hands so he could smell me because I know how to say hello to a dog. I told him I was sorry he had to be chained up all by himself, but that we were here now.

"Everything's going to be okay, buddy," I said.

I looked at his collar and saw his name stitched on it. It was Scooter. I said hello to him by name and "nice to meet you" and all that, and then I undid his latch.

I thought maybe he'd hang around with us or play with Buster for a little while, or maybe even join us on our adventures, but as soon as I unlatched him, he took off running. He ran as fast as he could, through the yard, and then across the street, and then into the field toward the mountains until he was so small we couldn't see him anymore.

Buster tried to run after him at first, but Scooter was a lot bigger and faster, and Buster gave up after not too long and came back to me.

We never saw Scooter again.

Buster and I went inside the house to see if there were more supplies we could take. I went upstairs this time and wasn't scared at all. I think it helped that it was daytime. I filled up our water bottles and put some water in a bowl on the floor for Buster. I found more food on the shelves. I got a box of cereal and some crackers. And we got a few more cans of beans, lentils, and something called artichoke hearts just in case we were ever starving to death and desperate. I also found a flashlight in one of the drawers and decided the next time I needed one, I was going to have one instead of being stupid. Especially since my phone didn't work anymore.

After that, we set out on the road. I decided we should walk back the way we came because the airport was in a city, and I remembered the name of the city. I saw it on my phone map. It was Sacramento. And I decided a city would have more supplies and more things for us to do. We could probably find a park with a lake to go swimming in. There might be a movie house so we could watch movies if we get bored and figure out how to work the projector.

The sun was getting higher, and it was starting to get hot again. I tried to remember how long we walked from the airport to the barn the night before so I could figure out how long it would take us to get back that way. I guess it was about three or four hours because we left when it was still daylight and when we got there it was dark.

We saw some little lizards on our walk back. Buster tried to catch one, but it moved too fast for him. We saw another one, and he tried again. He stopped trying when he realized he was never going to catch one, after maybe the third or fourth lizard.

The one thing about being the last person on Earth that takes some getting used to is how quiet everything is. There's nobody talking. Unless I talk. With no conversations, the world seems so empty. We walked along the road and heard a little bit of gravel from our footsteps, and maybe once in a while a breeze. And of course there's a bird here and there. But mostly it's just very, very quiet. I tried to have little conversations with Buster, but I gave up after a while because I might as well just be thinking to myself, since he doesn't even know what I'm saying.

"Buster, if you could be any other animal, what would it be? I would be a horse. Because then I could run really fast and I'd be really big and strong. I wouldn't mind a squirrel because they seem to be having a lot of fun. But I wouldn't want to be that small. I don't think I'd like that at all. I could definitely get excited about being a bird. Wouldn't it be fun to fly around? To see the world from high up like that? Do you have any dog friends, Buster? Do you ever hang out with them and do things? Have a few laughs? Do you know any cats? Did you ever make friends with a cat? Or do you think of cats as your arch enemy? What do dogs do with their friends? I suppose they just run around in a pack, huh? If their friends are other dogs, I mean. Like wolves. Is that what you'd like to do? If you could do anything, would that be it? Run around with a pack of wild wolves? Where do you think Scooter went off to? Is he running with wolves, do you think? Buster, do dogs ever get bored? What kind of things do you think about when you're bored? Maybe you're always bored. Unless you're chasing a lizard. Or barking at something. Did those angels scare you, boy? I thought they were kind of scary. Grandma didn't mind them, I guess. But they gave me the creeps, I have to admit. Especially after they took my mom away from me."

After I said that, I don't know what happened. I got really sad all of a sudden.

"Buster, I miss my mom." It felt good to tell somebody.

I started crying and stayed crying for a long time. I couldn't stop the tears or the wailing. They just kept coming. I wanted to hug her. I wanted to hug her so bad, but I couldn't. I knew I'd never touch her or hug her ever again. I'll never see her again. I'll never talk to her again. She's gone.

I miss how she always touched me and called me "honey." I miss her smell, and the way she looked, with her hair up, wrapped in a cloth. I miss how she would run around the house and be busy with things all the time, talking all the time. I miss having conversations with her. I like the way we talked. It was fun.

I wondered where she might be. I hoped she was okay. I hoped she was with Grandma and Jesus and they're all happy. But I didn't know. Who knows? That angel gave me a real spook. What if he was hurting her? I hated to think about that. But I couldn't help it. He held onto her too tight, and she couldn't get away. I didn't like seeing her fight against him like that. I didn't like him. I didn't like his face. I pictured my mom crying and being hurt and calling out for me.

After we walked for a while I took a little break because I got too sad thinking about things. I just sat on the side of the road and cried for a long time. Buster licked my face all up, and that helped me get over it for a spell. But every now and then the feelings would come back and I would cry more.

"Buster, we're going to have to get more water because every drop I drink is just pouring right out of my eyes."

The sun was really baking us now. I wanted to wrap some things on Buster's feet again to save him from the hot ground. I looked through my knapsack and found a pair of socks. I took mine off to make four. I slipped one over each paw. I just wore my shoes without socks after that.

I don't remember how long we walked before I started to hear the noise. It was a loud motor with a put-put sound. I looked around, and every direction was just flat ground except for the mountains to the side of us. But then I saw a black dot in the sky, coming from the direction we were headed. It was hard to see with the sun in the way, but it kept getting bigger. It was coming straight toward us. I thought maybe we should hide in case it was hostiles, but there was nothing anywhere you could hide under or hide in or hide behind. So I just stopped and looked up at it.

It got bigger, and pretty soon I could tell it was a helicopter. It was flying low to the ground, right along the road we were walking on. It was blowing up a lot of dust and gravel. I knew when it flew over us it was going to blow all that into our faces. I put my hands over my eyes.

But before it got too close, I heard it turn and fly over the field instead. I took a peek and saw it landing. It blew up a lot of dirt. Some of it blew towards us, but I could still see.

A man got out of the helicopter and walked toward us. I don't know what it was about the way he was walking, but I wasn't scared. He seemed friendly, just by the way he moved. And then he raised his arm like he was saying hello. He turned back and gave some kind of hand signal to the helicopter, and it started to get quieter. Pretty soon the motor was off and the man was walking close enough that I could see that he had dark black skin. And then I saw the white button shirt. And then I saw that it was Rene.

As soon as I saw that it was him, I felt like I wasn't floating anymore. I felt like the ground came back under me, and I was connected to the Earth. I felt like I had my balance and wasn't going to fall off the edge of it into space.

When he got closer, I saw that he was smiling.

"Hello!" he yelled.

I waved back, but I was surprised and confused, so I didn't say anything. I wondered if I was imagining him, like people in the desert see mirages when they're going crazy and dying from thirst.

Buster ran up to him. Rene bent over to scratch Buster's head and then stood up again and looked at me.

"Nice day, huh?" He was standing just a few feet away from me, wearing a mask.

If he was real, I almost want to say he's a gift from the heavenly angels. It's a thing I used to say. But I don't ever want to say it again because now I hate angels.

He tilted his head a little and looked at me.

"Are you okay?"

The way his voice sounded in my head was different than a daydream. It sounded real. So I decided this wasn't a daydream. I decided he was really here. I smelled the dirt in the air and felt the sun on my skin, and that helped convince me this was real.

I don't know why, but I started crying again. Maybe it's because he made me think of my mom. Other than that, I had no reason to be crying, and it was embarrassing because he was here now.

I didn't want to make him sick, so I found my mask in my pocket and put it on.

"It's good to see you, Patrick."

It took me a long time to get over my crying so I could talk without all the blubbering. And by that time Rene had us back in the helicopter and strapped in. He gave us headphones with little sticks in front of the mouth so we could hear each other while the helicopter was flying. We sat in the back and there was another man in front flying it. He was wearing a mask too.

I never flew in a helicopter before. It was like a carnival ride at first. I felt like my stomach was going a different way than the rest of me. And it was like seeing the Earth how a bird sees it.

The ground was made up of big squares, like we were flying over a quilt. We flew over the airport and I recognized it from when we were there. There weren't any people around it. I didn't see people anywhere.

"How did you find us?"

"Your tinfoil reflected the sun nicely."

I forgot I still had the tinfoil on me.

"Is that why you told me to wear it?"

"No," he laughed. "Not at all. I used your mom's last location on her phone to find you. It was from a few hours ago, but I figured we'd get close enough to spot you if you were still here."

I didn't know a phone could tell someone where you were.

"We have your dad to thank for that technology."

Every time someone makes me think of my dad, it feels like they're pouring boiling hot tar on me that glops all down my back and then dries and gets hard so that I can't move. I wish I didn't have to think about him, but I'm glad one of his inventions helped Rene find me. I was thinking just a few minutes ago that Buster and I would be alone forever and that there was no one else left on the Earth. So this time, I guess my dad did something good.

"I thought the angels took everybody."

"They took a lot of people. But not everybody. It's going to be a big project to make sense of it all and regroup and recover. A big project."

"What do you mean?"

"Well, there's people scattered everywhere. We have to bring them together. Cell phones are better now, but communications overall are not great. We have a lot to do to rebuild."

I looked at Rene. He was looking straight ahead out the front of the helicopter. He had a nose and a forehead that looked to me then like it was carved out of a mountain. He seemed bigger than any person I ever knew. The world was ending, and he wasn't scared. He wasn't crying, and he wasn't giving up. He was talking about building it up again like that was the only thing to do. He was talking about it like he thought he could do it. And I believed him. I wanted to be with him. I wanted to be strong like him. Being with him made me feel almost like Mom was back.

"Where are we going?"

"Headquarters."

20

The helicopter landed on a building that looked like a stack of big crooked bricks. It had a giant circle painted on top and the helicopter landed right in the center. I was glad to get off. I felt so sick from the ride, I decided I'd never ride in a helicopter ever again. I threw up in a paper bag Rene gave me, and then I cried some more. Buster didn't seem to mind the ride.

I didn't feel as embarrassed to cry and throw up in front of him as I did before. Maybe it was because of what happened by the barn, how I felt like a man now. Babies cry and throw up, obviously, but I know that Rene doesn't think of me as a baby. He seems to like me just fine, even though I'm always leaking or dripping or oozing some kind of liquid out of my face when he's around. He doesn't even seem to notice those things. He doesn't treat me like a little kid. He looks at me and talks to me like I'm just another person, which is just how I like it.

Rene asked me if I needed to use a bathroom. I told him I was okay. He told me he would take me to the bathroom anyway, and that I could relax and clean up and take a nice rest.

"Is this your house?"

He laughed. "This would be quite a house. I don't have money like your dad. This is where I work. It's a university."

I didn't want to say anything because I thought it might be rude, but I don't like that he keeps talking about my dad.

Rene explained how to get to my room, which is where the bathroom was.

"Where are you going?"

"I'll be downstairs in the lab."

Before we went inside, someone aimed a ray gun at my head and asked me to hold still. I stepped back and raised my hands to protect myself. Rene laughed and said it was okay. The person shot the gun. A blue ray came at me, but I didn't feel anything.

"Did that just fry my brain?"

"No, it took your temperature," Rene said.

"No fever," the person said.

I put Buster on his leash and we went down some stairs and into a room that had crooked walls like a stack of white blocks. There was a railing and a long window along the side of the room. We met a bunch of people there. They were all different kinds of people, different sizes and colors, some ladies, and some I couldn't tell which. They all wore masks, and some of them were wearing plastic gloves. They said their hellos to Rene and talked like grown-ups about a bunch of things that I didn't understand. The helicopter pilot walked by us and went down some other stairs. Rene waved at him, and he did a kind of military salute back.

Rene stepped beside me. "Everybody, this is Patrick. Patrick, these are my colleagues and my friends."

The other people seemed very happy to see me. They all said hello, and I suddenly felt like I was on the spot. One of them, a nice lady with golden hair and glasses like a cat's eyes, put her hands on her knees to get her face closer to me. She seemed very excited.

"Patrick, it is so wonderful to meet you finally," she said.

I wondered if Rene told them about me and that's why they

all seem to know me. I said hello back.

"I'm Dr. Neumuller. But you can call me Susan." She talked like an English butler.

She had a very nice face from what I could see around the mask, and I liked that she was so friendly.

"As some of you know, Patrick has been through a lot," Rene said. "I'm encouraging him to decompress awhile in the dorm."

Then Rene looked at me and said in a more quiet voice, "I'm going to be right downstairs, okay? You have my number. If you need anything, just call."

"My phone doesn't work. I think the battery died."

Rene wasn't worried about my dead phone. He asked the people to get a charger set up in my room.

"This is Buster," I said to the people, but maybe not quite loud enough. "He's my dog. I mean, I guess he's my dog now."

They heard me. Some of them laughed. I'm not sure why. Others said hello to Buster, "what a good dog," and things like that.

Rene made sure somebody got Buster a water bowl and some food for the room he was giving me.

Everything in this building was white and crooked. But the floors and stairs were gray. I think they were the only part that wasn't sparkling white. My room was white and the bedsheets were white and the pillow was white. There was a little bathroom with a shower. All those things were white. The room was just big enough for the little bed and table next to it. There were clean clothes just my size hanging on a hook in the room. They looked modern, almost like the boy I saw at the gas station, but not as colorful.

I got myself cleaned up and put the new clothes on, but I didn't like being alone. My phone was working now after they plugged it in, so I texted Rene and he reminded me how to find him. He asked me to leave Buster in the room. Buster wasn't too happy about that, but Rene said dogs weren't allowed in the lab.

The lab was at the bottom of more stairs with crooked white blocks above them. It had a big white wall in front of it with a long window where you could see inside. It looked like a scene from *X Minus One*. This must be where he builds robots because it looked like a robot factory or a place where new future gadgets are invented. It was ten times bigger than the gymnasium at my school. Maybe it was the size of an airplane hangar, but I wouldn't know since I've never been in an airplane hangar. I imagine they must be this big. Complicated metal machines hung from the ceiling, and more metal machines and metal boxes as big as an outhouse with dials and controls on them were spread out on the floor. Workers in lab coats and some in business suits walked around wearing goggles and masks and talked at big circular tables with black screens on top. And the sounds of the lab were like the sounds of the future. There were lasers and rivets, and they all echoed. Sometimes there was a computer voice announcing numbers. I looked up and around and took it all in like it was a fireworks show.

Rene met me at the door.

"What is this place?"

"Let me give you the tour." He walked beside me and explained everything in the lab. "This entire lab, in fact much of the University, is funded by the government. They finance research for things like space travel, robotics, and new technologies. A lot of what they do here, or used to do here, is large-scale physics experiments. There's an observatory where we can detect cosmic gravitational waves. The original application was for astronomy, but we're refitting it for, you know, what's going on."

I didn't understand all the words he used, so I started with the simplest question I could.

"Have you been to outer space?"

He smiled at that. "No. Not too many people have been to outer space. But we help think up and design a lot of the rockets and other equipment that take people to outer space."

We walked toward the center of the lab where people were standing over a table. Some of them were the people I met upstairs. They smiled at me, but they were mostly talking to other people.

"These large consoles are monitoring stations where our technicians figured out a way to track the sentinels and collect data on them, as much as we could, including the number of people they took or ki—" He looked at me before he picked his next words. "—or stopped in some way."

"You mean the angels?"

"Yes, we call them 'the sentinels.'"

"And you mean smiting people, with their fire?"

"Oh, you heard about that?"

"Yeah."

"It's a horrifying prospect. I wouldn't wish it on anybody."

"Me neither."

Rene rubbed his hand on his face around his mask and bent down to me.

"Patrick, we haven't talked about what happened to your mother and your grandmother. I don't want to—"

"The angels took them."

Rene nodded. "Okay. I wasn't sure. I thought as much. But I didn't want to bring up a painful subject."

"They took them to Jesus, didn't they?"

Rene nodded again. "That's what I'm thinking, essentially."

Rene seemed to know a lot, but wasn't telling me everything, just like Dad used to do. I wanted to ask him everything. He had these machines that could find angels like radar. I think he knew about Jesus. But how much did he know? I felt like an empty dog bowl. I felt dry and like I had nothing left in me. And the way Rene talks to me and listens to me and pays attention to me and tells me the things he was doing in his lab felt like fresh water poured in the bowl. I wanted to lap it up like a dog who's been running in the hot sun all day.

"I want you to tell me everything. My dad used to give me half answers, but I want the whole answers."

"You want to know more?"

I nodded.

He stood up and showed me a map on the wall. It was actually a TV screen as big as the side of a house, but it didn't have TV on it. It just had a picture of a map of the world. It was like the map on my phone. It had a lot of pink dots all over it.

"This live map updates where people have been taken or killed by the sentinels. You can see people were taken all over the world. And it separates out the people who went to the singularity in Israel by plane or other means versus by way of the sentinels."

He pressed some shapes on the screen, and the pink dots changed to blue dots. He pressed it again, and they changed to black dots. The dots moved around for each color.

"We thought this data may be helpful depending on the course of action or response by whatever is left of the government."

He pointed to the part of the map where I remember Israel was and said, "As you can see, there are still a lot of people crowding around the singularity."

"What's the singularity?"

"That's what we're calling it, the point of contact."

"You mean Jesus?"

He looked at me and then looked back at the map.

"Yeah."

I looked at the blob of dots by Israel.

"Can your machines tell who got sent to heaven?"

"We've had limited success with that. Although that's not what we're calling it. Since we don't have all the facts, we haven't named where they're going, but we're calling those taken 'the removed.'"

I wondered if Rene even believed heaven was real. Or if he

still didn't believe in God. I had to make sure he didn't think anything bad happened to the people who went there.

"Did my mom and my grandma go to heaven?"

"I don't know. My theory is that they're still alive. Well, it's more like a hunch. We're still working on it."

I had a terrible feeling the angel that took Mom was a bad angel, but I didn't know the whole story. Grandma's probably fine because she wanted to go, but Mom didn't want to go at the end. She could be in trouble. Maybe she's being hurt by that angel somewhere. Maybe her angel was sent by the devil and not Jesus. Maybe the devil tricked her like Grandma warned us about. Maybe he was going to smite her with fire. I started to breathe faster.

"Patrick, come sit with me." He held his hand out to some chairs around a little table.

We sat down. I was fighting back tears, trying not to think about where my mom was or what these angel sentinels might be doing to her.

"I apologize," Rene said. "There's a lot going on, and I know you've been through a lot. There are so many things I want to tell you, but—" He rubbed his chin like he was trying to think of what to say. "I don't spend a lot of time around kids, kids your age. I apologize if some of the things I'm saying are hitting you hard."

"It's all right. I like the way you talk to me just fine."

"Okay, good. That's very good to know." He sat back in his chair. "The world has been hit by an unimaginable, transformative event. Billions of people are unaccounted for. I—" He brought his head down and scratched the top of it. He had a crew cut of tight little black curls. "Where are my manners? Do you want something to eat, Patrick? There's a cafeteria."

I shook my head. After the helicopter ride, I was pretty sure I'd never eat again.

Rene leaned towards me in his chair. "One of the things I

want to tell you is about you, and your mother and father. There are some things I feel like you ought to know, that you have a right to know, especially after what happened to her. May I tell you about that?"

I nodded. I wanted him to tell me anything he knew about my mom and dad.

"Are you familiar with, you know, the birds and the bees, and all that?"

I nodded. "We had it in science. It's called 'mating.'"

He tapped the table a little bit with his hand and said, "Great. Of course. All right." He seemed nervous. I never saw him like this before.

"I met your mother when she was a senior in high school. I was doing advanced placement recruiting. Long story. We dated for a while."

"You mean mated?"

"No. I mean, well, of course. I mean no. We couldn't have any children. We wanted one. We were just a couple of lesbians who didn't know—"

"What's a lesbian?"

He paused like he wasn't sure what to say next.

"Uh, maybe skip that part. It's not important." He took a breath. "We were close, and we wanted to have a child together, so we visited a sperm bank."

"What's a sperm bank?"

"Hm. Okay, maybe we'll skip that part too." He lowered his head for a moment. "You were born, and your dad was—" He tried to use his hands to help him get his thoughts out, but then he dropped them. "He fathered you. Served as your father. But your mother and I were there for you, at first." He looked at me for a while without saying anything. "Are you following what I'm saying?"

I shook my head. He wasn't making any sense at all.

"The thing is, Patrick, one type of parent is the type of parent who is there for you, who raises you. Wakes up in the night when you cry and whatnot. Another kind is the kind—" He moved his hand around again like he was stuck on his words. "Do you know about DNA?"

I nodded. "You get the DNA and chromosomes from the parents when they do mating."

"Right. Perfect. So, another type of father is the type that gives you your DNA."

We sat there and looked at each other. I was waiting for him to finish explaining what he was trying to say. I still wasn't quite sure. It was a lot of science that didn't seem to have too much to do with me.

"You got your DNA from Mason Stoodle. Well, half from him, half from your mother. But your mother and I, we were with you as a baby, until you were 3 years old. They were three wonderful years. And then she wanted to exercise her right to meet the donor."

"What's a donor?"

"That's the DNA dad."

"Okay."

"And, that's kind of when things fell apart. He got this idea that he wanted to be the one to raise you. He didn't want us involved. He was the dad, and he had a lot of money and a lot of lawyers, and he sued the sperm bank and the state, and god knows who else. And here we were, just two poor mothers with our baby."

"You were a mother?"

"Your mother and I were like your mothers, yes. Like your mother and father. The parents that raised you."

I was starting to piece it all together, and I'm not sure why he was making it so complicated. I felt a million suns about to go supernova inside my body.

"Are you trying to say you're my dad?"

"Well, okay, yes. I guess that's what I'm saying."

I wanted to get up from my chair and collapse into his arms, but I forced myself not to. It took a lot of willpower.

"I want you to be."

"I am, Patrick. I will be." He looked at me with a smile in his eyes.

"Please say you'll never take that back, and you'll never go away."

He looked at me square. "Patrick, I will never take that back. I'm going to look after you now. And I'm proud to be your dad. I love you. I've always loved you. I'm sorry I couldn't be in your life these past ten years. They've been hard for all of us. You're so special to me. You're my child, and I'm very glad I finally get to be with you again."

I wiped my eyes. I only got a couple of tears. Not too bad this time. I felt like I just found a missing clue that I've been searching for forever, like that feeling when you put the last puzzle piece in its place after there was a hole in the puzzle for so long, and you couldn't find the piece. Rene is the dad I want. He's the dad I've wanted my whole life, but I didn't even know it.

"If you're my dad, I don't want to social distance from you anymore."

"That's understandable, Patrick. We'll take a test and make sure neither of us has the virus, and then you can be in my bubble. I'd like that."

"Your bubble?"

"That's what we call the group of people you don't social distance with, like with you and your mother and grandmother. That was your bubble."

"Now you and me, we'll be a new bubble?"

"That's right."

I felt like I went through a reverse atom smasher. All my atoms were where they were supposed to be. Rene knew so much about things, I knew he was going to be able to give me more answers and help me understand the world and how I fit in it.

I wanted to get started right away. I stood up and pointed at a giant box as big as a car with wires on one side and lights and dials on the other.

"What does this do?"

"That is a computer that's crushing a lot of data right now, trying to pinpoint the other end of the singularity."

"What does that mean?"

"It means, essentially, that we're trying to figure out where heaven is."

"Where do you think my mom is, really?"

"I really don't know. We don't have any data on it. She could still be in Israel near the singularity. That's where the sentinels are bringing everyone. Or she could have been taken up the stairs already. That's what we're calling 'removed.' I'm sorry, Patrick, but we just don't have any way to know."

"If there's a chance she's in Israel, we have to go find her."

"That's a real hot spot, Patrick. I don't think it would be a good idea."

"But she might be there."

"It could be dangerous with all the sentinels concentrated there. There's so much we don't know."

We walked to the end of the giant lab and down a long hallway. I stopped in the middle.

"Did they take everybody?"

"Not everybody. It seems they only took certain people. And they killed a lot of others, people who resisted them with any kind of violence. That seems to be the pattern."

"Who's left?"

"We're still collecting that data. Or trying to. We know it's a lot of kids. A lot of people who were in networks like mine—scientists, science hobbyists even, people who had done some of the research, or bought into my theory. I blasted it out. Remember that I asked you to wrap yourself in tinfoil?"

I nodded.

"It was just a hunch, but it looks like I was right about that one. We've known for a long time that a form of tin oxide can shield detection from infrared scanning. People have developed special clothes made from polyurethane composite fibers. Those have been around for a while. I'm wearing them now. Everyone here is wearing them. It's what the clothes you're wearing are made of. I knew tinfoil would offer at least some hope of protection in a pinch. I've been wanting to ask you if the sentinels seemed to notice you when you saw them, when they came?"

I shook my head.

"Could be because of the tinfoil."

"They didn't take Buster either."

He closed his eyes and nodded. "They've been leaving non-human animals, for the most part, and smaller children. But there were reports of kids as young as 10 and 11 being taken, so I didn't want to take any chances with you."

"I have another question."

"What's that?"

"You still don't believe in God?"

"No, I still don't."

I tried to figure out why he didn't, and then tried to figure out how to ask what I wanted to ask.

"But Jesus came back. The Bible and God and everything is true now, right? You said that would prove it if Jesus came back."

"I believe I said I would be more *likely* to believe. Sometimes you never know how you're going to react to something until it happens, you know?"

I understood what he meant, but I wanted the whole story. "So, what do you think really happened?"

He adjusted on his feet. "Okay, Patrick. I'll tell you. I'll explain my theory, and I'll explain why I think I'm right about it, and I'll explain why I think there's no God, no Jesus, and no angels. You deserve to know all that." He started walking down the hall.

I blocked his way. I was not going to let him avoid the more important thing, and I was not going to take no for an answer.

"No, wait. What if Mom is about to get taken away? First we have to go to Israel, and we have to hurry!"

21

WE WENT INTO AN OFFICE where I sat in a chair on one side of the room and Rene sat in a chair on the other side of the room. A nurse with a mask, gloves, and one of those blast shields stuck a cotton swab up my nose and then one in Rene's.

Then she stuck my arm with a needle. I had to scrunch my eyes and grit my teeth, it hurt so bad. I couldn't wait till it was out of me. But I was proud of myself for not crying. The nurse got the blood she needed. Rene didn't cry at all.

While she was doing her work, I kept trying to convince Rene to go to Israel.

"We can give Mom your special clothes so the sentinels don't see her. We can fly in your helicopter. I don't care if I throw up again."

"Patrick, I understand how important this is to you. I do. Unfortunately, it's very impractical."

"But we have to. She might be in trouble!"

"I understand. First of all, it would take forever to get to Israel in a helicopter. In fact, I'm pretty sure you can't even go that far in a helicopter. And none of the airlines are operating anymore. We'd need a private jet, which is expensive. I don't even know—"

"My dad has money. My other dad."

"That's true. I'm sure he has a fleet of private jets."

"We can ask him."

He took a big breath.

"I can try to get ahold of him. I don't know if he's removed or not."

"Yes, please. We have to try."

"Okay. I'll try. It's the least I can do. But I don't know what's going to happen. Try not to get your hopes up."

I couldn't help it. I got my hopes way up when he called my dad. It seemed like he had to talk to some other people first and explain who he was, and then I heard him say, "Hi Mason. It's Rene," and then I knew they were talking.

I wanted to get my mom back so bad I didn't care that I had to get my dad's help. The thought of seeing my mom again and holding her and being able to laugh with her again was an energy beam that melted off the crusted tar that got poured on my skin whenever I thought of my dad.

It was hard to be patient while they talked. I tried to hear what my dad was saying because I could hear his voice through the phone a little from where I was sitting, but I couldn't pick up much.

Rene stood up and walked around with his elbow bent to keep the cotton ball in place on his arm where he got stuck. I wanted to get up and follow him around to hear better, but I thought that would be rude.

Finally he said, "Okay, that works. We'll coordinate by text." Then he hung up.

"You're in luck, Patrick. He supports the idea. And he wants to help you. I think he feels guilty, honestly. He has a plane at LAX. He even has a pilot there. A lot of his people got wind of my theory and were able to avoid the sentinels. It actually kind of went viral."

He laughed at that, but I didn't get why it was funny.

"I almost died from a viral infection," I said, all serious.

Then he explained what he meant by "viral" and I felt better about it.

"One thing," he said. "I told him we both just took a test. He insists we're negative before we fly, for the safety of his staff. We have to wait until our results come back."

"How long will that take?"

"We have our own molecular analyzer. By the time we get to the airport, we should know if we can fly."

A molecular analyzer was a futuristic invention I hadn't heard of yet. It sounded like something out of *Buck Rogers*. I asked what it was and he said it analyzes the blood they took, which sounded a lot less exciting than I imagined. I thought maybe it would shrink us to the size of molecules.

Rene had to take care of some things, and I wanted to say goodbye to Buster. After that, we went upstairs to get in the helicopter again. I asked why we couldn't drive a car. The pilot said the roads to the airport were crowded with cars that people left behind. I could have figured that, so I at least begged him to try not to tip over and move around so much. He said he would do his best.

This ride was a lot shorter and I'm proud to say I didn't throw up. I felt sick and got another little paper bag, and it sure seemed like I was going to throw up, but nothing came out. I guess I got it all out last time and there was nothing left in me.

I asked Rene if the plane would make me throw up too, and he said it would be a lot smoother. I tried to think about seeing my mom again. That seemed to help my stomach settle down.

We landed at the airport next to the plane. We got off the helicopter and Rene took off his mask and held out his hand to shake mine.

"Congratulations. Neither of us have the virus. We can be in a bubble together."

I shook his hand back. "It's going to be a good bubble," I said. We had a little laugh about that.

The plane had a pointy front, and stairs that went up to a door. A man in a pilot hat and two other people, all wearing masks, said hello to us and invited us on. The inside of the plane looked like a rich person's living room. There was a couch and a TV and a work desk and everything. The ceiling was curved like the inside of an igloo. The pilot and one of the other people went into the cockpit. The other person said he would take care of us and bring us food. It was like we had our own butler on the plane.

After the plane took off, my ears got stuffed up like I was deep underwater. It was a strange feeling, and it hurt. Rene told me how to make it stop by opening my mouth as wide as I could. It turned out he was right about the plane too. It didn't twist and turn as much as the helicopter. It was kind of loud inside, is all, but not bad. We didn't even have to wear headphones to talk. After a while I even got hungry, and our plane butler brought us food. His name was Christopher. I got macaroni and cheese and an apple.

The pilot said we'd be flying for ten hours. My mouth must have dropped open when he said that because Rene smiled and told me it would go by fast because we could sleep. The seats on the plane folded out into regular-sized beds, Christopher said.

I tried to imagine the life my dad had when he wasn't in Cordial Falls with me. He went to work in San Francisco and played with futuristic machines and gadgets like phones, TVs, couches that folded into beds, and who knows what else. Then he flew around anywhere he wanted in these fancy planes. I felt left out of all his big-money fun. I don't know why he didn't just show me some of it. It would have been amazing to grow up so rich.

I must have been saying some of that out loud because Rene told me he was glad I didn't grow up around all this money.

"I'm thankful you had a normal childhood. Well, as normal

as can be expected when Mason Stoodle is your dad. It's good that you lived in a normal neighborhood with normal kids and rode your bike, skipped rocks, and all the rest of it. You might have ended up an insufferable, spoiled brat." He smiled at that. "That reminds me. I want to tell you what happened to the president."

I was curious about the president, but first I wanted to hear his theory of what was going on, and why he didn't believe in the Bible. I was a lot more curious about that.

He got comfortable in the couch across from me and said, "Okay, let's do this."

I rested my head in my hands and listened to his voice that sounded like a radio crooner.

"Are you familiar with the Aztec Empire?"

"I learned about them in school. They grew corn."

"That's right."

"That's all I can remember."

"I want to tell you a story about how the Aztec Empire fell."

I drank a can of soda pop Christopher brought me while I listened. He even brought a glass with ice to pour it in. I felt like a rich person getting told a bedtime story.

Rene cleared his throat and cupped his hands together. Even in the loud plane I could feel his voice vibrate in me like a long note.

"The year was 1519. The Aztec empire had a great ruler. His name was Moctezuma. He was powerful, maybe the most powerful ruler in the world. He went bare chested and had a magnificent headdress of rare feathers and finely threaded gold lace. He ruled over millions of people and reigned over a vast area that today is Mexico and a lot of Central America. In the center of it all was a spectacular city, a cosmopolitan trading center with the most magnificent, beautiful pyramids in the world, built from different colored stones and painted in bright reds and greens and adorned with flowers. The city was like a giant work of art. It was an incredibly wealthy kingdom, with so much jade and silver and gold. And corn." He pointed at me to give me credit for knowing about the corn.

"Moctezuma and many of his subjects believed in an ancient Aztec legend, a prophecy. They believed the end of the world was coming. And they believed a bearded priest from hundreds of years before was going to be reincarnated as a feathered serpent god who would return across the eastern sea as a savior who, legend foretold, would 'strike at kings.' The Aztecs were a very religious people, so they believed in things like serpent gods, signs, and dark omens. And Moctezuma was no different.

"One day, stories came out of the east of strange visitors from across the sea, people unlike anyone the Aztecs had ever seen. They had pale white skin. The Aztecs were more brown. Not as dark as me, but browner than you. The strangers had beards. They were sheathed in metal from head to toe, glistening like the scales of a great serpent. They rode horses, and they had deadly fire sticks that exploded like lightning and could kill a person from far away. The Aztecs had never seen anything like this before.

"Moctezuma was afraid. A lot of the Aztecs were afraid. But was this really the return of the reincarnated serpent god? No, it was Spanish Conquistadors, wearing armor and brandishing swords and rifles. They were led by a vicious conqueror named Cortes.

"Moctezuma offered Cortes gifts to appease him, but his men attacked with cannon fire. The Aztecs had never seen anything like cannon fire. They didn't have technology like that. Moctezuma invited Cortes to his royal palace, and offered him and his men hospitality. He offered them beautiful, handcrafted gold amulets and priceless treasures. Cortes and his men just took them and melted them down for the gold. Cortes spit in the face of Aztec hospitality, and then he took Moctezuma prisoner. He held him hostage in his own palace while his men plundered the great capital city. In just a few years, the entire Aztec Empire crumbled. The Spaniards cut Aztec citizens down by the tens of thousands with their superior weapon technology. And after that the Aztecs caught the Spaniards' disease, and millions died from smallpox. Only after it was too late did people realize these Conquistadors weren't gods. They were just men. It was all very predictable. Such a common story in history. Strangers from other lands come as brutal conquerors so often. There was no need to fear the superstition. Reality was the greater danger."

I let his story sink in, and I imagined the great pyramids he talked about crumbling to the ground, and the gold and silver treasures being tossed into the street and smashed. I saw the Spaniards slashing people open with their swords.

He had more. "In science, there are facts, which you can prove, and there are theories, which you try to prove, and there's also likelihood, which can inform a theory.

"Sometimes you have to ask yourself how likely something is before you can arrive at a good theory. The idea of a returning savior is a myth in a lot of religions around the world, not just Christianity. Cults with prophets and leaders who promise to return from the dead come up over and over again. But how often do they come true? By comparison, how often does one people conquer another people? All the time. So which is more likely?

"What's amazing is that this one prophecy from this one particular religion would actually come true. Why this one? Why would Jesus come down out of the clouds like it says he will in the Bible? Does this prove it's all true? That all the supernatural stories in the Bible are now scientifically factual? There are so many laws of biology and chemistry and physics that you would have to throw out the window for all of it to be true. We know that people don't come back to life after they've been dead. That's a scientific impossibility. Never mind about being born of a virgin, walking on water, or any of it. There's no such thing as miracles in science. So it's unlikely that this is the real Jesus coming back.

"And if it's real, there would be evidence, right? Extraordinary claims require extraordinary evidence. If someone is going to convince a scientist that they're a returning god, they'd better be able to prove it. So we studied the phenomenon, and we made some very interesting discoveries. We found evidence of a portal, a small wormhole in the opening where the Jesus image appeared. We found that the sentinels employ some kind of holographic projection technology that harnesses static electricity, which keeps them tethered pretty close to the Earth's surface in open areas, probably for the electron charge. We theorize that they use infrared scanners to locate people, and possibly some kind of algorithm that determines roughly the shape of a full-grown human as opposed to another animal or a small child. It seems they came here for people. Adult people."

I interrupted him while he talked, to ask what words like "holographic" and "algorithm" meant, and he told me. He didn't torture me and make me look them up in my dictionary like my dad used to. And I had more questions too.

"Who do you mean, 'they'?"

"I'm getting to that. Imagine if Cortes had known about the myth of the returning serpent god. In his case, he just got lucky that his arrival happened to coincide with the prophecy. But what if he could have used it to his advantage? Do you think he would have? Do you think he would have pretended to be that savior in order to trick the entire country into handing him the keys to the kingdom so he could conquer them without having to fight and risk his men?"

"I guess so," I said.

"Of course he would. Now look at us. We've been broadcasting radio waves and television signals into outer space for decades. Plenty of televangelists on those airwaves have told the story of Jesus and the prophecy of his return. What's the likelihood that an intelligence on a distant planet received those signals, and perceived that a good percentage of the population of our planet believed in this prophecy of the second coming of Jesus? If they wanted to conquer us without much of a fight, it wouldn't be difficult. They wouldn't have to invest in a lot of expensive space battleships. They could just make themselves look like Jesus, and collect as many people as they want."

"Aliens from another planet," I said, more to myself than to him. I was trying to fit everything he was saying into my brain. My brain was hungry for it.

"As unlikely as it might seem, it's the most likely scenario. No established science has to be thrown out the window in order for it to be true. Beyond that, it's supported by precedence."

"What does that mean?"

"It means a very similar situation has occurred in history at least once before. Cortes and Moctezuma. And one group with superior technology conquering another group happens all the time. And history tends to repeat itself. Or at least rhyme. The Spaniards came for gold. What do these Celestials want?"

"Celestials?"

"That's what we're calling them, the intelligent beings who harnessed the singularity and built and control the sentinels. It seems the Celestials want people. For what purpose, we don't know."

My chest was heating up. If Mom got taken by aliens instead of angels, she's in a lot more danger than I thought.

"Why do you think they want them?"

"I don't know. We have no way to know."

"But what do you think?"

"A scientist normally doesn't like those kinds of questions. But since it's just you and me talking, I'll throw out a few educated guesses. They might want to study us. Put us in a lab. The way you might collect bugs for a bug collection."

"Like an ant farm."

"Exactly. To put them in a big enclosure and study them and see what they do. Another possibility is, they might want a labor force. The precedent there is the way humans have rounded up people from other lands to use as free labor."

"From Africa," I said in a whisper. "To make them into slaves."

"Exactly. It happened to my ancestors, so I find this possibility particularly horrifying." He got a serious look on his face, like he wanted to stop talking about it. "Another possibility is too grim. I probably shouldn't say it."

"Tell me."

"No, they have your mother. It's too much. I'm laying a lot on you today, Patrick. I'm sorry."

"I know what you're going to say."

"What?"

"That they're going to eat them."

Rene dropped his head. "Okay, yes. That's what I was thinking."

"I've read comic books. I know what monsters from outer space do. They either blast you with a ray or they take you as a slave or they eat you."

"Your comics didn't steer you far wrong."

My hands were shaking, thinking about Mom in the clutches of some drooling alien. And my poor grandma, too. She never signed up for that. Things couldn't get more terrible. I just had to hope we could find them before they got taken to some other planet and we lost them for good.

"Patrick, we're going to do everything we can to find your family."

I believed him. He was the smartest person I ever met. Even smarter than my dad. He knew how to figure out what was real and what wasn't, and he used evidence. My dad tried to fool me with his lies and his big hoax, but Rene is trying to open my eyes and see this new hoax so I don't fall for two in a row.

The year 2020 keeps throwing things at me, and each new

thing is more strange and impossible than the last thing, crazier than anything from *X Minus One* or *Weird Fantasy*, things I could never imagine. These aliens pulled a prank on the whole world bigger than the one my dad pulled on me. And I would have fallen for it too, if it wasn't for Rene. He was the real Sam Spade. The real Sergeant Friday, searching for facts and telling it to me straight. And I was the blubbering client.

I looked out the window. We were a lot higher up than in the helicopter. I saw clouds below us. I couldn't even see the Earth. Everything seemed more real than ever. I grabbed my arm and pinched the skin. I was real, and this time was real. I really believed it.

Rene was still sitting in the same place, just looking at me.

"You okay?"

"So what happened to the president?"

"Oh, right. Well, there was a theory going around among some Christians that he was the antichrist. He fit so many of the prophecies. He proclaimed himself 'King of Israel' once, so that meant he exalted himself above God, which the antichrist is supposed to do. He mocked Christians, comparing the book he wrote to the Bible. He's a serial liar, and he's the most powerful individual in the world. So, that theory all lined up and made sense."

"Grandma thought my dad was the antichrist. My other dad."

"Yeah, that was the other theory, popular among a different group of Christians, the evangelicals. I hope you realize it's all nonsense."

"I guess so."

"I probably shouldn't be telling you this. It's pretty dark." He shook his head.

"No, tell me!"

"Okay, okay. You asked for it. The media that's still around has been talking about it all day today. Anyway, the president is not the antichrist, of course. A lot of people in the Pentagon looked at my infrared-scanning theory and thought my prescription was a reasonable precaution to take. They told him about it, but he ignored their advice, which he often does. He doesn't believe in science, as a rule, so he didn't protect himself. He was probably embarrassed to wear tin-oxide clothing. Maybe he thought it made him look fat. Who knows? A lot of his administration are evangelicals, so they got themselves to Israel. They were some of the first to go up the stairs, like the vice president and some others. But earlier today a sentinel came to the White House, and the commander-in-chief hid behind his desk. The last of his Secret Service agents tried to shoot at the sentinel with their guns, and it responded by smiting them with fire. Burnt them all to a crisp."

I felt bad for poor Dwight D. Eisenhower.

22

We didn't fold the beds out, but I fell asleep on the couch anyway. Rene must have been on the phone the whole time talking to the people at his lab because I kept hearing his voice in my head while I was dreaming. His voice turned into a big orchestra of voices. It was the people walking up the stairs to meet Jesus, mumbling to themselves. I saw my mom in the crowd, but she wasn't my mom anymore. Her face was torn up like shreds of paper, and her mouth was hanging open. Her eyes were just holes in her skull with no eyeballs. And then the other zombies around her closed in and crushed me until I couldn't breathe.

The pilot made an announcement on the speaker. "We're making our final descent to Ben Gurion Airport. We'll have you on the tarmac in just a few minutes."

His voice shook me awake. Rene put his phone away and asked me if I got a good rest. I said no, not really. I was just being polite. In fact, it was the worst sleep in history, but I didn't want to be so dramatic.

He explained to me that Israel is a country where Jews live, and Jews weren't Christians, so they didn't believe Jesus was the savior.

"A lot of them converted when the singularity appeared, but a lot more didn't want to go. We believe many of them were taken by the sentinels regardless."

He told me he wasn't sure what we'd find there, but that he'd stay with me and keep me safe.

"It might be an excitable crowd heading up those stairs."

The last thing I needed was another excitable crowd. I hope my dream wasn't a prophecy. I'm not ready for a herd of zombies.

The plane landed, and we got out. A big black car met us next to the plane. The driver said, "Welcome, Patrick," but I don't know how he knew my name.

Rene said, "Compliments of you know who."

Then I figured out my dad probably set up the car for us. He probably had Ubers all over the world. I thought, if I find my mom, I'll thank the actual heavenly angels my dad is one of the richest people there is. It would almost make up for him turning my whole life into a dumb prank.

We drove out of the airport and right away it felt like we were entering a different world. I opened my window. The air was hot and dry like California, but there were strange mountains and valleys, like we were on the surface of another planet. The car went up and down big hills and the driver drove wilder than a roller coaster. He swerved around other cars like the crazy black car we saw on the highway in California.

But my mind kept coming back to my mom. I held onto the thought that she was nearby. I wished she brought her phone so we could find her the way Rene found me. I kept looking at the blue dot in my phone, imagining it was Rene's map in the lab that showed dots where there were people. I wished my map would show the exact location of my mom.

I saw soldiers on the streets with big black boots and futuristic machine guns. There weren't many other people or cars on the street. It didn't look like too many cars got abandoned in

Israel like they did in California.

When we got closer to the singularity, we could see the light in the sky and the top of the stairs on the horizon. It looked like a lighthouse at the top of a building taller than the clouds.

"Spectacular," Rene said, taking pictures with his phone.

When we got closer, we drove by buildings made out of creamy stone that looked like big cliffs of sand, and a lot of tall palm trees just like in California.

We started to see some people walking toward the stairs. There were also all kinds of cats running around the streets. Everybody was walking in that direction. Except the cats. They seemed to be going wherever they wanted. But the people all moved toward the tower of stairs, and we started to see little blobs of light shepherding them.

"Sentinels," I said.

"Incredible." Rene took pictures of them too.

At first there were just a few sentinels, but the closer we got, the more we saw. Even though they were quite a ways away, the hair on my neck stood up when we saw them. I closed my window.

The stairs to Jesus looked more like a pyramid. It was a big triangle. We could see two sides of it, with stairs on both sides, filled with people moving up. Sentinels floated around the ground at the bottom of the stairs the way bees float around a beehive. I started to tense up, but Rene reminded me that they wouldn't pay us any mind with our clothes that blocked their rays.

The driver asked us where we wanted to be dropped off, and Rene asked him to let us out as soon as he couldn't drive any further.

I saw one or two more soldiers standing around, but they weren't holding machine guns.

"The police don't have their guns here," I said.

"They might have seen one too many armed comrades smote,

so they dropped their weapons," Rene said.

"Maybe they're wearing the infrared clothes too."

The car had to move slower when the people got closer together.

"I think we could walk faster than this," I said.

Rene asked the driver to stop and let us out. We got out and put on our masks.

"I don't expect people are going to be too careful here about coronavirus protocol," he said.

"Probably not."

The streets were made of stones. The city was creepy and quiet except for every once in a while a distant sentinel horn would blow. We walked through narrow passageways and up and down steps, through sand-colored old buildings that looked like they were straight out of *The Ten Commandments* movie. While people walked, they held up their phones to take pictures and movies of the stairs, Jesus, and the sentinels. Did they think they could take their phones to heaven? Rene took pictures too, but he had a good excuse.

"For research."

The stairs were so high you could barely see the top. I saw a lot of people walking who looked old and weak. Someone had crutches. I wondered how people could walk up so many stairs without getting tired. I thought of Grandma in her wheelchair.

Mom and Grandma could be anywhere. The base of the stairs looked as big as ten baseball fields. The crowd of people was too big, but they were getting on the stairs and disappearing at the top in good time. It was like everybody in the world was there. I could only hope we got lucky.

"Mom!" I yelled. "Grandma!"

"Marion!" Rene yelled.

We moved closer to the stairs, and the crowd got thicker. Rene asked if he could put me on his shoulders and I said yes, please. From there I could see the crowd stretched forever, all the way around the stairs. We kept yelling for her.

Some people looked at us and said, "Shh," but I couldn't stop yelling. I just wanted to find her.

"Follow me," came a big voice like thunder from the top of the stairs. A lot of people in the crowd yelled back, "We're coming, Lord," "We love you, Jesus," "Hallelujah," and things like that.

Sentinels floated by us, and I watched them fly over. From Rene's shoulders, I held on tight to his head, and he held on tight to my ankles. At least these sentinels weren't blasting fire or smiting anyone. Not yet anyway. In my head I thanked the real heavenly angels for our special clothes that made us invisible to the fake angels.

Being in the crowd, I felt an ache in my heart for all the people. They were walking up the stairs to get carried away by the aliens to get eaten, made into slaves, or wherever they were going, and they didn't have a clue. I wanted to scream at them and warn them all, but I knew they wouldn't listen. They were serious believers, like Grandma.

People were so close to each other now, it was a good thing we were wearing masks because there wasn't six feet of distance between anybody. We got close enough to the stairs that I could see people weren't walking up. They were just standing still, but going up anyway.

"The stairs are moving," I said, pointing. "So folks like Grandma don't have to walk up."

"An escalator. Of course."

We kept calling out for Mom and Grandma. My voice was getting scratchy from it. We walked all the way around the base of the stairs. They looked steep up close. Rene moved through the crowd fast with me on his shoulders. He looked at every lady who looked like the size of my mom or had the same hair, and every lady who waddled like Grandma. He wasn't yelling anymore. He was just saying, "We're looking for Marion Geddes.

Short, pretty woman with dark hair. Marion Geddes." That's the first time I heard her last name. I never realized it wasn't the same as mine.

After we made it all the way around the stairs and came back to where we started from, Rene looked up at me and said, "I don't think we should go up the stairs. There might not be a way to turn around if we go that far."

I didn't want to believe him, but I was sure he was right. We might end up like ants stuck to peanut butter. But finding Mom and Grandma in this big crowd was like trying to find a dust speck in a field of clovers a zillion miles wide. I thought she must have gone up the stairs. We probably got here too late and missed her.

But Rene didn't stop. He yelled louder. He walked around the stairs again and yelled to the new people moving in.

"Marion! Marion Geddes! Gail! It's Patrick and Rene! Are you here!?"

I yelled more too. I yelled until my voice was gone.

A man with dark glasses, a straw hat, and no mask, walked up to us and said, "Stop your damned yelling, would you please? Thank you." He was rude about it and it made my skin curdle up a bit. It gave me the double creeps because he was smiling when he said it.

"We're just trying to find someone," Rene said.

"No shit. We can all hear you. It's getting a little distracting."

A lady next to the man put her hand on him and said, "Stop it, honey. Don't make a scene."

Rene moved away from the man and yelled more. "Marion! It's Rene and Patrick!"

The man walked over to us again. "I got my family here all the way from Arizona. We'd like to enjoy this sacred moment without your yelling. Would you yell in a church? No, you wouldn't. It's the same thing. It's not respectful."

I was nervous for Rene to yell after that. Rene moved even

further away from the man and away from the stairs too, but he kept yelling, "Marion! Marion Geddes! It's Rene and Patrick."

More people around us said, "Shh!"

Someone said, "Shut up already."

I felt bad we were bothering people, but what did they expect us to do? How else could we find them? I wanted to explain to them that my mom didn't have her phone so they would understand, but there were too many of them, and I figured they wouldn't care.

Rene yelled for her more and the man in the straw hat came back and walked right up to him, blocking our way.

"All right, that's enough now."

"Okay, okay. No need to escalate this." Rene lifted me off his shoulders and put me behind him.

From back there I saw that the man was holding his vest open, and there was a gun in a holster on his belt. I held onto Rene's arm and got the distinct feeling I was about to get shot in the chest. My legs turned into macaroni noodles and the rest of me froze.

"You don't tell me what to do," the man said. His face was red, and he wasn't smiling anymore. "That's not how this works. There's no law no more, friend. World's over. All we got left is the Second Amendment and Jesus. And I'm your police, judge, and jury."

"You're absolutely right." Rene said. "You're the one with the gun. Whatever you say."

"Tell me why I shouldn't shoot you right here. You're probably not even a Christian. You a Muslim? You know they burned that Muslim garbage at Calvary, don't you?"

I didn't know what he was talking about, but I could tell he was trying to rile Rene up.

"Muslim!" someone yelled like it was a bad name.

"This ain't your staircase," someone else said.

I knew about Muslims from school. I knew it was another

religion, but that's all I remembered. Bad luck that these people seemed to think Rene was a Muslim because it was pretty clear they hated Muslims for some reason.

What I was more worried about was that the man said he was the police. Did that mean he didn't think Black lives mattered? Was Rene going to get shot just because he was Black?

A different man wearing a white muscle shirt with a painting of an eagle on it made his way toward us through the crowd and said, "What do you think you're doing here?"

A few people turned to face us. Suddenly we were the center of attention.

I could see Rene looking around like he was in a panic. I heard a lady's voice say, "Stone him!" Some people laughed.

Where were all the "God bless yous" like we got on the highway? People turned mean when they got this close to heaven!

An elephant trumpet blasted from behind me. I remembered what Rene said about the sentinels when they shot fire at people. I looked behind us and saw a sentinel coming toward us. He looked like the angel that took Mom in the barn, a man angel with a flowing beard. I looked ahead of me and saw the man's gun holster on his hip. It was right in front of my face.

The man was poking his finger in Rene's chest. "I think Jesus would thank me for shooting a Muslim on this special day."

I could feel the heat of the crowd and the feeling of being crushed again, and I didn't know what to do. I plugged my ears and closed my eyes tight.

There were too many loud noises and voices, too much heat, and too many people. There were too many feelings boiling up in me. I felt sure this angry policeman would shoot us. Or the crowd would move in on us and smash us with rocks. One way or another, I was dead, and so was Rene. All I wanted to do was make it all stop.

Without thinking, I reached my arm out from behind Rene really fast and lifted the man's gun out of the holster and dropped it. He tried to grab for it, backed up, and lost his balance. Rene stepped back too, pushing me with him. The gun clattered on the stone street. People in the crowd backed up, and the gun was just sitting there in the middle of a big empty circle.

The man ran for his gun. Rene ran for the man. They crashed, and Rene's shoulder hit the man like a linebacker right in the midsection. The man went falling backwards and landed on his back. Rene got his footing and stepped back by me.

The man coughed and scrambled for his gun, picked it up, and pointed it at Rene.

"You're going to pay for that, you goddamn ni—"

I braced myself for Rene to get shot right then and there. He turned his body sideways and stayed between me and the gun. A flash of light came from behind and overhead, and I felt Rene get shot. I felt the bullet go right through him and into me. This was finally the end of my life, and I knew it.

A short, loud sound like gushing water filled the air. It was like someone turned on an enormous hot water faucet full blast for a second and then turned it off. And at the same time a light flashed in front of me and I felt a heat so hot I thought my skin was going to fry right off.

I opened my eyes and saw the sentinel between us and the man with the gun. There was no blood on me or Rene, and I didn't feel shot after all.

Then I heard a little sizzling sound. The man wasn't in the center of the open circle anymore. There was just a pile of smoking ash about the size of the man, but slumped over. The air smelled like burnt hamburgers.

People screamed and cried. Rene put his arm around me and said, "Time to go," and worked his way through the crowd away from the stairs. Once we were a ways away, he took my hand and we ran.

I put the whole scene back together in my mind. I never saw anyone die before. If he'd only left his gun there, the sentinel probably would have left him alone. He didn't deserve to get burned. I could feel his skin burning. He died just like if an H-bomb got him. My knees almost gave out, and I wanted to curl up in a ball, but I had to admit it felt good to stand up to him. And I was glad Rene and I were alive. I didn't punch him, but I did the next best thing. I disarmed him. And that gave Rene the chance to knock him down. We stood up to that bully like Bill Cody of the Pony Express. The sentinel did the rest. It was like the time Cody tricked a bad guy's horse into kicking him and knocking him out. But the way we did it was even more amazing because we used an angel instead of a horse.

"I was just trying to take his gun away so he wouldn't shoot us."

"It's okay, Patrick. You didn't hurt anybody. We were just defending ourselves. That was a terrible tragedy what happened to that man."

"What was he about to say to you?"

"I believe he was about to drop the N-word."

"You mean 'Negro'?"

He laughed. "Negro. Right."

I felt safe with Rene. Now that he was my dad, I knew with him I would be strong enough and smart enough to protect myself from everything the end of the world might throw at me. H-bombs, viruses, killer angels, soldier-police, crowds of angry people, gunfighters, and everything else. I wanted him at my side for all of it.

Once we got out of the thicker crowds at the base of the stairs, we noticed the crowd thinned out quite a bit. There weren't too many people left on the ground. Most of them were on the stairs.

"We have to go back," I said. "We have to keep trying."

We stopped running, and I looked at every face in the crowd. We worked our way through as many people as we could. When we got close to the stairs, there was just a smattering of people. Most of them already went up the stairs.

That's when the stairs started glowing. We watched the last people go to the top, and then the rays of sun around Jesus got so bright you couldn't look at them anymore. The stairs lifted up off the ground and pulled themselves into the portal in the sky, and all the sentinels went with it.

The air was empty and silent. There were no more cries for Mom and Grandma. I looked at Rene and he looked back at me.

I sat down and cried.

He sat down next to me and put his arms around me.

I wish I could have stopped them. I wish I could have made them all sit down and listen to Rene explain it, then maybe they could have understood. I cried for Mom, Grandma, and all the people who marched to their doom when they didn't have to.

At least Mom didn't want to go, not at the end. She wanted to stay with me. And I kept remembering that. In my mind I saw her face looking at me, and her arms stretched out for me. At least she didn't leave me on purpose. She fought against that sentinel best she could.

I tried to imagine how I could ever find her. I tried to think of where she might be. She could be anywhere in the universe now.

23

The Celestials left the Earth to go back to wherever they came from. That's what Rene thinks. Or "theorizes," he says. His friends in the lab are trying to figure out where they went.

"So is the world over now?" I asked him.

"For some people it is."

"What do you mean?"

I was sitting on one of the couches on the plane back home. He was resting on his back next to me.

"Well, the world is ending because of a lot of different things, and has been for a long time. Decades."

I remembered he rattled off quite a list of terrible things when I first met him. "You said the oceans are dying, and the air is poisoned."

"Yeah, all those things."

"But when is the real end of the world going to happen?"

He sat up and looked at me. "Patrick, the world is going to be fine. The planet is going to recover and keep spinning long after humans are gone. It's barely going to notice we were here. How long humans last here is another matter. We've really messed it up."

"We did?"

He nodded. "We sure did. And the end of the world isn't going to be a single event that happens in the snap of the fingers where everybody dies. It happens so slowly, we barely notice it. For some people, it's already happened. People die every year from sulfur dioxide and nitrogen dioxide in the air. That's the end of the world for them. Anybody who got burned by a sentinel, that's the end of the world for them. The same goes for anybody who dies of the virus. We have more viruses now because of climate change. So, people who got the virus and died, that's the end of the world for them. Anyone who's been killed by a tsunami, or a wildfire, or a hurricane, it's the same thing. We're in the middle of the sixth great mass extinction on Earth, the Holocene extinction. Rare animals we haven't even discovered yet are dying out all over the world. The world ends for a different one of those species every day."

I let out a lot of air and tried not to feel the pain of all those people and animals dying all at once. It was too much. I had enough in my head already.

Rene kept talking. "Even before the world was ending, things were bad. Life has always been tough on this planet, and nobody knows when their time is up. It's good to know the science and what's really going on, but you have to live too. You have to enjoy your life, try to make the world a better place, try to fix the problems, try to leave it better than you found it, no matter when the end might come."

I looked out the window some more. There were a few clouds, but I saw some of the Earth this time too. It looked like it curved at the edges, so I could really tell it was a sphere in space. I never imaged I would see the whole planet Earth from so high up like that.

I couldn't stop thinking of all the people who got burned by the sentinels. I could still smell the man at the stairs. I couldn't get it out of my nose. I thought of all the people who got removed, who left kids and babies behind. A lot of those kids were probably just like me, alone, scared, and confused. I felt less alone thinking of them because at least I wasn't the only one who lost a mom.

I thought of my mom trying to get away from that sentinel's arms. And I tried to think about living without her and trying to enjoy life like Rene said. It's not easy. My mind went right to where she is now. Is she being whipped by that sentinel? Experimented on? Eaten? How do you not think about that? I guess watching the Earth turn real slow under you helps. It looked quiet. I could almost see it turning. And it looked like it would go on forever, just spinning around and around after all the people in the world die off and we're long gone. It's far into the future when all the pain and the sadness in the world is gone. It makes me feel light, like I'm the ghost of a bird, gliding through the clouds.

Sometimes people ask me what I want to be when I grow up. I guess it's something grown-ups like to ask kids. Maybe they think the answers are cute or something. But whenever a grown-up asks me that, my mind is blank. I never thought of growing up. I always figured the world would end and I would die like a sap before I ever got the chance to grow up to be anything. But when they would ask, I would always try to come up with some silly thing to say just so they didn't think I was being rude. I would say "astronaut" or "inventor" or something like that. But I never really gave any thought to doing those things. All I thought about was being blown to smithereens by an H-bomb.

But just now, after talking to Rene about the end of the world, somehow a new path opened up in my mind, and I could see myself going along that path and moving into the future. For the first time I saw myself as a grown-up who somehow survives the end of the world. And I actually thought of what I might want to be when I grow up. I thought about it and I pictured it like it could really happen. You want to know what I thought of? I thought of being a teacher. If I was a teacher, I could teach all the kids who don't have parents anymore. I could teach them reading, math, and things like that. But I could also teach them how to grow up without parents around. That's something I know a lot about. Maybe it's a job that's more than just a teacher. I don't know what the job would be called. But I liked the idea of it. I liked it real fine.

It was getting dark outside so I couldn't see the Earth so good anymore. After that, Rene pulled out the beds, and we slept.

Christopher woke us up to let us know the plane landed. The sun wasn't even up yet, so it must have been the middle of the night. We gathered our things. I yawned big, rubbed my eyes, and tried to keep my balance, walking to the door after waking up.

Rene stopped me before we got off the plane. "There's something important I want to share with you."

I got excited. "Is it a surprise?"

"Sure. Why not?" He got down to be at my level. "Actually, the only reason I didn't tell you earlier was that I didn't want to worry you. I know you're angry at your dad, your other dad."

I got unexcited. I wasn't that angry at my other dad anymore, mainly because I don't think about him much. But he was still kind of a sore spot.

"I think it would be good for you to thank him for letting us use his plane, and maybe you can even think about forgiving him for what he did. It might make you feel better about things."

What he was saying made me think of what the surprise was. "Is he here?"

"How did you guess? Yes, he's going to meet us outside."

My whole body went limp for a moment. I wasn't ready to see him. And I was still groggy. I might have let out a groan.

"I can understand why you would be hurt by what he did. But he did it with the best intentions. And did you know that after you left, he gave the same gift to some other kids from Cordial Falls?"

"He did?"

"Yeah, he let them ride in this mag-lev train to San Francisco and he told them it was a time machine, the whole thing. And you know what?"

"What?"

"A lot of them got a big kick out of it. That's what he was hoping would happen with you. He had no way to know you'd feel betrayed by it. He thought he was doing something really special for you. He thought he was giving you a big wonderful birthday surprise. But he made a mistake. He misjudged you. That's all."

I just stood there, trying not to breathe too loud.

"Did you ever make a mistake?"

"Sure. Probably."

"Don't you like when you make a mistake that might have hurt people, and they say, 'Hey, no hard feelings?'"

I looked down and nodded.

"And I want to tell you something else. You may not realize it, but he did give you a great gift. Your childhood made you who you are. And you're a great person."

His compliments felt as good as Mom's. I didn't say anything because I wanted to enjoy the bath and chocolate cake awhile.

"You're able to see the mess that we've made of this future with a perspective that other people don't have. If you'd grown up in 2020, you wouldn't know anything was wrong until it was too late. But through your eyes and your experience, you see the mistakes so clearly. And because of the person you are, you understand what other people are going through." He looked at me for a while. "Think about it, okay?"

"Okay."

"Because he's your dad. Just as much as I am." He stood up. "You've got two dads now. You're a lucky kid."

"I guess so."

"Also he's got an idea that I think you're going to like. It's an idea for something that pretty much no one else could have thought of."

"Uh-oh. Take cover," I said.

"Hey, you wanted a surprise." He smiled.

We put our masks on, and then he let me lead the way out of the plane.

There was a spotlight shining at us when we came down the stairs. It came from behind a bunch of dark outlines of people at the bottom. Sure enough, I recognized one of them as my old dad, short and a little bent over, with his stands of hair in the breeze. With the light behind him I could see the shape of his nose and his chin, and I could tell he wasn't wearing a mask.

"Dad, you should be wearing a mask," I said.

He reached in his pocket and pulled out a mask and put it on. "You're absolutely right. Patrick. Thank you for the reminder."

He glanced at the people he was with, and they all took masks out of their pockets and put them on. One man didn't seem to have one in his pocket and he was looking at the others, hoping they had one he could use. It didn't seem like anyone had a spare one.

We got to the bottom and people traded hellos.

"Thank you for the plane," I said to my dad. I forced it out, and it actually wasn't too hard.

"You're welcome," he said.

I wanted to tell him about Mom, even though I wasn't sure if he cared. I thought maybe he would care a little since she is my mom after all.

"We couldn't find her," I said.

"I heard. I'm sorry." He bent down so his face was at my level. "I wish I had a real time machine so I could go back and make her a part of your life. If I did, I would. I'd put everything I have into it. But I'm sorry I can't do that."

"I accept your apology." That one was a little harder to say, but I thought Rene was smart and I wanted to give his advice a good try.

"Thank you, Patrick."

We drove to Rene's building, Rene and I in one car, my dad in another, for social distancing. Rene told me they were going to have a big meeting, and I was welcome to come. I thought it might be boring, but I decided I'd rather do that than sit somewhere alone.

Dr. Neumuller came and sat with me in a room alone first. It was another white room with comfortable chairs and a window high up on the wall. There was a box of tissues on a table next to my chair and a big clock on the wall. I watched the second hand go around.

She asked me in her English butler voice all about what's been happening with me, looking at me like she really cared through her cat-eye glasses.

I told her a lot of stories, and I think I might have cried when I told her the sadder parts. She said she wanted to sit down with me more and talk things through. She's such a nice lady. She said I could stay here in the room in the lab for a few days, or I could go home with Rene, whatever I wanted, but that I could some and see her and talk whenever I wanted.

After we were done talking, she walked with me to the meeting Rene invited me to. It was on one of the top floors of the crooked building. It was a big room with a long white table and slanted white walls. The outside wall was one big window. The sun was just starting to peek out, making the bottom of the sky red and purple. And you could see the dark shape of trees and some smaller buildings on the horizon.

My dad, Rene, Dr. Neumuller, and some of the people I met before were at the meeting, plus some new people I didn't know. It was maybe ten or twenty people.

Dr. Neumuller started talking first. She stood and welcomed

my dad to the university, saying she was excited about partnering with him. I guess that means my old dad and my new dad were going to be working together.

She introduced someone else, a short man with a big bush of black hair on his head and sleeves all the way up to his fingers, which stuck out like budding plants. He stood up to read some numbers from his phone, which was bigger than a normal phone. He gave out numbers for the removed, numbers for the people still left, numbers for kids, and numbers for adults, and a whole bunch of other numbers. It was a lot of people. More than five billion people got removed. There were 500 million kids left. A billion people got killed by sentinels.

People got serious when he said those numbers because that was a lot of dead people. I could hardly bear the idea. I felt a heavy dark cloud come down on me that turned everything into fog. I heard all their screams as the parents were torn from the kids or burned in the fires. I thought of the numbers I first saw in the newspaper of people dead from coronavirus. They seemed so small now.

"It was a god-damned genocidal attack," my dad said.

"These are just estimates, compiled from satellite data and crunched by our computers here pretty quickly."

I knew that meant they were guesses.

"There are a lot of systems in disarray, so this is the best we can put together."

The man had more numbers. "In China and India and other major population centers that are not majority Christian, we estimate that approximately sixty to seventy percent converted and went willingly. The rest were taken by force or killed. This ratio is similar elsewhere."

While the bushy-haired man with the fingers talked, my mind wandered a bit. I pictured being outside. I saw myself taking my mask off and breathing in the fresh air. It was the future, and the killer virus was gone.

"In Washington there's no one left in the line of succession, in terms of the executive branch. There's essentially no one in charge. There are some groups at the Pentagon trying to build some kind of provisional authority. Dr. Hinkley and Dr. Neumuller have cautioned against that, against any kind of military rule, and we've put the word out on that and there's a great deal of consensus there thankfully."

People said "here, here" and "absolutely," and things like that.

"We're looking at the same situation played out in most other countries," the bushy man said.

Dr. Neumuller talked for a while. "Our network of scientists is one of the largest and most intact organizations remaining. So Luis set up a kind of online poll portal where everyone can chime in on the various challenges. They're looking to us for leadership. They're looking to Rene, frankly."

Then I imagined going around the world, meeting kids and asking them if they needed any help, just like Cody of the Pony Express checking in on homesteaders on the frontier. I gather them together and show them how we can rebuild and have a swell future. After I help them, I tip my hat and say, "Just doing my job, Ma'am."

Someone else said, "I set up Basecamp to manage some of the bigger things, like economic concerns, and some of the other functions that used to fall to local and state governments. There aren't a lot of people in remote areas."

"We're using project management software to run the world?" my dad asked.

A few people chuckled at this. Everybody's mood seemed better after that.

In my head, I was in a classroom a lot like this meeting room. I was explaining things to younger kids. And I was being all smart, like I knew what I was talking about, just like all the grown-ups in this meeting room.

Another person, a tall lady with long arms and a button

nose, said, "Just a brief update on the priority issues. These are the most urgent, but by no means is this list comprehensive. There has been a dramatic spike in temperature due to the aerosol masking effect. Our friends at Whitewater are tracking the DTR on that. We need to initiate a controlled shutdown of all the nuclear power plants. Many of them aren't manned, and so that's critical. The virus is still with us of course. We need to implement contact tracing and a real lockdown now to stop it. Thankfully, we have a lot of epidemiologists still with us who can lead on that."

My old dad stood up, and I popped out of my mind and listened. He talked low and fast with his head down. "Everyone, I appreciate your inviting me here and I appreciate these top-level updates. I don't know what good my money is going to be to address any of these peccadillos, or if money even works anymore." Some people laughed at that. "But it's available. We're clearly in a new world now, and who knows what's going to happen or how it's going to function? But I just have to say this. I'm not known for my tact. I sometimes say or do outrageous things, but I have to say, I'm with Jean here. Is it Jean?"

The tall woman nodded.

"That this is an opportunity to rethink. Of course we've been hit by an unprecedented, unbelievable calamity. So many people are lost. But if we put our thinking caps on, we see that for those of us left behind, the agnostics, the scientists, the clear-headed, this is a once-in-an-epoch chance to create a sustainable and empathetic recovery from this attack, the likes of which our planet has never seen. It's a dark and dismal time, I know, but we can affect real change, and I'm thrilled to be working with all of you on it." He sat down after that.

Then Rene stood up and held out his hand. "I appreciate your positivity, Mason. All of us are excited to partner with you and we're ready to do what we need to tackle every last issue we face. And there's a lot. The challenges are daunting. We've experienced no less than the collapse of industrial civilization. We have a lot of kids to take care of. We have to bring them together and take care of them and educate them. Dr. Neumuller is putting a plan together. We can and will rebuild this world and give us all the best chance to thrive in it."

Did you ever hum and feel the hum vibrate in your chest, and just let the sound of the hum calm you? That's what Rene's voice was doing to this big room. He talked like he meant what he was saying, like nobody could ever stop him from fixing the world and making it better.

"There's a word that's been lost in recent human history. I don't know the world is going to look like moving forward, but Mason, you said one thing that I want to second. You used the word, 'empathy.' And that's something you've inspired in others. And I see it in our son, Patrick."

He held his arm out towards me and I felt the blood rush to my face. But I didn't feel embarrassed. The bottom of the sky was turning orange, and it was like he was beaming this first bit of sunrise into me, and everyone looked at me and knew he was my dad, and that made me feel bigger and more grown-up than I ever felt before.

"Patrick is someone who cares. And that's going to be a cornerstone of everything we build. We may not have long on this planet. We may not be able to reverse all the damage that's been done in the name of so-called progress, but that doesn't mean we're not going to work till our bodies give out, and direct all our best minds to solve these crises, to confront them head on. Indeed, we're going to find a technological solution to the carbon in the atmosphere. We're going to clean our oceans. We're going to replenish our soil. We're going to stop the spread of new diseases. We're going to stabilize our habitat. We're going to unite as citizens of the Earth and defend our planet from unknown dangers from outer space. We're going to raise a new generation of passionate, free-thinking people to work with us.

We can, we must, and we will achieve all of these things."

The first light of the dawn was starting to poke through the window in long beams. It gave Rene a shining yellow edge along one side of his body. He stood with his head high, and his arm raised, his dark skin was glowing like a statue made of pure gold.

"The most monumental challenge is our ongoing project to analyze the data we gathered from the Celestials. We're going to use that data to mobilize a collective effort, an entire culture singularly focused, unlike anything this world has ever seen. With Mason Stoodle's help, his know-how, his finances, and his infrastructure, we're going to build. The hands of every person that remains on this planet will build. Our robots will build with us. We'll mine and we'll weld and we'll rivet and we'll hammer a fleet of magnificent ships capable of traveling far beyond where human spacecraft has ever explored before. We're going to target the Celestials. We're going to fight them. We're going to defeat them. We're going to gather up all the Christians, the believers, the 'saved,' and the captured. We're going to bring them back home, welcome them into the new world we've created on Earth, and we, the scientists, are going to save them."

24

WANT TO HEAR A GOOD ONE? Now that the world has ended, I finally feel like I have a future to look forward to. It sounds silly, but it's true. I know my two dads are smart enough to figure out how to build the spaceships we're going to need to travel all the way to the Celestials' planet, and I know they'll rescue my mom and I'll see her again before humans die off for good. I don't know how long it will take. Maybe I'll be a teenager by the time we do it. Maybe I'll be a grown man in my 20s. But I know it's going to happen.

After the meeting, I asked Rene if any of the people in his lab figured out what happened to all the people that got removed. He told me they had a theory. Just the sort of answer you'd expect from Rene. He told me they picked up a signal that the Celestials were using, and they found patterns in it. They were able to come up with a pretty good idea of what they were saying. They think the Celestials were communicating with a fleet of spaceships that was kept hidden from us that they parked right in our back yard, just a little ways from Earth. They opened their little wormhole at the singularity and only had to send people through it a short ways to load them onto their spaceships. And then he thinks they flew their ships back to their home planet. And he says they have some clues about where their home planet is, but they're still working on that. Rene's University has telescopes all over the world, some as big as a house. And they're studying space to zero in on these terrible aliens. And we're going to find them soon enough. And when we do, those outer space monsters won't know what hit them.

But the most important thing he found out is that one of his ideas from before was right. It was hard for me to hear about it, and I cried when I did, but I was already thinking about it, so at least it wasn't a surprise. He said they believed the aliens took the people so they could be their slaves. He knows that from trying to decode their communication. He thinks they do mining on their other planet. They mine for some kind of unknown mineral that they think is really valuable but that I say is probably worthless. And they want to use human workers to be slaves in their mines.

He said he doesn't know anything about how the people they removed are being treated, or how many of them will survive. My heart felt drained of all goodness thinking about my mom and my grandma being put in an alien mine and digging for some mineral on another planet. Their faces would get covered in the mine dust, and they'd cough, and who knows if they would live long. Especially Grandma.

But these Celestials were going to get a taste of their own medicine soon. We're coming after them and we're going to sock them square in the face and take our people back. That will show them. They'll learn it's wrong to treat people like that. If they think they can play a big joke on the entire human race, they've got another thing coming.

I talked to my old dad after the meeting too. I told him when he builds his rocket ships, he can't have any slaves. I told him it didn't matter what color they were, or what country they came from. The most important thing was that he had to pay them good, treat them right, and he can't make them work for free. He smiled and patted me on the head. But I wasn't going to let him treat me like that anymore. I told him I wasn't his pet, and he needed to listen to me. He still smiled, but he seemed a little surprised at that one.

Dr. Neumuller understood what I was saying because she heard me say it to him and said, "Universal fair labor standards is absolutely something we need to implement."

I didn't know what that meant, and I didn't want to go get my dictionary from my room or ask her too many questions just then, but she said the word "fair," so I figured it was a good idea. She patted him on the back and he looked at her like he was wondering why we were ganging up on him.

I was excited to go up and see Buster after the meeting. Dr. Neumuller told me they took good care of him while I was away. They took him on walks, and they even let him run around the hallways. They said he was a good dog. I can't argue with that.

As soon as I opened the door to my room, Buster came up to me and wagged his tail and licked my face. I scratched the sides of his head and said, "How would you like to go for a walk, boy?"

I attached his collar, and we went walking. The morning sun was making long shadows behind us.

We turned up a side street and passed a lot of houses. It was strange to see cars in front of houses and hear birds in the trees like it was a normal day, but no people. There was nobody picking up their newspapers, hosing off their cars, or taking walks. I was the only one. It seemed like all the houses were empty too. And everything was dead quiet. We heard a couple of dogs barking, but they sounded pretty far away.

We passed one house, and I saw the top half of the face of a little girl, maybe 5 years old, peeking out at me through the front window. I stopped and waved. She ducked her head down as soon as she saw me. I knew she was scared. Who wouldn't be? It's hard to say what kind of awful things she saw when her parents got taken. She was probably having nightmares about it. Or maybe they even got blasted with fire. She's probably crying all the time. I wanted to go in there and tell her, "Everything's going to be okay."

But I knew I couldn't do that. I knew she'd be as scared as a stray cat, and I'd only scare her more by trying to talk to her.

I thought of my cousins Emily and Liam. I knew they were out there somewhere, and I knew I'd find them soon. I could be Captain Patrick again and help them understand everything that happened.

Dr. Neumuller told me about her idea for how to talk to the kids. She's going to take over the TV stations and make special messages for all the kids, letting them know that there are people out there ready to help them and take care of them. She figures the kids all know how to turn on their TVs and phones, so they're sure to find the messages. Rene said she's a doctor of psychology, which is understanding people and how they behave. She especially knows about kids. So she'll do a good job. Besides that, she's a nice lady. I liked her right away, and I'm a kid, so that tells you something right there.

Buster didn't seem to be in any mood to go back to our room in the crooked building. I didn't feel like there was any reason to go back just yet either. It was a nice breezy day, so we kept walking. We walked a long way. I started imagining that I was alone in Indian Territory on the frontier, and Buster was my horse. An Indian would peek out at me from behind a rock like that little girl, and I would want to help him, but he wouldn't trust me because I was one of the White devils.

The Aztecs came into my mind. I imagined I was Cortes, coming through this strange new city with men, horses, and armor. Cortes would walk down the street I was on now and he would look into houses and see a little girl, and he'd figure she didn't have weapons as good as his, so he would bust the door down and slice her open with his sword and take her TV and any necklaces her parents had in their bedroom.

I watched my feet walk on the Earth, and I pictured how I saw it from the plane. I saw that it was just a blue ball with a sky around it sitting out there in space. And far away there was another planet. I pictured that planet as a dark place, with rain that came down that wasn't made of water. It was made of some kind of green chemical, and it stung your skin when it hit you. And I imagined my mom getting hit with that rain, chopping away at a pink sparkling cliffside with her pickaxe, sweating and crying and trying to chop out some precious rocks that these Celestials wanted so they could melt it down like Cortes.

One of the Celestials was watching her. I could see the Celestial clear as day. They rode some kind of dragon-type beast with a mean snarl. It was a black monster with green eyes and a spiky tail that whipped around like a snake's. And the Celestials looked sort of like blind moles with no hair. They were white and pink, had smooth skin, and beady little black eyes. They had all sorts of arms and legs, like a giant centipede. They cracked their whips at her. But it wasn't an ordinary whip. It had razors on the end, so it would cut deep in the skin every time it hit you. And they would work my mom and everybody else all day and all night. They would never let up. They would work them until they dropped dead.

My thoughts made me walk faster. My insides were bubbling up as goose bumps on my arm. But the thought didn't make me feel sad or helpless. It made me angry. It made me want to fight them. I imagined swooping in like Flash Gordon and cutting the Celestial down with a few punches, and then facing off against his dragon beast with my ray gun and blasting it dead. Then I grabbed my mom. She fell into my strong arms and I carried her back to my ship. I called to all the other slaves, "You're free! Follow me! We're headed home!" and they all tossed their pickaxes aside and cheered and ran behind me. Some of them carried Grandma. And they rose up and revolted against their Celestial masters, running them over in a stampede. The Celestials didn't have a chance. They were no match for the can-do spirit of us Earthlings.

There weren't as many houses on the road we were walking on after a while. And there were a lot more trees. We kept going up a hill. It wasn't very steep. It just kind of sloped up. Pretty soon there weren't any houses at all. We got ourselves on a dirt trail and saw a big wooden sign that said, "Eaton Canyon Natural Area." And under that it said, "All dogs must be kept on leash."

I looked down at Buster and said, "That's you, boy."

Then I had the thought that this sign didn't know the world ended. I had a little laugh about that. It's just a sign, not a policeman, so it can't tell us what to do. So I let Buster off his leash.

He ran ahead, and I walked steady. There was a creek bed along the path, and you could see brown mountains ahead.

We came to a split in the trail, and that's when I really felt like we were in the wilderness. It was just like the frontier. There was a sign that said the horse trail was one way and the canyon was the other way. I decided to go to the canyon. Maybe there would be falls there.

Now I was an explorer on a different planet. This was the frontier all right, but it wasn't the frontier of America or even of Earth. It was the frontier of a strange new planet far away from here. In a different galaxy. I was exploring it, just Buster and me. We had our own spaceship, you see, and we went on adventures together exploring new planets and finding new minerals and new chemicals that they could use back on Earth to make amazing new devices. And you didn't need slaves to get these minerals. You could build robots to do it. They'd work for you happily and would never complain. But don't give them emotions because then you'll have problems.

We came to another split in the trail, and there was another sign. "Eaton Canyon Falls, 1/2 miles." And below that it said,

"Life, liberty and the pursuit of happiness are right here. Please help protect it."

So there were falls ahead! We kept going. Up ahead was a tall gray bridge with a white picket fence across the top. We passed under it.

Suddenly our little walk became an adventure. We were hiking up an honest-to-goodness canyon, making our way around rocks and big tree roots, crossing from side to side through the rushing creek. The water was cold. Buster was scrambling right along with me like a trusted packhorse. He even had to dog paddle a couple of times through the water. I rolled up my jeans to keep from getting too wet. We walked across stones, a fallen tree branch, and through the water. My feet started feeling numb after so many crossings.

It was starting to feel like a real lost canyon on a distant planet. The canyon walls were high on both sides, but I imagined they were as high as the clouds. I imagined instead of the brown and sandy and green colors of Earth, it was black and red, and the rocks were sharp as glass, and we had to wear space boots to protect our feet.

Finally, after one last stream crossing, we came to a big pile of rocks. We could hear the falls and could even see a part of them through some tree branches.

"Be on the lookout, Buster. There might be hostiles."

I lifted my head above the rocks nice and slow, just enough to see the falls and make sure there were no aliens trying to drain the water out and suck this planet dry. The falls were strong, and about as high as a house. Ancient aliens posted a strange sign on the side of the cliff next to the falls. I aimed my deciphering machine at it, pressed some buttons on it, and it read back to me what the sign said: "Beware, all humans who enter here. The water is cold."

I scanned the area with my infrared scanner to see if there were any aliens. Once I got my reading, which was negative, I ducked down and looked at Buster.

"The coast is clear, boy. Let's go!"

We raced to the water! I tore off my clothes and jumped into the little pool under the falls. It was so cold I just about lost my breath. I decided it was just about the craziest thing I ever jumped in. But I stayed in long enough to throw some good splashes at Buster, have a laugh, and get some water sucked up my nose by accident.

After that I came right out and spread out flat on the rocks. Buster came out and shook himself, splattering water in every direction. Even with the warm sun on my skin, my whole body shivered like a rattle. I had goose bumps all over. I had to shift a few times to get a good spot that didn't have any rocks poking my back. Buster walked around some more and then finally stayed put next to me.

I looked up at the clouds. I couldn't see them very well because the sun was so bright, but they were like perfect white puffs of cotton. The water and the birds chirping and Buster breathing were the only sounds.

These falls were even nicer than Cordial Falls, I decided. First of all, they were real. They weren't built by my dad. They came out of the Earth and probably haven't changed for thousands of years. I could be in the Old West. Some Old West traveler probably stopped here and took a swim just like I did, and it wasn't any different.

I grabbed my pants and picked my phone out of the pocket and saw that Rene left me a message.

"How are you doing?"

I texted back, "Buster and I discovered a waterfall."

His dots came right away. "Nice! Have fun."

I looked past the falls and saw that there were more rocks and mountains back there that probably went on forever.

There was more exploring to do.

About the Author

Scott Dikkers is the #1 *New York Times* and #1 Amazon bestselling author of over two dozen books, inlcuding *Welcome to the Future Which is Mine*, *You Are Worthless,* and *Our Dumb Century*. He is the founding editor of *The Onion* and winner of the 1999 Thurber Prize for American Humor. For more, visit scottdikkers.com.

Acknowledgements

Liz Anderson, Ricardo Angulo, Nicholas Ball, Dandelion Benson, Dr. Bill Bradley, Captain Susan Brearley, Johanna Brown, Brooke Casady, Thavan Chantna, Fragnance Conchord, Elissa Cooper, Marina Cusack, Barbara Dee, Jon Desjardins, DM, Alexander Dolnick, Angela Dowdy L., Conor "The Baron Of Cheese" Duffy, Ken J. Evanchik, Dr. Chris Fleming, Ethan Freckleton, Ilana Freedman, Mark Freeman, Alyssa Gibson, Dan Greenberg, Helen Holmes, Keith Horvath, Jon Howard, Gerald Joseph, T. Donovan Keene, Keri Kelly, Hugh Kelly, Earnest Kinoy, Jim Koebel, Jim Kuenzer, Nick Leydorf, Amelie Lock, Z.P. Lovelace, Rachael Mason, Joel Mazmanian, Laura McCarthy, Kathy McIntosh, Gian Misso, Christina Anaya Mortensen, Michelle Nedelec, Irene Oh, Keith Patterson, Gordon Petry, Tavis Putnam, Dina B. Rodrigues, Madeline Schmidt, Simon Seline, Edgar Owens Snoke, Erik Sternberger, Robert Stinner, Karen Sullivan, Erik Thornquist, Jaymie Todero, Kyle Towers, Zachary Truran, Matt Visconage, Brooke Washington, Huxley Westemeier, William Whitaker Darrah, Elizabeth Willard, Wendy Wilson, Phil Witte, Mike Wollaeger, Kristopher Michael Wood, Sara Zadrima, Sam Zee, and a very grateful pupil.

There's more to the story...

Years ago, 8-year-old Patrick Stoodle discovered that something wasn't right with his family—something mechanical...

Don't miss *Patrick Stoodle's Completely Awesome Army of Killer Robots*, the exciting prequel to *The Joke at the End of the World*.
Get it FREE before its official release!

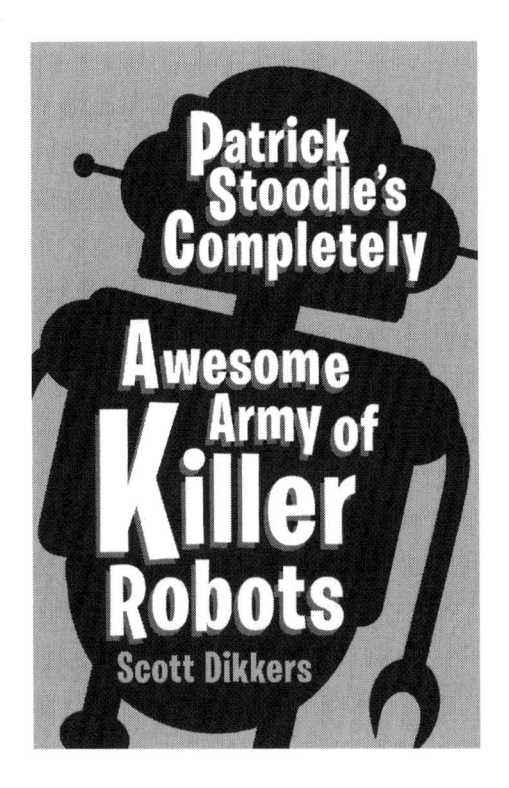

visit scottdikkers.com/robots